ATTACK OF THE WYVERN

Kham heard the hissing bellow of the wyvern, saw its snakelike body and bat wings. It was headed straight toward him and the elves.

The beast swooped up and its serpentine body writhed as it twisted in a tortured spiral, higher and higher. Then it snapped its wings up and darted its head down. The wyvern came screaming like a speeding bullet train, jaws gaping wide, wings beating, as it dove on the elves.

Kham's suddenly sweaty fingers fumbled with the magazine. He couldn't get it loaded in time. Turning, he readied himself to barrel through the elf's position. Maybe he could carry them both out of the beast's line of fire if he was fast enough. Seeing that the elf was standing still, staring up at the beast, his hands glowing with arcane energy, Kham rethought his plan; he didn't want to get caught between fire and magic. He turned again and raced away. If the elf wasn't bright enough to take cover, Kham knew one ork who was. . . .

SHADOWRUN 6:

NEVER TRUST AN ELF

ROBERT N. CHARRETTE

A ROC BOOK

ROC
Published by the Penguin Group
Penguin Books USA Inc., 375 Hudson Street,
New York, New York 10014, U.S.A.
Penguin Books Ltd, 27 Wrights Lane,
London W8 5TZ, England
Penguin Books Australia Ltd, Ringwood,
Victoria, Australia
Penguin Books Canada Ltd, 10 Alcorn Avenue,
Toronto, Ontario, Canada M4V 3B2
Penguin Books (N.Z.) Ltd, 182-190 Wairau Road,
Auckland 10, New Zealand

Penguin Books Ltd, Registered Offices:
Harmondsworth, Middlesex, England

First Published by Roc, an imprint of New American Library, a division of Penguin Books USA Inc.

First Printing, August, 1992
10 9 8 7 6 5 4 3 2 1

Series Editor: Donna Ippolito
Cover: Keith Birdsong
Interior Illustrations: Jeff Laubenstein

ROC REGISTERED TRADEMARK—MARCA REGISTRADA

Printed in the United States of America

To Ruth and Paul Johnson,
thank you

PROLOGUE

''Pain is a useful tool, Mr. Kern.''

The muscles of Kern's neck complained as he turned his head to look at the speaker, who was tall and thin, suspiciously thin. Kern could distinguish little else because of the way the other man stood silhouetted against the light. Squinting against the glare, he made out the elongated shape of the man's ears and the slant of his eyes, and knew that this was no man but an elf. Kern spat at him, but the sputum sizzled and vanished without ever touching either the impeccable suit or the dark skin of the elf. Protective magic, no doubt.

''An unnecessary display, Mr. Kern.'' Those dark, slanted eyes twinkled for a moment. ''I am aware of your antipathy.''

Kern was restrained in some fashion he could not see, but nothing seemed to restrain his voice. ''Slot yourself, elf.''

''My name is Urdli, Mr. Kern.''

That didn't mean anything to Kern. The name might not even be real. The face certainly wasn't familiar. The sure thing was that this Urdli had Kern at a severe disadvantage. But that could change.

''We are going to get to know each other quite well, Mr. Kern. Or rather, *I* am going to get to know *you*. Through pain, I will come to know you.''

''Know thyself, weedeater.''

''A clever play on Aristotle's maxim, Mr. Kern. Perhaps you will be comforted to know that this course will not be without pain for me as well.''

Somehow Kern doubted that. ''My heart bleeds.''

"Not yet, Mr. Kern. Not yet."

The elf's matter-of-fact tone seemed a promise that Kern's offhanded remark might become a literal truth. Kern's body tried to shudder, but was balked. Neither could he act on his desire to leap up and run. Though he could sense his limbs well enough, he had not the slightest command over them. He was helpless, held immobile by the elf's magic.

Well, at least the elf had left him his mind and his voice. Too bad he wasn't a magician himself. But then, Kern supposed, the elf would not have left him his voice.

"You're looking for trouble messing with me, weed-eater. Don't you know who I am?"

"Of course I do, Mr. Kern. That is why you are here."

Kern felt a strange sensation on his feet. A light touch, then another, and another. The sensation spread, flowing up his legs like worms crawling over his flesh. There seemed to be dozens of them squirming invisibly over him. The phantom slithering advanced past his knees, up his thighs, and then the first of the ghostly worms reached his crotch.

Then they all bit him, and he screamed.

The ghost worms vanished at his shout. The pain they had caused was minor; Kern had been as much surprised as hurt. He was in darkness, and he realized that time had passed. Opening his eyes, he stared venomously at the elf. Urdli regarded him blandly as if he were some sort of experiment.

"You have a strong will for a mundane human, Mr. Kern. Your master chose well."

"If you know who I work for, then you know you're in deep drek."

The hint of a smile touched Urdli's wide-lipped mouth. "Do not comfort yourself with the false hope that you will be rescued, Mr. Kern. No one knows that we have you. Your associates at Saeder-Krupp believe you dead."

Kern told himself that the elf's assertion was unlikely. His people would know, wouldn't they? Suddenly he wasn't sure. How could he be? He didn't remember much of his capture. A flash and some thunder, or maybe the loud noises echoing in his head had come from gunfire. He remembered Eunice screaming, her face all bloody. Was she still alive, too, another of the elf's prisoners? They'd been on a trip. Obviously, they had not reached their destination. His people had to know he had been taken.

"They'll come for me."

"As I said, Mr. Kern, a false hope. To them you are no more. Your only hope of life lies in cooperation."

Not bloody likely. If Saeder-Krupp thought him dead, he might as well be dead. Without the support of his corporation, he had no protection and no one to avenge him. This elf would have no fear of killing Kern once he got what he wanted. No matter what hints Urdli threw out of letting Kern live if he cooperated, Kern could tell that the elf was lying. If he had intended to permit his captive to live, he would never have started with torture.

As if the thought had given them birth, new ghost worms began to crawl up Kern's legs. This time they touched his hands as well, curling around his fingers and slithering up his arms. He tried to steel himself for their bite, but they only continued crawling. Another moment, and he readied himself again, certain the time had come, but still they just crawled. It was a cruel game, but he played it anyway. When they finally bit, he had no time to feel surprise that he had misjudged the timing. He only had time for the pain.

The darkness and dissociation came again. He knew time had passed. He had been thinking of his job with

Saeder-Krupp. His own thoughts, or the results of Urdli's probings? Had he talked? If so, about what?

When he opened his eyes again, another elf was present. Kern didn't remember his arrival.

This new elf was neither as tall nor as thin as Urdli, but he would never be mistaken for an ordinary human. His face was handsome, almost beautiful. His hair was spun of fine silver, his eyes a molten gold, and his fair skin almost alabaster in its sheen and tone. He had that ageless look of the classic elven metatype. He might have stepped from a fairy tale save that, like Urdli, he wore a business suit of the most fashionable cut.

Kern didn't want to believe that he recognized this elf. The implications were too much.

The worms came again, squirming up his limbs.

"Strip him." It was the new elf who spoke.

"You are impatient," Urdli said, his tone that of a teacher's commenting on a student's performance.

"Maybe I just don't like playing with him."

"Playing?" Urdli turned to his companion and the worms vanished. "I am not playing. There is an order to all things, even to what we do here."

"Just hurry up," the silver-haired elf snapped, his expression stony.

"If I were to 'hurry up,' the knowledge this man carries might be damaged. He is only a human, after all."

"We must know."

"And we shall," Urdli assured him.

"Soon," the newcomer insisted.

Annoyance crept into Urdli's voice. "Would you care to do this yourself?"

The silver hair was barely ruffled when its owner shook his head. "You have far more experience in these matters."

"Then perhaps you will trust me to know the best course."

The fair-skinned elf said nothing. Instead he turned and stalked from the room.

Kern watched the retreating back of Glasgian Oakforest, Prince of Tir Tairngire. Glasgian was son and heir to Prince Aithne, a prominent member of the Tir Tairngire Council of Princes. If Glasgian's presence meant the council was involved, there would be only one release for Kern. Death. His last hope for salvation departed with Prince Glasgian.

The worms returned.

* * *

Glasgian did not like waiting, but he liked being present even less. Three days passed before he reentered the darkened chamber. A long time of enforced patience, considering the nature of the information the man could provide. And, given the possibility that an investigation could uncover their deception, time might be in short supply. If the master of Saeder-Krupp became suspicious, he would act and they would lose the prize. The sooner they had what they wanted from this Saeder-Krupp tool, the sooner they could act and, thereby, avoid any interference from the tool's owner.

He found Urdli stripped naked and sitting in the center of a chalked circle. The Australian elf no longer looked like a dapper businessman; rather he looked like an aborigine from some old vid documentary of the last century. On thongs around his neck and waist he wore bones and other scavengings of the natural world. More danced on bracelets when he waved his arms. Stripes and whorls of ocher and drab gray stood out against the darkness of Urdli's skin, the paint streaked where sweat had carved channels through the symbols.

In the center of a chamber stinking of incense, hu-

LAUBENSTEIN·92

man sweat, excrement, and other odors that hinted at even less savory things, Kern hung suspended. Mundanely, Glasgian could see no supports. It was only by concentrating on his arcane senses that he could perceive the tall, gangly-limbed beings that held the man. The human in their grasp was covered in segmented things that glowed in an eerie blue color as they slithered over his body, occasionally gnawing their way beneath the skin and disappearing even from Glasgian's astral sight. Seemingly aware of his observation, the beings holding the human turned their narrow, solemn faces toward him. Discomfited by their stare, Glasgian shifted back to mundane perceptions. He took a moment to compose himself, then addressed Urdli.

"Has he talked?"

"Quite a bit."

Not a useful response. "What we want to know?"

"Much that touches on the matter."

Exasperated, Glasgian prompted, "And?"

"It is as we thought."

"Then let's get on with it."

"In time," Urdli said. "In time. There is an order to all things."

Urdli gestured and Kern screamed.

The human's screeching clawed at Glasgian's spine. If he had talked and told Urdli what they needed to know, what was the point? There was no time for self-indulgence.

Glasgian looked down at Urdli. The dark-skinned elf was concentrating on the human, whose screams changed tone each time the dark elf gestured. But Urdli was asking Kern no questions.

Stepping up to Kern, Glasgian lifted one hand toward the man's head as a blade hissed out from its sheath in the cuff of his jacket. The next instant he drove the tapered steel into the man's eye, through the socket, and into the brain. The screaming stopped as the man spasmed and went limp.

"Ill-done," Urdli said softly. "I was not finished."

Glasgian stared at the old elf. "This is not the time for fun and games."

"Indeed. It is not."

Urdli's midnight eyes bore into Glasgian's with an intensity Glasgian had only ever seen among the elders. There was challenge in those dark pools, challenge and reproval. Glasgian bridled, his anger stiffening him. He had no need to bow to this elf; he was a prince of Tir Tairngire, the scion of the Oakforest line, with a heritage as old as Urdli's own. One day he would sit on the council. Who was this Urdli to question that? True, Urdli was an elder, but age was not everything. They were working toward the same goal, and Glasgian's methods were as valid as Urdli's. Perhaps more so. The old elf only seemed interested in plodding along, but the Sixth World was not one to reward dawdlers. Whatever Urdli might have been once, he lived in the Sixth World now. Being born of that world, Glasgian knew it better than did the Australian.

"When you're cleaned up, join me upstairs," Glasgian said, breaking off his stare.

Without waiting for a reply, he turned and left the chamber, wanting only to be out of there. For one thing, he had to change his own clothes; the stench of the chamber permeated them. Not only that, but the damned human had bled all over his sleeve.

Easy Money

1

The haze over Puyallup Barrens was thick, as usual. The sun, sinking toward the Olympic Mountains on the other side of the Sound, was already starting its evening display. Kham squinted at it. The sun was playing hide-and-seek among the clouds, but dark would not come for an hour or so. Not that he was worried—he was ork and orks were made for the night—but if he kept on now, he'd be home before dark. He wasn't sure he wanted to get there so soon.

Slowing his pace, he looked around for a patch of quiet, a doorway or an alley mouth with a good view of the street. Halfway down the block he found one, an old theater complete with a marquee that would shelter him in case of a shower. He scanned the graffiti on the wall. Hotbloods turf, by the signs. Zero sweat. He was neutral to them right now. They wouldn't mind him taking up their space, as long as he was ready to vacate the moment they showed up. He moved into the shadow under the marquee, feeling the coolness of the coming night already hanging in the darkened air. Settling in, he leaned back against the chill stone.

Things hadn't gone well today. Not that they'd been bad, but not good was bad today. No nuyen to dump onto Lissa's credstick. Everything was dry. Dry, dry, dry. Nobody talking and nobody doing. Worse, nobody running. Leastways, as far as his contacts could tell him. To go looking daywise had been an act of pure desperation, but he still had not turned up a speck of work, and no work meant no cred. The prospect of going home to Lissa without fresh cred was not very appealing.

She would be all over him about it. Probably start ragging him again to sign up with a corp or the fed army. Didn't she know that either of those options would mean he wouldn't be around much? Yeah, he supposed she did. Maybe that's what she wanted. She hadn't eased off since he came back from old Doc Smith's place with the replacements.

He looked down at the chromed cybernetic hand protruding from his right sleeve. It wasn't state-of-the-art, but it worked. He had almost died the day he lost that hand. What would have happened then? Where would that have left Lissa? Worse, what about the kids? At least he was still around, still able to protect and provide for them. *Right,* he thought, *like today.* Well, most of the time anyway.

He stared sullenly down the street, watching the locals and the daytrippers. Cullen Avenue was one of the nicer parts of Carbonado, lots of well-fortified shops. The business day was coming to a close, and this stretch of Cullen was a real nightwise place. A few of the daywise folks were starting their scurry toward their nice, safe homes. He could see in their hasty pace and frequent glances at the sinking sun that they didn't find the prospect of gathering twilight nearly as comforting as he did.

The streets were crowded still. Most of the folks were still just folks, going about their business, but a few among them were heralds of the nightwise types that would soon haunt these same streets. A beefy ork girl was hooking on the next corner, while across the way a trio of bedraggled chipheads were begging. There would be more of both soon. Then a knot of leatherclad dwarfs came strutting past. Dressed in

Ironmonger colors, they scoped Kham out as they approached. He gave them a smile, showing just a little of his upper tusks, and rubbed his broken lower tusk with a chromed thumb. The short, burly one behind the leader whispered something into his warlord's ear and they kept on moving.

By far the bulk of the crowd were breeders, stupid, puny, thin-skinned norms. They and the occasional elf scurried along the sidewalk, heading for whatever they called security for the night. The norms were being bright, since they weren't nightwise. Elves could see in the dark as well as any ork, but Kham supposed they were being bright, too. None of the Barrens that hedged in any of the megacity sprawls were kind or gentle places after dark.

And Puyallup Barrens, one of the two spawned by the Seattle sprawl, was no different. An urban backwater like Puyallup was nobody's first choice for a home, maybe everybody's last. That's why so many orks like Kham ended up here. Forced into the places nobody else wanted. Forced to scratch and scrape to get by. Forced out of the nice places because they weren't powerful enough to object. Or didn't have enough political clout. Or firepower. Or whatever it took to hold onto the good places.

Kham had grown up here and survived. So far. He had survived the gangs, the hate, the riots, and everything else the Barrens had thrown at him. And he'd thrived, clawing his way to the top of the gangs and eventually putting together an alliance of gangs that had ruled Carbonado. Past history, he mused. Gangs were kid stuff, and he wasn't a kid anymore. He had reached his full growth and would be twenty in a few years.

Twenty!

He didn't really want to think about that. It was much better to dream of the day he'd be living in style. But style meant nuyen, which again brought him back to the reality that he'd not done very well at collecting any today.

There weren't many ways for an ork to pile up the nuyen. Sure, he could have gone into the fed army or one of the private corp ones, something he'd considered when younger, much younger; but hearing Black Jim's stories when Jim came home to the neighborhood on leave from the feds, Kham knew that the regimented life was not for him. He'd thought about it long and hard, and the only conclusion he could reach was that if you can't make your nuyen legally, you gotta do it illegally.

Once he'd reached that conclusion, he hadn't wasted time. He'd started to put the gang to decent use and done a few small jobs, smart stuff that was practically built into the system, like looting the corp trucks running along 412, and only taking what couldn't be traced. After they'd made a couple of hits, his fixer had realized that Kham wasn't just another stupid ork kid out to break some heads, and so he'd turned him on to Sally Tsung's ring. Lady Tsung introduced Kham to the lucrative life of shadowrunning, and one payoff was all it took for him to see the light; corp snitching just couldn't compare. He'd dropped the gangs and signed on with Lady Tsung.

His hard-built alliance had crumbled while he attended to other matters, but he hadn't cried. He'd worked to build the gang, using it to his advantage while still the boss, but he didn't need it anymore. Nothing wrong with that. That was the way the world worked. You grabbed what you could, held on as long as you needed it, and when something better came along, you grabbed that instead. Had to keep the nuyen flowing in. Had to look out for yourself.

Shadowrunning offered almost everything the gangs had. There was action, excitement, and firepower—lots of firepower on the right run. The only thing missing was the power and the respect, the chance to make a difference on your turf, and all the chummers looking up to you. Then again, maybe running the shadows did offer those things, but in a different way. A runner could make a difference, but it was subtler, excepting of course the differences to your cred balance. Those differences were truly truly sig—at least when the nuyen was rolling in. And the respect was there too. The scuzboys and streetrats like those Ironmongers gave wide berth to Kham now that word was about that he played in the big leagues. It was the personal stuff that wasn't there. Sure, he had his guys, and they were some of the best rocking orks ever to pack big guns, but they were runners like him and mostly loyal to the biggest buck. They weren't *his* the way the gang had been.

Drek! He was supposed to be thinking about the future, not the past. Only old guys found the past brighter than the future and Kham was not an old guy yet!

Kham heaved himself up, ready to be on his way, when some old fool plowed into him. Kham swung a hard backhand, then realized halfway through the swipe that the idiot wouldn't have gotten close enough to collide if Kham hadn't already dismissed him as a threat. Kham pulled his punch, but he still bounced the guy into the wall. Catching him on the rebound off the brick, Kham recognized the slag, and his condition.

"You're blasted, Kittle George."

"Huh?" The gray-haired ork frowned as he tried to bring his vision into focus. "Kha—"

Kham heaved him upright in time to avoid getting splashed when Kittle George started to vomit. Kham watched in disgust. This was how old orks ended up.

Kittle George swayed erect and staggered on down the street. Too drunk to walk a straight line, he caromed off the street folk he passed as he stumbled along the sidewalk. Kham caught up with him in a few strides, grabbed an arm, and hauled him erect.

"Ya oughta go home, Georgie."

"Am goin' home," Kittle George slurred.

"Yer home's da odder way."

Kittle George looked around confusedly, then squinted at Kham. "I knew tha'."

Kham shook his head sadly. "Ya want me ta walk ya dere?" He didn't really want to, but he thought he should offer. Kittle George was ork, too, and orks had to stick together. Besides, walking Georgie home would mean putting off going home himself for a bit longer.

They strolled along the streets, Kham keeping his pace to something Kittle George could manage. Taking the offered bottle, Kham took the swig required of friendship, then managed to drop the bottle. Accidentally, of course. Then he had to drop it again before the brittle plastic would shatter. Georgie cried over the loss, embarrassing Kham, but fortunately he didn't recognize anyone in the crowds that flooded around them. He got Kittle George underway again.

The old ork started mumbling a long list of complaints. Life hadn't been treating him very well. But that was no surprise. He was ork. What did life have for orks besides trouble anyway?

They had reached Kittle George's place, a condemned tenement just like the others lining the streets. The Seattle metroplex government had condemned it, then left it; lacking the money to trash it, they certainly did not have enough to replace it. People still lived there because it offered a roof and walls. The rent was cheap, too. Kittle George had prime space in the basement, the warmest spot in an unheated building during the winter. Kittle George had company then; but it was still autumn and the neighbors hadn't moved in yet.

''Ya gonna be okay, Georgie?''

''Yeah. Gonna get some sleep. Wish I had a bottle, though.''

''Sleep's good, Georgie.'' Hoping the old guy would forget about the bottle, Kham pointed him toward the stairs and made sure the drunk had a grip on the rail before urging him down into the darkness. ''Just get some sleep.''

The old man mumbled something as he went down the stairs, but Kham didn't understand a word of it. Booze and age, the bane of an ork's life—if despair and drugs didn't get him first.

As Kittle George disappeared, a shadow fell over Kham. He turned slowly, careful to avoid sudden moves. The big troll he found grinning at him was familiar. Grabber worked as a bouncer at Shaver's Bar; he also was a small-time fixer. The troll's operational area ran about five blocks north and south of Kittle George's, along Cullen, and out west all the way to the wall that marked the Salish-Shidhe boundary with the plex. The troll was rumbling with a deep chuckling.

''Hoi, Grabber. Whuzzappenin' down at Shaver's?''

''Hoi, Kham,'' the troll boomed. ''Bodyguarding these days, chummer?''

Kham shrugged.

For a troll, Grabber was moderately bright; the troll picked up on the fact that Kham didn't find any humor in his poor joke, and so tried some more innocuous small talk. ''Been quiet at the club. Just the usual. No sweat 'cepting Saturday night.''

Kham had heard about the riot. ''Local scuzboys giving ya trouble?''

''Nah.'' Grabber cracked his knuckles, and smiled. ''Just a workout. Ain't seen you lately.''

Kham shrugged again. He hadn't worked Grabber's turf in a while—and after what had happened the last time, he hoped he wouldn't be anytime soon, either. Who could say, though? Things had been pretty slow lately. "Been busy."

"Not what Lissa says. Says you been hanging home a lot. Things slow?"

Did everybody know? He stifled a sharp retort. *Gotta stay chill*, he told himself. If you say you ain't doing biz, you don't do no biz. Nobody wanted a washed-out runner. For the third time, Kham shrugged, but this time he added a raised eyebrow to let Grabber know he'd listen.

The troll made an elaborate affair of checking the now sparse street crowd to see if anyone was close enough to hear. "Jack Darke's running. Looking for muscle, I hear."

"Solo, or he need a whole gang?"

"Solo."

"Personal interest on Darke's part, or will any ork do?"

"Must be personal, chummer. Otherwise I'd be running it instead of shopping it to you."

Kham hesitated. Once he would have jumped at the chance. Drek, maybe he *should* jump at it. He could convince himself that he needed the work, couldn't he? That the other guys didn't matter. But he didn't spend a lot of time thinking about the offer. "Ain't interested," he said sourly. "Ain't no room in da run for my guys, ain't no room for me. When ya got a crew ta worry about, ya got responsibilities."

"Responsibilities tie a man down, chummer."

"What would ya know about dat, Grabber?"

It was Grabber's turn to shrug. "I hear things."

Kham was annoyed by the turn of the conversation. "Well, ya ain't hearin' yes from me. Darke'll have ta find his muscle somewhere else."

Grabber squinted his larger eye almost shut, and leaned down. His voice was modulated to a conspiratorial tone, which meant it could probably be heard only half a block away. "Last chance. Good money, all certified cred."

"Some odder time."

Straightening up, Grabber said, "You called it, chummer. Maybe some other time. Maybe not. Stay chill, chummer. Careful you don't get so cold you freeze."

"My worry, Grabber."

"Like I said, chummer, you called it," the troll replied. He eased his way down the street, amusement rumbling deep inside him.

Angered by the troll's reaction, Kham watched him go. Did it really matter what the troll thought? Grabber was small fish. But then, so was Kham. Darke, now. Darke was a bigger fish. Not as big as Sally Tsung, but bigger than Grabber and Kham. But Darke was running and Sally wasn't, which meant Darke was paying and Sally wasn't.

Drek! If he didn't take it himself, he might have hired out one of the guys. Rabo had kids, too, and was as hard up for cash. They all needed to score. So why was he worrying about the guys when he had troubles of his own? Why didn't he just take the job and put the nuyen in his own pocket like any corp putz would do? Responsibilities? Drek! He hated being grown up.

Grabber was almost out of shouting range. It wasn't too late to call him back, and Kham almost did. Then he thought about how that would look to the fixer.

Besides losing face, Kham was sure that the pay offered for the run would now be less than it was. With Darke's personal interest, that price would have been Kham's going rate. Calling Grabber back, making himself look hungry, would drive the fee down. If he took the run at the lower price, word of it would get around and that would also be bad for business. Once a shadowrunner's price starting going down, it wasn't likely to go up again. The jobs would get cheaper and cheaper and eventually you'd face a dirty run for dirt and then you'd end up under the dirt. Kham wasn't ready for that, so he let the troll go on walking.

But maybe he was ready to go home. It was almost dark, but still early enough that Kham didn't feel underarmed with his Smith and Wesson .45 in his side holster and the Walther in the underarm sling. His thirty-six-centimeter survival knife slapped against his thigh, reminding him that he had blades as well: two cutters in boot sheaths and a half-dozen shivs in various other concealed sheaths. He had a pair of knucks in his jacket pocket, too. Not much, but then he'd be home before the real predators came out.

The people on the street were mostly orks now. Kham tried to tell himself that there were no more chipheads on the street than before, that it was just a change in the proportions of straight to chipped. But he knew better. There really were more of the simsense addicts and most of those new addicts were orks. Chipheads were lost in their simsense fantasies and rarely showed the caution a straight—norm or ork—would show. Day or night, they lived somebody else's life inside their heads. Who knew what time it was in there?

Kham buzzed. He kept aware of his surroundings, as was prudent, but he tried to tune out the chipheads. He wasn't very successful. Too many of them had his brother's face.

By the time he hit his neighborhood, he was really sour. He checked his stride as he turned onto Greely and saw three orks of his crew gathered in front of Wu's grocery. The guys were obviously keeping watch on somebody down the street. Kham cheered up; maybe there would be a little action to make him feel better. He started forward again, his step livelier. John Parker was the first to notice him coming.

"Hey, hoi, Kham. Where ya been, bossman?"

"'Round." They went through the ritual punching and tussles. "Whuzzappenin'? Got hostiles on the turf?"

"Nah," Rabo whined. "Nothing so much fun. Then again, maybe there will be fun. Got a suitboy looking for you by name."

"He's hanging over there," Ratstomper said, pointing with her head. A man stood in the shadows at the mouth of the alley, next to a fire-gutted tenement in the next block down. "Told him to wait. We knew you'd be along."

Kham looked and noted that the man was unfamiliar. He was also a stranger to Orktown. Though he was wearing a long coat, lined with armor no doubt, thrown open and back to reveal street-smart leathers, he was clearly not at home on the streets. He looked too nervous. Kham thought that he'd probably smell that way close up. This slag was a suit, no doubt about it.

The man was tall and on the thin side. Though too bulky for an elf, he might be mistaken for one by a less astute observer. He didn't fool Kham, though. He wondered if the suit knew how dangerous such a resemblance could be. If he did, he had plenty of reason to be nervous. The Ancients, an elf biker gang with no permanent territory but claiming all of Seattle for their own, had rumbled through two nights ago. Those elves had no friends in Orktown and had used their visit to make a few more enemies. Tempers were still up, and any elf, or even a human who looked like one, could end up the target of well-deserved hate. If the suitboy knew what had gone down, he was brave to come around without backup. It was surprising he'd gotten this far unmolested. Maybe the fact that Kham's guys were watching him had kept the other locals off the suitboy's back.

The man had noticed Kham's arrival and was trying to watch the orks without being obvious. The attempt was pathetically inept. The suit might be able to see them if his shades were set for light amplification or if he had enhanced eyes under those dark lenses, but his continual fussing said that he couldn't hear the orks.

"Let's see what da man has got ta say fer himself."

The guys trailed along with Kham, bouncing and hooting, in high spirits. They thought they were going to get work. Kham didn't want to let himself believe that just yet. It had been too long and disappointing a day. He walked right up to the suit and thrust out his chin.

"Hear yer looking fer Kham."

To his credit, the suit did not back away, although his nose wrinkled at Kham's smell. "Yes. Are you he?"

"Are you he?" Ratstomper said in imitation of the man. "Fancy, fancy for Orktown, chummer."

The others laughed at her remark, but the man held onto his calm. "Can you take me to him?"

"Might," Kham replied.

"There is remuneration in it for you."

Fancy words. Upscale words. The suitboy needed to be reminded of where he was, so Kham asked, "Re-what?"

"Money."

"Dat I understand." Rabo was nudging John Parker and grinning. "How much?"

"That depends on how quickly you take me to him."

"Dis is hot biz, den."

"There is a time element."

Turning, Kham backed up half a step, letting the man relax, then swung back. "Why Kham?"

Startled, the man was silent for a moment before blustering, ''I'll discuss *that* with him.''

Kham leaned into the man, eye to eye. His bulk was impressive and he let it have its usual effect on a norm. ''Ya tell me, or Kham never hears.'' The gang snickered behind him. Kham was hoping the man would take it as a threat. ''Well?''

The man was breathing heavily, and, yes, he did smell nervous. ''There is to be a trip. The persons taking it want protection. They are looking for discreet escorts who are able to handle themselves in case of trouble.''

''A muscle job.''

''As you say.''

''So ya come looking fer Kham. Maybe somebody else'll do?''

''Highly questionable. It is reported that this Kham leads an efficient group experienced in such matters and able to respond on short notice. In any case, my principals specified his group.''

The gang broke out in guffaws.

''Drek, Kham,'' Rabo burst out, ''if we used them big words ourselves, we could charge more.''

''You're Kham?'' the man stuttered.

Kham gave him a toothy grin. ''Whatsamatta, suitboy? Didn't dey give ya a pic ta spot me?''

''Of course, but I . . . I . . .''

Dropping the grin, Kham snarled. ''Yeah, right. Us orks all look alike. If ya ever bodder ta look. Let's get one ting straight, suitboy. We don't gotta like each odder ta do biz. And I don't like ya. Straight?''

Nodding, the man said shakily, ''I understand.''

''I doubt it,'' Kham said with a snort. ''What's yer schedule?''

''That you will have to discuss with, er, Mr. Johnson.''

Ratstomper piped up. ''Johnson? Johnson? That

name's familiar. Hey, John Parker, you ever hear of a Johnson doing biz in Seattle?''

''Johnson? Yeah I heard of him. He's the short, tall, fat, skinny guy, ain't he? A real Mr. Corp.''

''I tink ya may be right, John Parker.'' Kham poked the man with a horny-nailed finger. ''Okay, suitboy, when do we meet yer Mr. J.?''

''Ten o'clock at Club Penumbra. Back room three.''

Kham grabbed the man's shoulder and thrust him out into the street. ''Ya said yer piece. Vacate.''

Catching himself before he fell, the man straightened up, stiff with repressed anger, or maybe fear. His eyes would have told the tale, but they were hidden by his dark glasses. He mumbled something, then set about straightening his clothes. By the time he'd arranged himself to his satisfaction, a black Ares Citymaster was rolling down the street toward him. It didn't have Lone Star markings, but that didn't mean it wasn't the cops. The twin machine guns in the turret said that; police-issue cars mounted water cannons.

The armored riot vehicle stopped behind the suit. He gave the orks a last hard, unfriendly smile, then climbed in. Kham and the others didn't bother to watch the Citymaster roll away, but they stayed quiet until it was gone. John Parker was the first to speak.

''Hey, Kham, Penumbra is Sally's territory.''

Kham shrugged. ''Dis ain't Sally's kind of job.''

''You don't know dat,'' Ratstomper said.

Kham cuffed her. ''Lady Tsung ain't muscle. We're muscle. Dey's looking fer us. Dat means da Club's okay fer a meet. Even an elf-brain like you should be able to put dat tagedder.''

''So we taking it?'' Rabo asked.

''Maybe. Call Sheila and Cyg. And have the Weeze check the armory.''

Kham didn't know what the job was yet, but he knew

he needed it. They all did; it had been too long since their last run. And they needed more than the money; they needed a boost in their rep and a new chance to show just how tough they were. A good run now would start the biz rolling in again. Then let the other runners in town look out. He'd show them all that he could run a gang as smooth as Lady Tsung herself. He might not have the ju-ju Sally brought to her team, but his guys had plenty of firepower, and he hadn't yet met a wage mage who didn't bleed when you shot him. Guns were still a good way to take out opposition magicians. A bleeding mage had a lot more on his mind than backing up the rest of the corporate goon squad with magic.

This job was muscle spec and his guys were primo muscle, something the shadow side of Seattle was going to know real soon. But first they had the meet, and he had to get ready for that.

At long last, Kham was ready to go home.

2

Meeting face to face with a client was not business as usual for Neko Noguchi. Personal contact between principal and runner was a rare thing in the shadows of Hong Kong. That was what made this intriguing.

Most of those who employed him preferred to work through virtual conferences such as Magick Matrix offered. It was a clean, safe way to do business. No one need be concerned for personal safety, because the participants did not physically attend the meeting. They sat around the virtual conference room in the form of computer-generated icons of themselves, running no risk of physical or magical danger. No concern for eavesdroppers, either, as long as one trusted the Magick Matrix staff. And that was reasonable enough because Magick Matrix employed some of the best deckers in the world and their entire livelihood depended on their integrity. The firm was something like an old Swiss bank, except they dealt in conversations instead of money. Magick Matrix didn't care who you were, who you were talking to, or what you talked about; your conversation was the "money" they were safekeeping. All they asked was a fee for the service. Not always a small fee, either. That was something Neko understood; how could you trust someone to do something for you if he asked no compensation?

This meet had been arranged through just such a conference at Magick Matrix. Usually by now Neko would be running, or looking for another Mr. Johnson, but he had to be philosophical about it. The retainer that appeared on his credstick after the conference had, of course, made it much easier to be philosophical about the delay in getting to the heart of the matter.

Though meetings were intriguing in their own right and the byplay between prospective clients and him could be highly entertaining, he wasn't used to more than one interview for a run. He couldn't decide if he found the necessity for a second interview an insult, or a goad; the unusual always made him want to know more. A second layer of security might mean that the principal was paranoid, a not unlikely scenario in this world. It could also mean that this matter was one of import. Either way, there was business to do.

Without a doubt, his rep was spreading, and that pleased him.

Pleasure always came after business, unless it was a part of the business—as satisfying his curiosity would be. Having reached the place appointed for the meet,

Neko had the urge to stop and consider it for a moment, but if he stood in the middle of the street staring up at Logan Tower, the crowds bustling around him would probably either bowl him over or sweep him completely away. At the very least, some minor predator would mark him as a target and try to lighten his burden by removing valuables from his person. Though he had no fear of the second possibility, Neko was concerned about the first. The crowd was beyond his abilities to control. To remove their threat, he stepped out of the traffic flow into the lee of a vegetable stand. The scrawny, over-priced legumes had no interest for him, but the cart on which they were piled shielded him from the torrent of humanity surging along the street. He looked up.

Logan Tower was one of the newer buildings on the island, and one of the tallest in the world. As one of the new skyscrapers of the new world, it had few rivals. Even the previous century's giants like the now fallen Sears-IBM Tower and the Empire State Building could not have matched it. Logan Tower had been built after the megacorporations had asserted their control over the Hong Kong territory and disposed of the British stalking horses who had led the re-separation of Hong Kong from China. The tower was an arrogant spire, thrusting like an angry finger from the fist of lesser skyscrapers and pseudo-arcologies. It was a gesture to the mainland, made by defiant corporate interests.

Logan Tower embodied the open and free commerce of the city. Though no single megacorp owned it, or even occupied a majority of its space, many had offices there. Even the frail and self-important local government was housed among its many levels. But commerce was Logan Tower's reason for existence and commerce was its lifeblood. Commerce, of a sort, had brought Neko here today.

He thought about checking his appearance, but could see no effective way to do so. He had to take it on faith that the suit he wore for the meet was as impeccable as when he'd put it on. It was a salaryman's suit, the uniform of a corporate drone, and Neko had arranged the rest of his appearance to match. As his master had so often said, "To blend, everything must appear as it should, nothing must be out of place." Including attitude. He assumed the self-centered, casually arrogant stance of a moderately highly placed corporate wage slave, and strode through the crowd.

The crowd accepted him, the lesser strata parting in deference and those of his apparent rank accommodating him wordlessly into their own navigation plans. The guards at the tower's entrance let him pass without a glance, but those at the second barrier, who controlled access to the lifts serving the upper reaches of the tower, were less nonchalant. Nevertheless, the identification and access cards he offered them were satisfactory to their computers. They passed him through.

Neko relaxed a little when he was safely into the elevator. There had been a small possibility that the cards he had been provided at Magick Matrix might have been designed to entrap him here. That possibility still remained, for a bad interview might see the cards cancelled before he could ride the lift back to ground level. A paranoid thought, perhaps, but then paranoia was life in the shadows. Surreptitiously, he checked the hidden pocket where he carried a second set of cards, courtesy of Cog, his fixer.

The car stopped on the seventy-fifth floor, a floor devoted to an exclusive club. Neko exited, crossing the Persian carpet and then through the wood-paneled foyer to the podium. The man standing behind it was well-dressed and groomed, in an oily sort of way. He would be the maitre d'. He spoke as soon as Neko had closed to a reasonable distance.

"Good day, sir. Welcome to our establishment. You are . . . ?"

"Watanabe," Neko replied, using the name on the identity card he carried.

"Ah yes, Watanabe-*san*. You are expected. Please follow me."

The restaurant was mostly empty, no surprise, as it was only late afternoon, well before the corporate crowd would be dining. Neko knew at once which table the maitre d' was leading him toward. It was the only occupied one in the section.

Two persons sat there, a shapely young woman with ash blonde hair and a slim older man. The woman was discreetly dressed, her clothes of excellent cut and material. Golden bangles sparkled from her ears, fingers, wrists, and neck, but on her they did not seem ostentatious. Neko judged the woman to be an aide to the man, but her beauty made him wonder if she was skilled in other duties as well. Her eyes lifted to meet his and he immediately sensed the animal sensuality about her. She whispered to her companion.

The man looked up and fixed Neko with a stare. Like his companion, he was Caucasian, and by his dress and appearance, a gentleman in the European style. Neko found it hard to judge his age; the man's gray hair was cut in an outdated style and the poise of his movements suggested the casual confidence born of decades of cultured living. Yet his face showed few lines, and barely more on the generally more revealing hands. Of course, there were techniques to hide age, but Neko's sharp eyes saw none of the usual marks. Neko placed the man as a well-preserved fifty. Unlike his companion, he wore only a single piece of jewelry: a silver ring wrought in the shape of a dragon adorned his right hand. The man smiled, revealing gold incisors. A curious affectation, Neko thought.

"Your guest, Mr. Enterich," the maitre d' announced, then left.

Enterich rose and started to extend a hand, then stopped himself and bowed in the oriental fashion. A shallow bow, Neko noted, one suitable for a superior upon meeting an inferior. Neko made the proper complementary bow. Then he made one to the woman, the kind suitable to another of equal stature. She merely inclined her head, remaining seated and dazzling him with a smile.

"Please be seated, Mr. Noguchi," she said. "Or do you prefer to be addressed as Neko?"

Had he misjudged who was the superior and who the inferior? The maitre d' had referred to Neko as the man's guest, but that could be merely an assumption on the headwaiter's part or a deliberate deception for the benefit of observers. Caution was indicated until he understood the situation better. Neko smiled at her, and him, as he took a seat. "Here, either will do. As I am a guest, I surrender my preferences to yours."

"Neko, then," she said. "We wish this to be a friendly arrangement. My name is Karen Montejac."

"And I am Enterich."

"You are free with your names," Neko observed.

The gold flashed in Enterich's smile. "As are you, Neko. Also like you, our names are not to be found in any public database."

An assertion Neko would test after the meeting. He'd try a few private databases as well. But that was a matter for later consideration; Enterich was still speaking.

"Business can wait until after we dine, can it not? As I understand it, that is the practice in your native Japan."

"It is the practice," Neko said, leaving unsaid the

fact that he was Japanese, but not a native of Japan. He would let them believe otherwise; such a false assumption on their part might be useful later.

The meal, unsurprisingly, was superb, and the talk, though remaining inconsequential, pleasant. Both Enterich and his—as became obvious during the course of their dinner—aide were facile and engaging conversationalists, well-acquainted with the region's folklore and history. Neko even thought he detected a glimmer of more than professional interest in Ms. Montejac's eyes. *Perhaps later,* he promised himself, with a reminder of pleasure's place in business. When the last plate of empty lobster shells had been carried away and a fresh pot of tea brought, Enterich spoke seriously.

"I am looking for a person of discretion, Neko. Are you that sort of person?"

"Great discretion is available, Mr. Enterich. For a price."

"Cannot indiscretion be bought as well?" Karen asked.

"From some, perhaps, but not from Neko. There is some honor in the shadows."

"That is the answer I expected from you, Neko," Enterich said. "You are well-spoken of in certain quarters."

Neko inclined his head in acceptance of the compliment.

"We shall proceed, then." Enterich's finger absently traced the dragon design on the teacup before him. "Though you have likely concluded that I am the principal in this matter, I should tell you that I am only acting as an agent. Others are seeking to assemble a team for a certain operation, a bit of business in which they anticipate some danger. I believe that your credentials as part of the force used by Samuel Verner uniquely qualify you to become a part of this team."

Caught off-guard by the reference, Neko blurted out, "You know of that?"

Enterich's gold teeth flashed. "I have had dealings with Mr. Verner in the past and retain an interest in his doings."

So ka. Was this another of Verner's runs? Or was this just a result of Neko's growing rep? Either way, Enterich had sought Neko out specifically, but there was still a hesitancy here, a caution. A probe was called for. Neko restored calm to his voice.

"If you are aware of that run, you are aware of the kind of results I can achieve."

"You will not have Striper at your side," Karen said.

"I have worked without partners before."

"This is not a solo run," Enterich said quickly.

"Then I must confess to some confusion," Neko said. "Your approach implies that you believe me to be the person you seek, yet your tone suggests some uncertainty about my qualifications."

"It is not my wish to confuse you, Neko. Nor to suggest that you are unqualified. Qualifications are not at issue, nor is interest. Say, rather, that any hesitancy on our part is born of concern over willingness."

"Price, then."

Enterich laughed. "You are unusually direct for a Japanese. But price is a matter for later discussion. I speak of a different sort of willingness." He paused, making a show of seeking the right words. "It is well known that most, ah, persons of your trade wish to operate exclusively where they have a secure net of contacts and intimate knowledge of their territory. I'm afraid that this job will require some travel on your part."

"Paid for, of course."

"Of course," Enterich said. "Your involvement with Verner suggested that you had a wider outlook than many of your colleagues."

"Competitors," Neko corrected.

"Competitors." Enterich accepted the correction with a nod. "This matter will require that you travel to Seattle."

Neko leaned back in his chair. He could feel his excitement and hoped he was hiding it well enough. As if there were any doubt that he would agree! Seattle meant North America and an entry into UCAS, the United Canadian and American States. He had always wanted to see the States. Aloofly, he said, "If I agree."

"Yes, of course." Enterich smiled at him. "If you agree."

Neko's mind raced. America! UCAS, with its spy nets, the quixotic southern Confederated American States, the exotic Native American Nations, and the sinister Atzlan! Such fertile ground for shadowrunning. The big-league shadowrunner circuit. Once in the States, he would find many opportunities to employ his skills. He would make a name for himself in the land that had spawned modern shadowrunning. He'd meet the legends of the trade. Maybe even meet the elven decker Dodger in person or even the shadowy Sam Verner himself.

He raised his teacup and said, "The European custom involves a drink on agreement, *so ka*?"

"It does, but not usually tea." Despite his words, Enterich raised his cup and touched it to Neko's. "Let us drink, then, and get down to details."

3

A bunch of half-grown ork kids from the hall, Kham's son Jord among them, tore past Kham as he turned the corner onto Beckner Street. They were chasing something that yowled when the leader of the pack struck it with the stick he carried. Each yowl from the prey brought a chorus of jubilant hoots from the pursuers and a change in the leader of the pack. When the leader missed his stroke, the hoots were derisive and the failed swinger dropped to the back of the pack. Kham watched them for a while, smiling. The prey was quick and agile, so the kids' reflexes would get a good workout before they brought whatever it was home for the stewpot.

Food, especially for the crew that filled the hall, was always a problem. Beyond what they could buy, scrounge, or catch, they had access to government rationing, thanks to the widow Asa's pension. The beef-soy cakes they got for the coupons were far more soy than beef, but that was not surprising. The Native American Nations controlled most of the prime beef-land, and though the federal government had culture tanks, the corps usually raided them for their dependents well before the government got its share. Wherever the beef went, it wasn't into the soy cakes they gave to the good, but poor, citizens of UCAS. The beef-soy they got for the widow's coupons might be okay nutrition-wise, but it tasted like ashes and there never was enough. Any meat the kids brought in would flavor and add more protein to the stew.

If they'd had more SINs in the hall, they'd have more

food, but they didn't. Asa was the only one with a SIN, a system identification number, which she needed to get her government pension and the ration coupons. The disenfranchised, like Kham's family and the rest of the hall's residents, were not even entitled to that. They weren't in the computers: numbered, tagged, and ready to be processed. Without a nice corporate system identification number neither were they eligible for the government dole or even any of the corporate ones. They were outside the system, scraping up what they could to get by.

Sure they could buy meat in a store just like anybody else, if they had the money. Or they could go to the black market, where the meat was cheaper but you never knew how safe it was. The net result was that fresh meat was a luxury they couldn't afford except when somebody made a score or the kids brought something home from the alleys. Kham hadn't gotten a good look at what they were hunting, but he hoped it wasn't cat again. He hated the taste.

Thoughts of food made his stomach growl, reminding him that supper time was near. He sauntered on down the street, sniffing the air and checking the signs. There were no strange odors, no new marks of violence, no signs of alarm. His neighborhood was as quiet and as safe as it got. There were still some kids from the hall across the street playing around the wrecked or nearly wrecked vehicles that lined the sidewalk. Here in Orktown, there was no towing for the junkers or off-street parking for the workers. Everything was left until it rotted away, like the garbage.

Like a lot of the orks in Orktown, Kham and the others called their communal house a hall. Word on the street was that the ancient Vikings used to live all together in a hall, and everybody knew Vikings were tough; orks were tough, too. Calling their places halls made it a little easier to deal with the squalor, Kham supposed. If you couldn't live in a palace, at least you could pretend you did. Kham's hall was a run-down structure that had once been a store. His family and the half-dozen others of his home group lived there, bedding down in the upper stories and doing most of their day-to-day living in the lower story, which was mostly kitchen and open space.

As he turned off Wilkerson Boulevard, Kham could see that the hall was lit. A trio of young orks, all wearing Black Sword colors, waited idly near the front steps. Like the kids from the other halls in the neighborhood, kids from Kham's hall joined a gang when they were old enough, or good enough. The gang provided local security, more reliable than the police, and halls that had kids in the gang didn't even have to pay for the service.

The biggest of the three, the obvious leader, straightened up when he saw Kham approaching. That was Guido, one of John Parker's brood. Guido was a shadowrunner wannabe, always trying to act like he thought a runner ought to.

"Hoi, Kham," he said in a casually familiar drawl. " 'Zappening?"

"Hoi, Guido."

A little miffed by Kham's ignoring his question, Guido tried again. "Got work?"

"Could be."

Guido elbowed one of the others and gave him a conspiratorial wink. "Better, or Lissa'll have your balls for breakfast."

Kham was too tired to play games. His response caught Guido totally off-guard. The young ork made only a feeble, futile effort to block the paw that reached for his throat. Exerting a mere fraction of his strength, Kham lifted the boy off the ground. Guido struggled to take the pressure from his throat by keeping his balance on his toes. Kham smiled grimly into Guido's purpling face and said, ''Watch out *your* balls aren't on the menu.''

''Hey, he didn't mean anything by it, Kham,'' one of the others pleaded.

''Yeah,'' the other chimed in. ''Everybody says that, ya know. Like it's not a secret.''

Giving them a squint-eyed stare, Kham said, ''Yeah? Well, if everybody knows, ya don't need ta say anyting about it.''

''Chill, man,'' Guido choked out. ''I'm a sphinx.''

''Nah. Ain't good-looking enough,'' Kham said, releasing the boy. ''Or tough enough.''

''Hey, man, I'm tough,'' Guido whined, rubbing his throat. ''Take me on a run, I'll show you.''

Not if you can't take a little rough treatment. ''Gotta walk before ya can run, Guido.''

Recovering his former bravado, Guido straightened up and said, ''I'm ready. You got a job and need some more muscle, I'm the orkboy for you.''

Guido's quick recovery was a good sign. The boy was still a little young to move up, but he had talent. Maybe in a year or two. Kham decided to be encouraging. ''Could be. Keep hanging till I call ya.''

Kham walked up the steps, listening to the gibes of Guido's companions as they started in on the boy. They'd sort it out. If an ork couldn't survive his own gang, he didn't have any business looking to tackle *anybody* else.

As he stepped through the door, the familiar scent of ork and old food washed over him, blotting out the refuse scent of the street. The light was brighter than in the street, but not enough to bother him, nor was it enough to really illuminate the squalor. The main room, what had once been a show room, was littered with debris and randomly scattered piles of bedding, but, he was pleased to see, no garbage. The chamber was furnished in early junkyard; its broken-down chairs, stained and ripped couches, and tables of jumbled scraps gave it an air of bedraggled but comfy chaos. In one corner an unwatched monitor, the coils of its illegal cable hook-up snarled around its base, blared out the latest video from Maria Mercurial, courtesy of one of the music channels.

Someday, he promised himself. Someday they wouldn't have to live here.

He could hear shouts from the kitchen. Teresa was calling one of the kids down for snitching from the pot. Almost immediately a knot of kids came brawling through the archway. Catching sight of him, one of them shouted, ''Kham's back!'' As the brawl tumbled past him and into the stairway hall a small missile launched itself out of the melee. Kham caught the hurtling ork child, his oldest son Tully, and pivoted in place, swinging Tully at arm's-length. The child squealed in delight.

Twice more around, then he tossed Tully high, catching him under the arms and lowering him to the floor. ''More!'' the child yelled. Kham complied, as always. Out the corner of his eye, he could see Shandra, Tully's littermate, staring from the doorway. Setting Tully down and tousling his hair to stifle his cries of ''More!'', Kham spoke to his daughter. ''Hello, Shandy.''

''Hello, daddy.''

Crouching closer to her height, he said, ''Come give me a hug.''

Shandra hugged herself and shook her head.

It was the way she was most of the time now. He hoped it was just a phase. He straightened and took off his jacket, hanging it on a peg and slinging his weapon belt over it. He held his arms out to his daughter. ''Come to daddy.'' She remained where she was, staring. He followed her gaze, dropping his eyes to his artificial hand. The chrome gleamed softly in the low light, a shiny ghost of the flesh that had been. He took a step toward her and she bolted back to the kitchen.

"You don't need her, Daddy," Tully said, affixing himself to Kham's leg.

Kham scooped him up. The boy gave his father a squeeze around the neck, then settled back to nestle in the strong sweep of Kham's arm. Tully reached out a hand and ran it along the smooth plastic of the flesh-metal interface and down over the rigid alloy of Kham's hand. "It's hard, Dad. Like you."

"Ya gonna be hard when yer big, Tully?"

"Uh-huh."

"That's my boy," Kham said, with a delighted smile.

Kham heard familiar footsteps approaching. Lissa. He turned to face her. She was as beautiful as ever, if a bit tousled from her work in the kitchen. Her tusks, delicate and fine, gleamed like old ivory. They showed particularly clear when she was frowning, which she was now. She stopped about a meter away and put one hand on her hip while the other unconsciously caressed Shandra's head. Clinging to her mother's leg, the girl sobbed softly. Lissa said some quiet words to her before looking at Kham.

"About time."

"Had a meet."

She looked at him for a moment, then bent down and whispered to Shandra. The girl nodded her head and ran toward the kitchen. Lissa straightened to face Kham again. "You've got a run then."

"Most likely. Got another meet tonight."

She folded her arms. "This better not be another story, Kham. We need the money."

"We'll get it."

"And I don't need the grief." Taking a step forward, she tugged Tully from his arms. Setting him down, she said, ''Get along, Tully. Teresa needs your help in the kitchen.''

''Aw, Mom.''

''Go!''

Tully sulked off.

''We were playing,'' Kham said.

''He's got work, even if no one else around here does. You think this hall runs itself?''

Kham knew from experience that she didn't really want an answer to that question. In fact, she went on to answer it herself in an all-too-familiar tirade. He shouldn't have been gone so long. He shouldn't get in the way around the hall. He should've brought home some money. He shouldn't keep the kids from doing their chores. And on and on and on. He nodded in the right places and shook his head in the other right places. He lost his appetite as his stomach went sour. Why did it have to be this way?

For all her harping, he still loved her. He wanted to tell her that. He reached out a hand to gather her to him, realizing too late that he had reached out with his right. She flinched away from him, a flash of horror reflected in the chrome of his hand. Then she stood her ground and let him gather her in his arms.

''I love ya,'' he said.

She said nothing.

''It's gonna be all right.''

''How can you say that, Kham? Everything's different now.''

Her voice was shaky. He knew she was worried, scared for the kids mostly. That was what made her shrill so often now. He caressed her hair with his right hand and she shivered, so he stopped. ''Nuttin's changed.''

''It has,'' she said softly.

He knew her words for truth. Ever since he'd gotten his cybernetic replacements, Lissa had been different, cold and distant. She shuddered when he touched her with the replacement hand. It was easier sometimes not to touch her at all.

"Dere's lotsa guys wid enhancements on da streets. Orks, too. Their chicas don't got problems wit dem."

"It's not real."

"But I ain't no vat-grown corp monster. I'm still me. Kham, yer husband. An artificial hand and syntetic muscles in my leg don't change dat."

"I haven't left you, have I?"

"No."

"I've been a good wife, haven't I? I take care of the kids. I feed this crew and run herd on this brawl you call a hall. You can't say I don't."

"No, I can't." They both knew that the street was not a nice place, and there were damned few shelters that didn't want a SIN before they did anything for you. It was all part of the system, which didn't work for orks like them.

"If it wasn't fer da implants, I'd be a crip. I wouldn't be able ta take care of ya and da kids."

"I know that."

"I still love ya and da kids."

"I know that."

But Lissa didn't sound like she really believed it. "I didn't abandon ya, like John Parker did his woman when he took up shadowrunning. And yer not a widow, like Teresa, Asa, or Komiko. What if I'da died on dose runs last year fer Sam Verner? What if I'da died aboard dat damned, drowned sub like Teresa and Komiko's men? What woulda happened ta ya and da kids den?"

"I don't know."

"An honest answer at least." He held her tight, careful to keep his replacement hand from touching her flesh. "But I did survive dose runs even dough da first cost me my hand and part 'a my leg. Drek! I survived da run and was back up in time ta go on annoder inta dat damned bug-filled submarine fer da dogboy. It takes a tough guy ta get back up dat fast, and I'm tough. I'm a survivor, babe. I'm a rough, tough ork like I gotta be."

"Not every ork is as tough as you," she said, breaking free of his embrace.

"Don't I know it."

"Well, you don't know everything!" She ran away, crying.

Kham just stood there, confused and frustrated. He never seemed able to find the words Lissa wanted to hear. He thought about going after her, but what good would it do? After the meet, when he had some money, things would be better.

As he stood there lost in his thoughts, Jord and the rest of the hunters came into the hall, prancing and shouting. "Hey, dad! Look what I caught," Jord yelled, swinging his prize by the tail. A cat.

Kham looked at it with distaste. "Take it inta da kitchen, boy."

"Sure." The victorious hunters continued their parade toward the back of the hall. Jord looked over his shoulder. "You coming, Dad?"

"Ya go ahead, Jord. Dad's gotta do some biz."

Facing Lissa over the table would be bad enough. But cat, too? He strapped on his weapon belt and ripped his jacket from the peg and slung it over his shoulder. He stomped up the stairs to the room his family used for a bedroom. From the locked case in the bottom of the closet he took a skeletal-stocked assault rifle, an AK-74 special. Working with sure hands, he broke it down and concealed the parts in pockets sewn to the lining of his jacket. He had a meet tonight at ten and he might need a little extra insurance. There wouldn't be time to come back here if he was to make a stop before the meet. He stomped back down the stairs and out into the street.

The third pay phone he tried was working. He slipped in his credstick and punched in the telecom code. The line opened and a recorded voice started speaking. He waited a moment, then tapped in a code that Sally Tsung gave to only a few people. The code patched him through to another line. The voice that answered this time was live, female, but not Sally herself.

"Hello."

"Dis is Kham. Sally in?"

"She's not here right now. May I take a message?"

"Gotta talk wit her."

"Business?"

"Looks like it."

A moment's pause, and then, "She'll be at Penumbra tonight. Around eleven."

"Club's okay but da time's no good. Need ta see her 'fore dat."

"When?"

"Nine."

"I'll tell her when she checks in," the voice said, then the connection broke.

Kham slammed the receiver down. Drek! There was no way to know whether Sally would get the message in time to meet with him. There was nothing to do but go to the club and hope she showed.

* * *

It was quarter past nine when Sally Tsung walked into Club Penumbra. She strolled in like she owned the place, a common enough attitude for top-rank shadowrunners. Her armor-lined coat was of real leather, stitched with arcane symbols and fringed along the arms and lower edges. Billowing out behind her, the coat opened to reveal what she wore underneath, which wasn't much: a halter top, cut-off jeans, and knee-high boots. Crossed weapon belts rode low on her hips, a pistol holster on one and a scabbarded magesword on the other. She nodded to Jim at the bar, her shock of blonde hair bobbing over her forehead. The rest of her hair was bound back into a rat-tail braid that snaked around from behind her neck and slithered down between her breasts to lie over the constraining strings of her leather halter. She was a street mage, as lean, hard, and dangerous as they came. And she was every bit as beautiful as the day she had first recruited Kham, and more unreachable than ever. Still, he couldn't help grinning at her as she slouched into the seat across the table from him.

"Hello, Kham. How's my favorite hunk of ork flesh tonight?"

"Hello, Sally. Doing okay. You?"

"Living the life, doing the scene." She shrugged her shoulders with casual negligence. "Hear you got a party starting."

As he'd suspected from seeing her in her working clothes, she was in a business frame of mind and not interested in social chat. So, he complied. "Looks dat way. Got a meet fer da job here at ten, muscle only on da spec, but ya taught me shadowrunning too good. I want an ace in da hole, a magical ace."

"I understand the lay of the land, Kham." She gazed off across the bar. "But I'm afraid I can't help. I've got something cooking myself."

"Ya didn't call me."

"Nothing personal, Kham." She still didn't look at him. "It's just not your sort of biz."

"What about my run?"

"Null perspiration, chummer. There's lots of magic children on the streets these days. You can take your pick."

Sure there were magicians out there, but she was

the only mage he would trust. Without magical aid, he was left to rely on his orks and their mundane firepower. Magic might not be common everywhere in the world, but shadowrunners had a tendency to run into it, and that was the possibility that worried him. "Maybe I only want da best."

She faced him, a wide, warm smile on her face. "Ooh, flattery. You tempt me, chummer, but a girl has to honor her commitments and I've already got one. Tell you what, though. Just for old times' sake, I'll run cover for you at the meet."

"No cost?"

Her smile was sweet. "I could ask for a percentage, but you're a chummer. Besides, I have to be here anyway."

* * *

Kham's guys arrived in a bunch only half an hour after the time he had told them. Not bad for them: they were only ten minutes behind the time he wanted them there. Punctuality before a run was always a problem with them. Fortunately, that problem disappeared when things got warmer.

They joined him and started drinking. Just beer, nothing to queer the meet. With each round, Kham watched the tab go up, but the job would pay for it, he hoped.

Sally was hanging out at her usual table in the back, screened from most of the noise of the dance floor. It was still early and the crowd was light. Big Tom the sasquatch was doing the warm-up show, all instrumental pieces that he could imitate with amazing facility. The club's real action wouldn't start until later.

A pair of rough boys walked in. They were real hard cases, razorguys with lots of obvious cyberware. Both wore patches from a half-dozen mercenary units, implying that they'd seen action in some of the corporate

CATS
IS
GOOD
FOOD
LAUBENSTEIN · 92

fracas of the last ten years. One was a blond and the other a brunet, but otherwise they were identical. Cosmetic surgery probably. Something in their body language also made Kham wonder if they were lovers. The razorguys looked around, scanning the place. The blond said something to Jim at the bar and Jim nodded toward the back room. Kham was sure these two weren't the employers, so they had to be other applicants. Was there to be a bidding war for a place on the run?

A dwarf was the next runner Jim sent to the back room. Kham recognized him at once. The dwarf was Greerson, a West Coast heavy-hitter who spent most of his time down in California Free State. His presence definitely meant that others had been contacted about this run, and raised the odds of a bidding war. But any Mr. Johnson who wanted it discreet would be making a mistake to start taking competitive bids. The losers would have word of his run on the streets in nanoseconds.

Kham nodded to Rabo. Time for the guys to go in and show the flag. He hoped Sheila wouldn't let Greerson goad her into causing trouble before Kham was in there to keep her temper cool. There had been trouble between the two of them before.

Kham waited a while longer. He was almost ready to go in himself when another stranger approached Jim. This one was a small Asian, Japanese maybe, who was no taller than the dwarf but slighter by a wide margin. Young, too, for a norm shadowrunner. The Asian had a whispered conversation with Jim, who then sent him on back. Another runner, definitely, but what sort of specialty? Maybe a decker? He sure wasn't big enough for a frontline fighter and he didn't have the look of a magicboy.

"Your Mr. Johnson's an elf," Sally's voice whispered in Kham's ear a few minutes later as a tall man in a long trench coat approached the bar.

Confident that she would hear, Kham whispered his thanks and rose from his seat. He caught up with the elf before he reached the door to the back room. He didn't surprise him, though, because the elf turned as Kham approached. With a wide, toothy grin Kham said, "Evening, Mr. Johnson."

"You're Kham."

"Right."

The elf looked over Kham's shoulder. "You are alone?"

"My guys are waiting inside. Along wit a few other people. I wasn't told dis was a joint venture."

"You cannot expect to know all the details. I was informed that you were a professional. Professionals understand that secrecy is a necessity of business."

Kham leaned toward him. "Professionals expect fair deals, too."

The elf turned his head to the side as if offended by Kham's smell, but he didn't retreat. "I am prepared to offer a fair deal. To all. However, I am not prepared to cut separate deals with overly pushy persons of inflated ego. You will hear the deal along with the others, or you will not hear it at all."

Pulling back and allowing the elf his personal space, Kham said, "Yer gonna be late fer yer own meet, Mr. J."

"Perhaps you would care to precede me," the elf suggested.

Kham shrugged. "Ain't worried about having you behind my back, Mr. J."

Yet.

Kham opened the door and entered the room. The elven Mr. Johnson followed.

4

The runners gathered for the meet were a mixed lot, but that was no surprise to Neko. Mr. Enterich had said that this was to be an ad hóc team. He surveyed each runner carefully, trying to assess his or her role and potential value to the team. Many showed obvious cybernetic enhancements and all carried weapons. All the orks, save for one, seemed to be muscle types, too. The odd ork, Rabo, had datajacks in his head and a variety of logo patches on his jacket, most advertising manufacturers of automotive or aeronautic equipment. There seemed little doubt that the ork was a rigger, a vehicular technomancer.

Neko found the preponderance of orks curious, even a trifle unsettling. Until now his contact with runners of that metatype in Hong Kong had been only the most cursory; the less beautiful metahumans were not much welcome in the island's corporate enclaves. It was not that Neko himself felt any distaste; he had dealt with far less savory metatypes in his shadowy business. He watched the orks curiously. Their easy familiarity with one another led him to conclude that they had run together in the past.

The orks named the dwarf for Neko: Greerson. Though they obviously didn't like him, Neko could see that they knew him, possibly had even worked with him in the past. Greerson's name was not unknown to Neko, and he knew that a runner with the dwarf's reputation within the international shadowrunning community would not come cheap. Mentally, Neko raised his own price for any upcoming bargaining; one could not afford to be seen as of less value than one's fellows.

The other two runners were a matched pair of heavily modified norms, "razorguys," in common street parlance. One was a blond and the other dark-haired, but the faces beneath their thatches of hair were identical. That need not be natural; Neko thought it more likely that they had chosen to have their features altered to match. Such artificiality would seem to be to their taste. Neko found their reliance on machinery more distasteful than the brutish forms of the orks, and so, like the others, he mostly ignored the razorguys. Such division would not serve on the run, but neither should he be forced to accept unpalatable companions in circumstances unrelated to the biz.

The door opened and admitted a blast of noise from the band starting to warm up in the main room. The sound was muffled briefly as a burly ork squeezed through the doorway. Dressed in leathers and fatigues, the metahuman entered and looked around with an air of casual caution that marked a man who was no stranger to dangerous places. Following hard on the ork's heels was the elven Mr. Johnson who Neko had met briefly upon his arrival in Seattle. The elf's clothes were different now, as were his hair and the fashionable face paint. Despite the superficial differences, the frown that darkened the slimmer metahuman's features when the ork put an arm around his shoulders told Neko that this was the same elf. It was not a lover's embrace, more a possessive statement of control. The elf was clearly discomfited by the contact, but the ork was only amused, to judge by his half-concealed grin.

"'Bout time," Greerson grumbled.

The elf ignored him and shrugged away from contact with the ork. Unfazed by his rejection, the big ork joined the others of his kind, with shoulder-slapping and arm-punching all around. The others addressed him as Kham, another name Neko recognized as associated with that of Sally Tsung, a runner and magician of no little reputation in certain circles. Neko had once heard the ork mentioned as muscle for one of Tsung's operations. As he recalled, that run had been successful, but one run did not a career make. Perhaps Kham's presence meant that Sally Tsung was involved in this operation, or possibly Tsung's decker Dodger. That would shift the balance in this muscle-heavy crowd. If one or both of them were on the run, Neko decided it would be a good omen.

The elf walked around the table and took the empty seat at the head. "Good evening, gentlemen, and lady," he said, with a condescending nod to Sheila. A broad-shouldered female ork the others referred to as The Weeze snarled, and the elf amended his salutation. "Ah, excuse me, ladies. I'm glad to see that you are all punctual."

"Unlike some people," Greerson said.

Neko noted that Kham glanced openly around the table, obviously assessing the gathered runners. The ork stared curiously at Neko for a moment, a slight frown on his face. He seemed puzzled by Neko's presence in this crowd of heavy muscle. Neko offered him a slight smile. Let the ork wonder.

"I have for each of you a paper describing the deal," the elf said, passing a sheet to each of them. "Please read it quickly, as the paper is unstable and will decompose in a few minutes."

Greerson barely glanced at his sheet before tossing it to the table. "Price is too low."

Neko checked the compensation line on his sheet, and surreptitiously compared it to the sheets held by one of the razorguys and The Weeze, on either side of him. Both were the same as his. Likely, Greerson's was too. Though the sum was more than Neko was used to receiving for a simple bodyguard run, he said, "Greerson-*san* is correct."

The elf's stony expression did not change. "The fee was previously agreed upon, Mr. Greerson, Mr. Neko."

Greerson raised one stubby leg onto the table's edge and levered his chair back until it rested on two legs. "First price is always negotiable, especially when you got this many bodies involved."

"The number involved is not your concern. You were informed of your remuneration for this run. If you had a concern regarding compensation, you could have expressed it earlier."

"If I'd had any idea how many bodies you were talking, I would have. The money's definitely too low for me to play traffic cop."

Kham addressed the elf. "If da dwarf won't play, we can replace him wit anodder of our guys."

"Replace me?" Greerson laughed. "I didn't know you had fifty more warm bodies, orkboy."

"Don't need fifty to replace you, halfer," Sheila growled. She was the ork who had shown blatant dislike upon seeing Greerson. Clearly, the two had a history.

"You're right, orkgirl. If you're a typical example of the quality, you'll need more."

Kham gave Sheila a look that quieted her, then said. "Look, Greerson, ya don't wanna work, dat's okay. Buzz, and let da rest of us get on wit da biz." The dwarf tried to start a stare-down, but Kham turned and addressed the elf. "Look, dis crew's all muscle. We facing any magic in da opposition?"

"Do not concern yourself," the elf replied quickly, having apparently anticipated such a question. "Any magical problems will be more than sufficiently countered."

"Heard that before," said the blond cyberboy.

"And it was a lie then, too," his dark-haired companion added.

The elf gave them a plastic smile, shared it with the rest of the runners, and said, "Gentlemen, and ladies, I assure you that this run has a low probability of trouble."

Greerson spoke for them all. "Then why so much firepower?"

Again, the elf answered rapidly. "Insurance only. My employer is a cautious sort. You are all to be present simply as fire support in case of trouble. Trouble, I might add, that is most unlikely to come."

"And if it does?" asked the raven-haired cyberboy.

"What then?" the blond cyberboy queried.

"Then, you perform as per contract."

"For which we will receive a combat bonus," Greerson stated.

The elf stared at him. "That is not stipulated in the contract."

Making a sour face, Greerson said, "Maybe you ought to think about putting it in."

Narrowing his eyes, the elf spoke through gritted teeth. "There are other runners."

"Which you won't be able to line up on your short fuse, elf. You've got top talent here." Greerson paused to scan the orks. "Well, mostly, anyway. You won't be able to match this line-up in your time frame."

"Your suggestion has the smell of extortion, Mr. Greerson." The elf's voice was low, almost threatening.

"Call it what you want, elf. I'll still only think of it as good business."

"I am not authorized to increase the up-front payment."

"That's fine. I'm not a bandit. Deposit a suitable amount in a secured account and I'll be satisfied," Greerson offered cheerfully.

"I must confer with my employer."

"You do that. But confer to a substantial monetary conclusion, otherwise you may find nobody to dance with you when it's time to rock and roll."

"You realize that all participants must share in any increase, Mr. Greerson."

"Sure. I ain't greedy. So long as there's a double share for me, everything will be fine."

Sheila snorted. "Double for a halfer? Seems like that only adds up to a single share."

Without looking at her, Greerson said, "Did I say double? I meant triple. I forgot the charge for excessive aggravation."

Sheila started around the table, but Rabo and The Weeze scurried around to block her. Greerson remained seated, unflappable. The cyberboys watched tensely, though their placid expressions did not change. The elven Mr. Johnson looked on with detached amusement. As the orks restrained their own, Neko wondered if his trip to America was turning out to be what he had hoped. A dead runner had no prospects, and an unstable team made for dead runners.

The fair-haired cyberboy asked for a clarification on one of the points in the synopsis, and Mr. Johnson elaborated. There were a handful of other questions, Johnson fielding each in turn and dismissing the runners' concerns. Sometime in the middle of a discussion of the timing for the rendezvous with Johnson outside the city, the papers started to crumble. The meeting followed suit. After going around the table and asking each runner if he or she agreed to the run, the elf left. Greerson and the cyberboys vacated the premises with identical dispatch, leaving Neko alone with the orks. Neko took the opportunity to approach Kham.

"I thought we might coordinate efforts to cross the border to the rendezvous point."

The big ork looked down at him, the expression on his misshapen face slightly quizzical. He rubbed the stub of his broken lower tusk. "Ya wanta cooperate?"

"That is a wise course, is it not?" Neko said, giving his most polite smile.

"Yeah, sometimes." The ork nodded. "Why ya talking ta me and not dem odder guys?"

"You are the Kham who has run with Sally Tsung and The Dodger?"

The ork's expression changed to a frown. "Ain't seen ya around town before."

"I have only recently arrived."

"So how da ya know who I run wit?" the ork asked suspiciously.

"I am in the biz."

The ork didn't like that answer, for his eyes narrowed to slits. "You know da dogboy?"

"I do not understand your reference."

"Verner." At Neko's blank look, Kham added, "His street name is Twist."

So ka. This ork was smarter than he looked, to turn the probe around so quickly. Would the ork prefer an affirmative or a negative response to his question? The metahuman's physiognomy was different enough that Neko could not easily read his expression. Let the truth serve. "I have been involved in some of his biz."

The ork's smile was particularly toothy. "Den maybe ya won't be a liability."

Neko had been thinking reciprocal thoughts about the ork. "You need have no fears in that regard."

"Confident pup."

The comment seemed uncalled for. "Pup is slang for a young dog, is it not? My name means 'cat' in English, so that makes your remark inaccurate. And if I understand the contextual use correctly, it is doubly inappropriate."

"No need ta get in an uproar, catboy." In a bewildering shift, the ork's mood changed and he laughed. "Why'd ya wanta know if I know Sally and da elf?"

"A personal matter."

With another mercurial shift, the ork became serious. "Look, kid. I may not like da elf much, but I ain't gonna set him up, and if yer looking ta make trouble fer Lady Tsung, yer gonna be lying in da streets instead of walking on 'em."

There was no mistaking the ork's fierce loyalty to Sally Tsung. Perhaps it was even more than loyalty. In any case, mollification was in order. "It's nothing like that, I assure you. I just want to meet them face to face."

"Don't know where da elf is. And da Lady's busy." The last was said with a frown. Kham was obviously unhappy about something to do with his relationship with Tsung.

Further elaboration might be enlightening. "I would especially like to meet Lady Tsung."

That earned Neko a sidelong glare from the ork. "What are ya, a fan?"

"After a fashion."

"Yeah, well, she don't like fanboys."

"I assure you, it is not like that."

"You do an awful lot of assuring."

"I merely meant to be polite."

"She's still busy."

"Perhaps after this run?" Neko suggested.

"Yeah, maybe." Kham's mood shifted again, going pensive. "If we all survive."

Neko accepted his response with a bow of the head. There was always the matter of survival. The ork took the gesture as a sign that the conversation was closed, and told his group to meet him at a specific time and place. Neko was not specifically addressed, but he was allowed to overhear, suggesting that Kham expected him also to show up on time at the named location as a test of his suitability and reliability. The move was neither unexpected nor unacceptable.

Neko watched Kham and his orks leave, then sat down at the table. Idly he blew the ashes of the decomposed briefing across the table. He would sit and wait a while to see how long it took before the proprietor evicted him. If he was going to operate here in Seattle, he was going to have to learn all the finer points of its shadow world.

5

Kham slipped loose bullets into a spare magazine as he scanned the woods around him. With clouds scudding along on the night wind, the moonlight was fitful. Not that he really needed it; he was used to the slightly greasy feel of the caseless ammunition, used to loading by feel. But tonight the slickness of the ammo made him think of other slippery things. Like Mr. Johnsons who sent you out on runs in which they didn't have to risk their own necks, and runners who had better things to do than get ready for a run.

So far, there had been no problems. He and most of his guys had made it across the wall and into Salish-Shidhe territory without a hitch. By going over the wall, they had avoided the roadblocks on the highways leading to and from the Seattle metroplex, points where a bunch of orks with heavy weaponry would attract a lot of attention. Climbing the wall had been a sweaty and nerve-wracking effort, but they had gone over it without incident. In some ways, the wild lands out here were just as sweaty and nerve-wracking. The lack of concrete under his feet made Kham nervous.

He could tell that the guys were nervous, too, but nervous runners were alert runners, so maybe it wasn't all bad. The guys would keep their eyes open, and trouble was never as bad when you saw it coming.

The border between the Seattle metroplex and the S-S Council was too long, and the Salish tribes too shorthanded, to watch all of it all of the time, but there were still occasional patrols to worry about. None of Kham's team had travel passes for the tribal lands, so their guns would be their only tickets home if they ran into any Injuns. There had been no trouble so far, not even when Greerson had come sneaking in from the woods. Even Sheila had stayed chill.

Kham wouldn't be happy until Rabo and the Jap kid arrived with the Rover, however.

"Rabo's late." The Weeze coughed when she made her comment, sounding like she had some deadly lung disease. The cough came from a genetic defect, the same thing that made her voice a breathy squeak, but she was a good hand in a fight and that was what counted.

"He'll be here," Kham assured her.

Sheila fingered the stock of her AK, absently tracing the woodgrain pattern. "That Jap kid probably tipped off the Injuns."

"Why do you say that?" asked John Parker.

"Dunno. That kid gives me the creeps. It's like he knows something you don't, ya know? How come he's along anyway? He ain't muscle. Ain't magic or a Matrix runner neither."

Kham had wondered the same thing, but hadn't thought it politic to come right out and ask Neko. The elf hiring the runners had obviously thought Neko worth including, and the kid had kept up with the guys in the one drill they'd been able to manage. At least the kid had worked out with them. That was good, wasn't it? None of the others had been interested in working with Kham and his crew to get ready for the run.

Kham hadn't been able to track down Greerson or the cyberboys after last night's meet, so they never made it to the drill. But they probably wouldn't have come even if he'd been able to find them. Kham didn't like going out without knowing how they would play it if the drek hit the fan. Without knowing their styles, he might position his guys wrong or shoot one of them by accident. Too dicey not knowing your team. It was true that Greerson was a pro, but Kham had never worked with the dwarf before, and the razorguy twins were total strangers. This kind of random mix wasn't the sort of thing Kham would have worried about in the past, but leading his guys had made him think about things like that. The elf had assured Kham that only seasoned professionals were involved, which was good. If trouble came, professionalism was the only thing they had going for them. Maybe it would be enough to keep them from screwing up. Maybe it wouldn't.

The sound of a vehicle engine drifted through the woods. Kham signaled for his guys to take cover, and they scattered into the darkness under the trees. Greerson and the cyberboys faded on their own, raising Kham's hopes that the run wouldn't be a disaster after all.

The wait was short and their precautions proven unnecessary when Kham recognized the battered green Chrysler-Nissan Rover bouncing its way up what passed for a trail. While Rabo was shutting down the vehicle and jacking out, Neko slipped out of the passenger side and reported no problems crossing the border.

Rabo was grinning when he climbed out of the Rover. "Good idea the kid had, making like a tourist. The Injuns scanned the disk he gave them and waved us on through. Smooth quicklike. We coulda had all of you guys in the back.''

``Then what took so long?'' Sheila asked.

Rabo looked sheepish. ``Got lost.''

``The link to the Navstar was out,'' Neko offered in Rabo's defense.

Kham was unhappy. ``I tought I told ya ta check everyting out before ya left.''

``I did,'' Rabo protested. ``It's not the Rover. It's the fragging sat.''

``The Navstar's down?'' Greerson asked.

``Ain't broadcasting,'' Rabo said.

``Gonna be a lotta unhappy people,'' John Parker opined.

``That is not your concern,'' said a voice new to the conversation.

The voice was Mr. Johnson's. The elf had turned up without Kham hearing him approach. From the surprised reactions of the other runners, no one else had heard him either. Kham noticed that one of the razorguys was tapping his ear as if to check its function, but Neko was already looking in the direction of Johnson's approach. The kid had seen Johnson, or heard him, or known he'd be there, and he had said nothing.

Annoyed, he growled at Johnson. ``So what's da deal?''

``All in good time, Kham. Gentlemen, and ladies, my role in directing this affair is nearly complete. I will leave any further instructions to the principals for this run.''

With that remark, two tall, thin figures emerged from the growing gloom. They stood silhouetted against a pale rockface, but Kham could have sworn they hadn't been there a moment before. From the height and build of the newcomers they were elves like their Mr. Johnson, but that was the only clue to their identity. Also like Johnson, they wore nondescript camouflage coveralls but, unlike Johnson, they had no recognizable features. Above the upturned collars, there were no faces, only shimmering ovoids of flickering colors, a magical disguise to conceal their identities. One or both of them would be the promised magical support.

Kham had been around enough magic to know that they could easily have disguised themselves totally, looked like anyone they'd wanted. Hadn't Sally arranged numerous magical disguises for Kham on their runs together? He also knew that such magic took effort and concentration. No magician had an inexhaustible supply of either, so they often skimped. He remembered Sally saying that a partial disguise or a false face based on a person's real one was less taxing, a good choice when there might be other needs for her magic. With their nothing faces, these elves were totally unrecognizable. If holding the blanks was easier than maintaining a made-up collection of features, the magician might be hoarding his power the way Sally did.

The disguises had two implications. The first was simple: somewhere these two elves were important people, and their faces were well-known. At the very least, one of the runners might recognize one or both of them. The second was more disquieting: the magician who cast the disguise spell was concerned about conserving power while protecting the identity of these important people. If that magician was here for the run, the magic man seemed to be expecting to need all his juice, suggesting that the runners might be facing a serious magical threat. And if the magician wasn't here, that meant no magical support, which was its own problem.

On the other hand, the principals—if that's who these two elves really were—were risking their own butts on this one, so maybe things might not get too hot.

Only one thing was very clear: whatever was going down was pretty fraggin' important to these two.

6

Neko was only slightly surprised that they traveled toward their destination without incident, suspecting that they were traveling under magical protection. Mr. Johnson's vehicle had arrived cloaked in a silence spell, and the other two elves had appeared with what could only have been magical aid. Because the two elves who were apparently Mr. Johnson's principals were magicians of some power—or so their assured stances would have onlookers believe—it was unlikely that they would take chances with their persons. The magicians would be using their magic to conceal the tiny caravan and ward it from arcane threats. They had also shown concern for mundane threats by their selection of runners for this still mysterious task, but nothing had yet materialized to justify such precautions.

Neko had chosen to ride with the orks, a ploy that gained him some measure of respect from the orks at the cost of disdain from the other runners. His choice had possibly alienated him from the other runners, but the importance of the change to the group dynamic would only be revealed with time. Accordingly, he dismissed such concerns from his mind and turned his attention to studying the countryside.

The forest was fascinating and frightening all at once. Despite Neko's training in less urbanized areas, he was a child of the city. To the despair of his teachers, he had always felt most at home surrounded by manmade structures. The giant trees that ruled here looked ancient, but he knew better. He had seen the videos depicting how the Native Americans had restored the Pacific Northwest and most of the other lands in the Indian-controlled territories to a primeval state. They had done so by obliterating all traces of man and by accelerating the natural growth process of the remaining vegetation and wildlife, but somehow Neko hadn't really believed it. According to those vids, most of the trees were magically grown after the triumph of the Native Americans and the return of much of North America to their control. As a child he'd believed it all wholeheartedly, but later he began to doubt that such magic was possible, assuming instead that the images in the vids were the result of mere technical wizardry. But here, among the trees themselves, there could be no doubt. This forest was real. It might have taken great effort, using both magical and mundane means, to achieve this end; but it had been achieved, and supremely well. Neko would have liked to have more time to simply appreciate the wonder of this place.

The vehicles moved stealthily, without noise and without light. They passed the dark boles of immense trees, moving along paths skirted in a green profusion of plant life. All was accomplished in darkness, the drivers using no more than the scattered moonlight. Norms could do it with light amplification goggles, but using such tech was tiring. The elven and ork drivers didn't need such technological aids; they guided the vehicles unerringly as they bumped along.

At length, the lead vehicle carrying the elves rolled to a stop at the edge of a stream. Rabo pulled the Rover into the space between the elves' vehicle and a rocky outcrop. With a caution that Neko admired, the rigger situated the truck so that its headlights would sweep a different part of the clearing should illumination be needed. Upon disembarking, Mr. Johnson gave orders to set up a perimeter, explaining that what they were about to do might attract hostile attention. The orks and the razorguys dispersed across the clearing and into the trees to secure the area. When all were in place, Greerson toured the perimeter, critiquing the layout and suggesting improvements. At one point Johnson had to step in to prevent an argument between Greerson and Sheila from escalating into a fight. Neko watched the proceedings patiently; he would find the best position for using his skills once he knew where the others would be. Just as he had decided that he would fill a hole between the positions of The Weeze and the blond razorguy in the northwest perimeter, one of the elves restrained him with a feather touch on his shoulder.

"There is another task for you," said a voice distorted and toneless behind the disguise spell.

The Dark One, Neko noted, as the dark-skinned hand dropped from his shoulder. The other elven principal, the Light One, was Caucasian. Skin color and a slight difference in size and build were all that distinguished them visually, but Neko was beginning to pick out characteristic gestures and stances. Soon, he would be able to distinguish easily between the two without the need to refer to the color of their skin. That was good; skin color might be an additional part of their disguise, although he doubted that; it was inconsistent with the featureless faces and distorted voices.

He watched the elves as they unloaded cases and satchels from their vehicle, noting every subtle difference in the way they moved. He was fascinated that although Mr. Johnson showed a deference to both, his attitude displayed more than ordinary subservience to the Dark One. Neko thought he detected a hint of fear.

The equipment emerging from the unloaded cases

caught Neko's eye. It was obviously occult apparatus. Rarely had he seen magicians at work and never had he beheld such marvelously constructed ritual paraphernalia. The craftsmanship was of the finest quality and the materials exquisite. This would be interesting.

Noticing his attention, the Light One said, "You observe our work with an interested eye, Neko."

"No disrespect is intended."

"No, I did not think so. But do you understand what we are doing?"

Neko thought it best to be honest. "No."

"Does it frighten you?"

"No."

"An almost honest answer."

Even without seeing it, Neko knew that the elf smiled in condescension. Neko decided that he didn't like the Light One's attitude, but he said nothing. His silence had no effect on the elf. The Light One continued speaking, a pedantic tone creeping into his voice despite the magical disguise.

"For the work we are attempting, all the elements must be aligned precisely. Due to certain obstacles, we are unable to place one of these elements ourselves. It is you who must achieve that." The elf pointed to his left. "Two meters to the left of that tree, the one with the lightning scar, is a hole. It is in the side of the stream bank, invisible to the unaided eye. It is quite a small hole, but not so small that you cannot pass through. Once we show it to you, you must enter it, carrying an item we will give you."

An unusual task, Neko thought. "Where does this hole lead?"

"To a cavern," the Dark One said as he joined them.

"Are there no other entrances?"

"None available to you, or to us," the Light One said.

''Are you prepared to do this thing?'' the Dark One asked.

Neko was not; at least, not yet. ''What will I be facing? In the way of defenses, that is.''

''We know of none that will affect you. Here, the primary defense is camouflage.''

''You suggest that there remain secondary defenses.''

''Yes,'' the Dark One confirmed. ''Magical ones.''

''That is why you must be blindfolded to ensure your safety,'' the Light One said. ''The cave will be dark anyway, rendering vision useless. We cannot allow you to carry or use illumination because of the adverse effect of light on the magic we will be performing. This might be a handicap to others, but we were informed that your skills will allow you to function effectively in such an environment.''

Neko nodded affirmatively, but said nothing. His own safety might depend on these elves not knowing all of his abilities.

''Good.'' The Dark One held out a satchel. ''Once you are inside, you will know where to place the object by the vibration you will feel once it enters proper alignment.''

Neko took the offering; it was heavy for its size. Slinging it over his shoulder, he found that it was hard, as well, and that its weight unbalanced his stance. He shifted the strap over his head and onto his other shoulder, settling the burden more comfortably against the small of his back.

The Dark One offered him a cloth with symbols painted on it, telling him that the symbols were the sigils for a protective spell. A spell it might be, but Neko felt no different when the Dark One tied the blindfold around his head. The lack of any kind of sensory effect was unusual, judging by past experience with magically imbued artifacts, but to question the elves would be an insult he thought it best not to give.

"Time is of the essence," the Light One said as they led Neko to the dark, musty-smelling hole in the streambank. Taking that as an order to proceed, Neko suppressed any final reservation and climbed into the hole. What lay below was unknown. Others might quail before the prospect of crawling blindfolded into the unknown, but to Neko a mystery was always compelling. For the moment he might be deprived of the use of his eyes, but he had other senses, and he trusted those implicitly.

The opening was naturally small, but the passage opened up almost immediately. For a while. He soon discovered that the elves were correct about the tightness of the way, but tight passages were Neko's playground, and making his way through them was how he had earned his living and no little part of his reputation. In darkness, he crawled deeper into the earth, scraping through ever smaller spaces that made his burden even more an inconvenience than the blindfold. To deal with that he unslung the bag and pushed it ahead of him as he went.

The air was at first cool and damp, but no more than was natural. As he progressed, however, it became drier and warmer than it should be. His skin began to prickle.

At last, Neko emerged into an open space. It was large, but he had none of the sense of vastness he had felt in other caverns. A hint of light touched the edges of the blindfold. His skin began to itch, and he wondered if he was feeling the workings of the place's defensive magic. Was the blindfold doing its work? He would know if he removed it, but then he would forfeit the protection the elves had said it offered.

Neko felt a sense of peace in the chamber, not the sort of thing one would expect if magics were seeking

LAUBENSTEIN·92.

to deny an intruder. Curious. The satchel in his hand vibrated slightly, the object reacting to something in front of him. He took a step forward and the vibrations increased. Step by cautious step, he moved forward, following the ebb and flow of his burden's vibrations, always moving in the direction of the strongest. He finally noticed that at one spot any movement seemed to result in a lessening of the vibrations. This, then, was the spot.

He lay the satchel down, opened the flap, and reached in. Without removing the object, he began to unwrap it. The sense of peace lessened as he peeled away layer after layer of what felt like cloth wrappings. Something felt wrong. Fearful that he was opening himself to danger, Neko reconsidered the wisdom of trusting the elves.

Lacking sight, he was at a disadvantage. But lacking the blindfold, he was at the mercy of the defensive magics of this place. Or so the elves had said. Even though he was supposed to be in danger here, somehow Neko did not feel threatened. The elves hid their faces, preventing him from seeing their true appearance, and in here they had him wearing a blindfold. For what reason? To protect him, they had said, but might they not have other reasons as well? A blindfold, whether magically endowed or not, served a mundane purpose; it deprived the wearer of sight. Perhaps there was something in the cavern that the elves did not wish him to see. But what?

And to whose benefit was it that he did not see whatever it was?

Theirs, most likely.

Perhaps it would be more to his advantage to see what he was not supposed to see, even though removing the blindfold might forfeit his magical protection. Having already penetrated to this place, Neko decided that he no longer needed protection against the magics that would have denied him entrance.

Also, he had achieved what the elves had asked of him; he had fulfilled his job, one might say, and was now on his own time. Curiosity overcoming the last shreds of caution, he decided to remove the blindfold. Before doing so, he focused his *ki* as he had been taught. If this course of action were rash, he wanted to be as ready as possible. When Neko was satisfied that he was attuned to his surroundings, he stood, readying himself for the worse, then he pulled the rag away from his eyes.

Nothing happened.

He opened his eyes and immediately squinted to protect his dark-accustomed eyes from the light in the chamber. Through slitted lids, he marveled at the sight of a cavern swirling with eldritch light. Strange hues sparkled and glimmered on fantastic rock formations, colors drifting across the scene like strands of fog across a lake. As his eyes adjusted somewhat, Neko could see that he stood near the center of the open space, next to a large plinth of some sort. He turned his attention to it.

Sitting atop a carved wooden framework was a large, faceted crystal of remarkable clarity, its top more than a meter above his head. Each face of the translucent stone was carved with strange symbols and pictures. Though Neko did not recognize them, the symbols seemed regular enough to be writing. The pictures were strange, too, stylized in a curious, elongated way. Some were simple geometric shapes and others were complex interweavings of line that hurt his eyes when he tried to follow their convolutions. A few were more representative and seemed to be beasts of many forms, including several dragons. Curiously, the carvings on the wooden framework that supported the stone seemed cruder, as if a less skilled hand had copied them from those on the stone.

He knelt by the satchel and felt the object the elves had given him. Yes, it too was faceted and carved. Removing the last layer of wrapping, but careful to keep the object within the satchel, he held it in his hands and peered into the bag. It was another crystal, almost a miniature version of the one that dominated the cavern, except that the elves' stone was tinted slightly red. Like the larger one, it was carved; some of the images were similar, but most were very different from both the framework carvings and the emblems on the great crystal. The arrangement and subjects of both stones suggested that each had a different purpose. Carefully, Neko removed the stone from the satchel.

Nothing happened.

He rotated the elves' crystal until its long axis was vertical, like that of the cavern's crystal. Moving it back and forth until he could ascertain the place where the elven crystal vibrated most strongly, he placed it on the cavern floor, propping it upright by tucking the satchel around its base. Then he stepped back in wonder as the crystals began to sing to each other.

7

Kham's position let him look down into the clearing where the elves had set up their magical apparatus. He watched as they blindfolded the Jap kid and led him over to the stream. Then he watched Neko squirm down into a hole and disappear. Seeing the performance Kham wondered if the kid didn't have a separate deal with the elves.

Once Neko had disappeared underground, the elves returned to the clearing, where they fussed with their magic junk for a while. One of them, the more angular one who Neko had dubbed the Dark One, squatted down in the center of a triangle marked out by three tall poles. After setting up some occult devices of crystal and silver wire, the elf began to chant over them while his partner walked around the poles shaking a wand and scattering powder. Magic stuff, no doubt about it, but it didn't look to Kham like anything he'd ever seen Sally Tsung do.

The Light One finally settled down halfway between one of the poles and the hole where Neko had disappeared. As the elf crossed his legs and stretched his arms wide, Kham thought he could see a faint green light outlining the mage's hands, but he couldn't be sure. The Dark One remained squatting in the center of his triangle, singing. Kham could make out the tune, a strange awkward thing, but none of the words were clear; they sounded foreign.

Kham knew that magic rituals sometimes had to be performed in certain places and at certain times. Sally had told him. So, this crazy run was starting to make sense, as much as anything connected to magic made sense. These elves wanted mundane protection while they did their stuff. The spells would warn them of magical trouble, which was just as well because they were the only ones out here who could handle that drek, and the runners would cover the real world, protecting the elves against any mundanes butting in.

Kham couldn't see the connection with Neko crawling into the hole, though. Maybe it had some kind of ritual symbolism.

The glow around the Light One's hands became definite. With a flash that startled Kham, a spark leapt from each of the elf's hands and converged on the pole behind him. The crystal at the top of the pole kindled to life, flashing beams of jade light to the crystals topping the other two poles, kindling them also. In the glow of the crystals, the clearing was bathed in a wan, iridescent light, as the strange assemblies of silver and crystal situated at the midpoints between the poles began to hum. Kham had the sense of a generator sparking to life.

"I got movement out here," John Parker whispered excitedly on the radio link. He was on the eastern edge of the perimeter.

Kham tore his eyes from the spectacle of the ritual working and tried to see John Parker's position, but trees blocked his line of sight. Out beyond the perimeter the forest seemed quiet. "Injuns?"

"Naw," John Parker responded. "Not unless they're coming to visit in a tank."

"If dey was in a tank, we'd hear it. Can't be."

John Parker sounded unconvinced. "Whatever it is, it's big enough to be a tank."

"Maybe it's a tank stealthed like the elf car," The Weeze offered.

Greerson broke in. "If it *is* a tank, they been listening to your chatter. Dump it until you've got a good ID." Kham watched Greerson cut across the clearing and disappear into the woods in the direction of John Parker's position.

"Everybody hold yer position," Kham ordered. "Dwarf's right. Keep it down till ya know what yer lookin' at."

Kham considered swapping the magazine in his AK-74 for the one with explosive bullets. If it was a tank coming, the shells wouldn't penetrate the armor, but they might decouple a tread on a tracked vehicle, or jam a thrust vent if it was a hover type. If it wasn't a tank, then it was trash; the shells would wreak fine havoc with anything unarmored. On the other hand, maybe it was just that John Parker was jumpy and the explosive shells overkill, and overkill was expensive. Before he could decide, Sheila was on the radio net.

"Got an aircraft coming in from the southwest," she reported.

"That ain't a plane," one of the cyberboys contradicted. "It's organic."

"Movement on the west," the other cyberboy reported.

That could be bad. John Parker was on the eastern perimeter and Sheila to the southwest. They had activity in at least three directions. If they were all hostiles . . .

"Fraggin' drek! It's a wyvern!" Sheila yelled.

Kham heard her without benefit of the radio. He also heard the automatic weapons fire and the hissing bellow of the beast. Tracers lit the sky to the southwest with trails of orange fire. In their light, Kham made out the snakelike body and bat wings of the creature. It was headed toward the clearing, straight toward him and the elves.

Kham didn't bother climbing down from his perch; he just jumped. His heavily muscled legs took the strain with ease and he bounced up and ran for the clearing. He hit the open space just as the monstrous beast cleared the treetops opposite him.

The Light One spoke without turning from his work. "Do your job, ork."

The wyvern swooped up, rising high over the center of the clearing. The serpentine body writhed as it twisted in a tortured spiral, higher and higher. Then it snapped its wings up and darted its head down. Body followed head in a rush like a speeding bullet train. The beast screamed as it came, its jaws gaping wide. Wings beating, it dove on the elves.

Kham fired, and the slugs from his AK ripped divots

from the beast's flank, but still it came on. Behind him Kham could hear the elves talking.

"Deal with it," the Dark One said.

The Light One's response sounded worried. "But the spell?"

"I will manage."

His weapon dry, Kham fumbled for a clip with one hand while he popped the release lever to eject the empty. As his fingers closed on the magazine with the explosive shells, he heard the elf moving behind him. The wyvern slapped its wings down in a mighty stroke, suddenly arresting its progress. Wind tore at Kham, staggering him. The beast pulled its head back, neck arching in a sinuous curve.

"Drek! It's gonna breathe."

Kham's suddenly sweaty fingers fumbled with the magazine. He couldn't get it loaded in time. Turning, he readied himself to barrel through the elf's position. Maybe he could carry them both out of the beast's line of fire if he was fast enough. Seeing that the elf was standing still, staring up at the beast, his hands glowing with arcane energy, Kham rethought his plan; he didn't want to get caught between fire and magic. He turned again and raced away. If the elf wasn't bright enough to take cover, Kham knew one ork who was. As hard as he could, he ran for the trees, his precious magazine of explosive shells clattering on the ground behind him.

Turning his head to look back as he ran, Kham stumbled and fell. He twisted, trying to get his shoulder under him into a body roll, but he didn't make it. He hit hard and flopped on his back, stunned.

Above the clearing the wyvern seemed to fill the sky.

Flames and a billowing cloud of sulfurous smoke burst from its open maw. The Light One stood firm as the fire crackled toward him. Then he raised his hands, the arcane energy around them shooting out to form a barrier between the elf and the monster. The beast's flames hissed as they struck the faintly glowing shield, rivulets of flame sliding along the surface of the magical barrier and falling to scorch the earth in a circle around the elves and their ritual apparatus. Smoke roiled above the clearing, boiling up in a cloud that hid the wyvern.

Kham scrambled to his feet, grabbing the AK from where it had fallen. The sounds of weapons fire and strange crashes and howls were coming from the woods to the west of the clearing. That had to be John Parker and Greerson engaging whatever had spooked John Parker. Kham could also hear fire and bestial roars from the cyberboys' position on the west.

With a thunderous noise, something large and armor-plated smashed through the last trees and bushes on the east, bursting into the clearing. It might have been a tank, but Kham had never seen one so big nor one that ran on four legs. The new beast halted, seemingly taking in the scene before it. Its toothy jaws gaped wide, dripping with saliva. Above them the beat of the wyvern's wings sounded like thunder. But, for a moment, nothing happened.

The respite gave Kham a chance to slap in a new magazine. Ordinary rounds, but better than nothing. This new creature was alive, which meant it had to have some soft parts; the eyes at least.

Firing, he dodged as the beast charged. As expected, his slugs had little effect. The beast crashed into the arcane barrier the Light One had erected. It howled in fury and lashed its tail. Too close, Kham was caught by the tail and lifted from his feet. He sailed through the air, directly toward the center of the clearing. Expecting to be smashed into the barrier, he was surprised as he flew through its perimeter in a flicker of green light, landing ignominiously on his butt next to the dark elf.

The Dark One's magical mask was gone, and Kham could see his features contorting with the effort of his concentration. Despite his earlier casual assurance, he was having trouble maintaining the spell he and his companion had set into motion. Kham checked the other elf. The Light One's mask was gone, too. The conjuring the two elves were now doing obviously required all their strength and concentration, leaving insufficient energy to maintain their disguises.

Neither was familiar to Kham, but he marked their faces.

Greerson appeared at the edge of the woods, his weapon raised. Though he was aiming at the armored beast, Kham could see that Sheila, emerging from the trees on the opposite side of the clearing, was in his line of fire. Kham shouted a warning, but it was drowned out by the beast's bellowing. The scene flickered before his eyes, lit by the strobe flashes of the Light One's lightnings as the elf scoured the sky and ravaged the wyvern screaming overhead.

The dwarf fired.

Sheila fell howling. Flesh and blood exploded from the armored critter's neck in a fountain, covering Sheila's prone form with gore. Unmindful of his previous bashing by the beast's tail, Kham leapt over the thrashing member and ran to her side. She was alive. Scorched by the explosion of the dwarf's rocket, but alive.

"You crazy halfer, you could've hit me!" Sheila screamed.

"I didn't." The dwarf popped the one-shot launcher from his weapon and replaced it with another. "If you'd been doing your job, you wouldn't have needed my help."

"I was handling it."

"Your version. Looked otherwise to me." The dwarf shrugged and inclined his head toward the center of the clearing. "I suspect it looked that way to our employers as well."

The three all looked to the elves as if expecting confirmation.

The elves, no longer engaged with their magic, said nothing, but they seemed to chafe under the stares the runners were giving them. The Light One muttered something under his breath and the variegated colors again sheathed the elves' faces.

There came one last burst of fire from the western perimeter, then silence descended over the clearing.

8

The elves' crystal was some kind of magical conduit, linked to the magical apparatus the pair had set up outside. Through it, Neko could see the Dark One as though through a fog. Behind the elf, Neko also saw flashes of gunfire and the darting shape of a wyvern. When the Light One joined the fight, pale semblances of his lightnings flashed upon the cavern walls. Neko gauged that the fight would be over long before he could return to the surface, so he merely sat back and watched. Nothing he did now could affect the outcome.

He didn't have long to wait. As expected, the runners' firepower and the elf's magic finished the wyvern and the other beast in short order. He saw the faces of the elves before they hid again behind their magic and returned to their ritual.

The cavern walls echoed with the musical tones from

the elven crystal, now joined by lesser voices from the smaller stones in their cages of silver wire. The song was an inviting, beseeching melody. At the edge of his awareness he thought he detected a sour tone, but he couldn't be sure. Light sprang forth from the elven crystal, flooding the chamber and overcoming the ambient reddish glow with its harsh green fire. A stronger, more coherent shaft arrowed out to the cavern wall, opening a path through the earth to the surface that was at once there and not there. The Dark One, arms held wide, walked through that tunnel of light to join Neko in the underground cavern.

The Light One was hard on his companion's heels. Remaining outside, but reflected in the elven crystal, the orks and the dwarf stood scattered around the ritual circle in the clearing, watching their patrons disappear into the hillside.

A sudden roar shattered the tableau.

"What is it?" Kham bellowed, as though he'd forgotten he had a radio link with the others still in the woods.

"It's another fraggin' dinosaur!" John Parker yelled back from somewhere in the woods. His voice was faint in Neko's ears; the ork might have been a half-kilometer away.

"Dracoform, you stupid tusker," Greerson grumbled. "Ain't no live dinos."

"Don't matter what it is. Get it before it clears da trees," Kham ordered.

The runners scrambled, converging in the direction of the new threat. Neko heard the beast's bellows, the runners' gunfire, and the single whoosh of the dwarf's rocket launcher. The dwarf boasted over the radio link that his shot had killed, but Kham heard other screams before the beast died, the kind that only mortally wounded persons make. Neko had heard such screams before and knew that one of the runners was dead, or soon would be.

The elves stood, looking back along their magic tunnel to watch the conflict. They did nothing to help. Unsure whether he could use the magic tunnel, Neko hesitated.

Silence returned as suddenly as it had gone. A few moments later, a bloodied Kham reappeared in the clearing. He peered into the tunnel and announced, ''John Parker's dead.''

The elves looked at him wordlessly for a moment, then the Dark One said, ''The large crystal must be removed from the chamber.''

Kham didn't take their cold attitude well at all; rage flamed in his eyes and he went rigid. In the magical light, Neko could see the whiteness of the ork's knuckles as he gripped his automatic weapon. Neko edged to one side, away from the line between Kham and the elves. To his surprise, the ork seemed to slowly master his emotions. The Light One, apparently oblivious to his danger, snapped an order.

''Well, ork. This is what you are being paid to do. Come within and remove the crystal from the frame.''

Kham stood frozen for only an instant longer, then he slung his weapon in short, violent motions. Beckoning two of his gang forward, he strode into the tunnel, eyes focused on the great carved crystal to which the Light One pointed. Rabo and Sheila were the ones who followed Kham. Unlike him, they glared at the elves as they passed, their eyes full of disdain.

Kham rattled the frame when he reached it, assessing its strength. The highest crossmember was at the height of his shoulder, too high to lift the massive crystal over it. Rabo and Sheila joined him and they set to work. Neko gave the Light One a shrug of helplessness when the elf turned to him. The crystal was too heavy for Neko, and he'd just get in the way of the burly orks. He caught the bag the elf tossed to him, but its contents were neither hard nor heavy the way the satchel had been. In response to the elf's gestures, Neko dumped the contents out, making a pile of the straps and cloth inscribed with arcane symbols.

The orks worked in uncharacteristic silence, no talk, no jokes, only grunts of effort as they attacked the frame containing the great crystal. When their knives failed to cut the frame's bindings, they worked the structural members, pulling and tugging on the old wood. Under the assault of their brute strength, the wood cracked and the crystal rocked precariously.

"Careful!" shouted the Light One.

Kham glared at him, but said nothing.

As the orks increased the violence of their assault, one of the vertical supports broke with a crack, sending slivers of dark wood flying in a hundred directions. Neko saw one of the splinters pierce Kham's arm, but the big ork only grunted and tugged harder on the rest of the frame until the remains of the crossmembers that cradled the front of the stone broke away.

Neko stepped up and offered the straps, which the orks took and fastened into a carrying sling. The wrapping cloths Neko handed to Kham, with the comment, "You're bleeding."

Kham looked down at his arm. A fragment of dark wood protruded from the wound. The ork snapped it off and tossed it away. "Ain't nothing compared ta what happened ta John Parker."

"A piece is still embedded in your arm. It could get infected."

"Den let it! If I'm gonna die, I'm gonna die."

"I was just concerned for—"

"Look, catboy. I'm a big tough ork. I don't need any mothering from a half-pint Jap."

Neko took the insult in stride. The ork was distressed at the loss of his friend; the lack of control was understandable. Still, Neko stepped back. There was no need to press; the ork might decide that a ''half-pint Jap'' was a suitable target for the rage still boiling within him.

* * *

''Well, the hard part's over,'' Greerson said to nobody in particular as the orks finished loading the crystal into the elves' vehicle. In the silence that greeted the dwarf's remark, the elves checked the bindings, satisfying themselves that their prize was secure.

Mr. Johnson called the runners together. ''Your services are no longer required.''

''What about an escort,'' the blond razorguy began, and his companion finished, ''back to the plex?''

''Yeah,'' Greerson seconded. ''Don't you want help getting that thing home?''

''No.''

Greerson slapped his rocket launcher. ''What if some more of the local wildlife want to play?''

With a disdainful stare, the elf replied, ''My principals do not consider that a significant likelihood.''

From the back of the group, Rabo asked, ''Hey, Greerson, what was with those critters anyway? Why'd they attack like that?''

''How the hell should I know? What do I look like? A parabiologist?''

Neko took the opportunity and suggested, ''Maybe you've got an explanation, Johnson-*san.*''

The elf shrugged. ''Magical operations sometimes rouse the local wildlife into an unreasoning rage.''

Rabo nodded as if he understood. ''And that's why you wanted all the firepower.''

''It seemed a reasonable precaution,'' the elf agreed.

''An expensive one,'' Greerson said. ''Cost-effective, Johnson?''

The elf's look of disdain shifted to one of distaste. ''That is not your concern. Our association is terminated.'' He turned toward his vehicle.

''So you're just buzzing,'' said the raven-haired cyberboy.

''And leaving us here?'' concluded his buddy.

The elf replied over his shoulder. ''Your companions' vehicle is large enough to get all of you back to Seattle in reasonable comfort, especially now that you've got one less ork.''

Neko sensed the reaction in the orks, saw their tenseness. He spoke before any of them could. ''A cold-blooded evaluation, Johnson-*san.*''

''Practical, Mr. Neko. As anyone who works the shadows must be.'' For no apparent reason other than that Neko had been the last to speak, Mr. Johnson tossed him a datadisk. ''If you are prompt in returning to Seattle, you will be able to reenter with your vehicle through the disrepaired section of the wall in the Tacoma district. You may expect the Council border guards to be distracted at four-fifteen this morning, thus leaving several of the old roads open. I can't be sure how long that condition will endure, but you should have at least a thirty-minute window.''

Neko handed the disk to Rabo. ''We are supposed to trust your word on this, Johnson-*san*?''

''As you think prudent,'' Johnson replied, his back to the group and not deigning to turn toward them.

''Wouldn't do his bosses' operation any good if we were picked up.'' Greerson's comment was directed at the other runners but clearly meant as a warning to Johnson. The elf continued toward his vehicle, then climbed into it. The other elves must have already boarded, for they were nowhere in sight. The engine started with a barely perceptible sound, then even that was silenced as the stealth spell was reactivated. The vehicle pulled away, leaving the runners with little choice but to leave as well.

For a few moments, however, no one moved. The cyberboys stepped away from the group, each plugging one end of a double-ended datacord into a jack on his temple, linking for a private conference. Most of the orks looked at one another, then at Kham. Their leader ignored them, wandering about, gathering up pieces of the late John Parker's equipment. There was not enough of John Parker to pick up.

Greerson looked at the sky. ''Just about time to get to Tacoma if we leave now.''

''We leave when Kham's ready,'' Rabo told him.

There was an awkward few minutes in the clearing until Kham finally gave the order to get under way. The back of the Rover was cramped, but the elf was right; there was room for all of them since there was one less ork than had set out. The orks were subdued and showed none of their usual rowdiness, which Neko realized he missed. Shadowrunning wasn't supposed to be glum. It was supposed to be the adventure of a lifetime, a testing of one's skills, with survival the prize. If that was the measure, then they had done well, for most of the team had survived.

Greerson also seemed to find the silence unsatisfactory. He mumbled a bit to himself after failing to get the attention of the raven-haired cyberboy, then addressed the group in general. ''This run was easy enough. We made meat out of a few animals and that was it. Didn't have to face any real opposition. I'd say we were really overgunned out here.''

''John Parker died.'' Kham voice was hollow.

The dwarf shrugged. ''Everybody dies sooner or later.''

''Fer a stinking elf rock.''

''Rock's not what was important,'' Greerson said.

"Those elves are playing games with themselves. Somebody somewhere is going to be upset that our twosome has got that rock."

"How do you know that?" asked Neko.

The dwarf eyed him, evaluating his curiosity. "You don't know, you don't need to know. Just as well. Sometimes it's better not to know what you get involved in."

Kham growled deep in his throat. "And what ya die fer?"

"You're really hung up on that, aren't you, tusker?"

"Leave him alone, halfer," Sheila snapped.

"You prefer I pick on you?"

"Yeah." Her grin exposed her upper tusks as well as the lower.

Greerson folded his arms and cocked his head back to survey the roof of the Rover. "Well, too bad. I ain't the least bit interested in you, sow."

Sheila lunged at him.

Kham caught her by the arm, holding her back from reaching the dwarf. Neko saw that the dwarf had been expecting her attack—naked steel jutted from his forearms, shining blades that would have gutted Sheila as she closed. In the close quarters of the vehicle, Sheila's size would have been a disadvantage against the compact dwarf. Greerson was also heavily augmented. Though Sheila was an ork, she was virgin of the cybernetics that would have given the dwarf further advantage in a fight.

Sheila let Kham quiet her down, and the Rover proceeded on its bumpy way. After a while the dwarf started up again. "Maybe the elves was expecting more trouble. Must have been; they hired me, after all. Rest of you are probably just as glad no real opposition showed up. That way you didn't have to face real problems. Especially you orks. You guys were pathetic out there in the woods. Don't you ever see trees in Orktown?''

Sheila growled and Kham elbowed her.

''Hey, tusker, let the girl talk. She needs to express herself.''

''Didn't you get enough killing?'' The Weeze asked Greerson.

''The dracoforms? You got to be kidding. They're just animals. Where's the sport in that?''

''You kill for sport?'' Neko asked him.

''Me? Hell, no. I'm in it for the money. That's why this was a good run. Easy money.''

''Easy money?'' Kham said incredulously. ''Not fer John Parker. Never again fer John Parker.''

The Weight of Time

9

The hall was as riotous as ever and Kham almost felt relaxed. The running and shouting kids made a lot of noise, and the noise filled a void in him. John Parker had been the first of his runners, and somehow his death was different from those that had occurred on other runs. Not that any of the losses were trivial. A ringleader had to take care of his crew, *had* to, or he wasn't going to hold on to a crew worth anything. The first law of the streets was that you took care of your own. He'd learned that in the gangs.

Gorb and Juan had died on one of his runs, but he hadn't taken it as hard as this time. He had done his duty by them and taken in their widows and kids. They all lived in the hall now, a part of the tumult that made the place home. Now Kham would also have to look after Guido and the rest of John Parker's brood, at least until they could make their own way on the street.

Lissa emerged from the kitchen and chased the kids outside, telling them to take advantage of the dry weather. With winter coming, there wouldn't be many more nice days. She smiled at Kham, a sign of her improved attitude since he had turned over the credstick from the elves' run. Less to worry about, he supposed.

They were set for awhile, although he, too, had been worried about getting paid for the run. That worry nagged at him even after Rabo pumped the access codes for the certified cred memos on Johnson's disk.

Elves were known for paying with fairy gold, phantom credit that wasn't there when you tried to spend it. Not until Kham got word from his fixer that the transfer had gone through was he satisfied that the creds were good. Well, as good as any Matrix money could be—what with all those cowboy deckers playing games out there.

With the kids out from underfoot, Kham could no longer ignore that he had a visitor. Neko. The Jap kid—the guy was so small that Kham kept thinking of him as a kid, although he had learned that Neko was at least as old as he was—was as curious and self-possessed as his namesake. He prowled the hall, poking his nose into everything, or sprawled in one of the chairs, looking like he lived there. He made himself every bit as at home as one of the gang. Now that the kids were gone and it was quiet, the catboy would be after Kham again, badgering him for an introduction to Sally. Just like he'd been doing for the past two days.

Neko smiled at him from across the room, but just as the catboy was about to speak there came a hooting from outside, the standard signal that someone was headed for the hall. It wasn't the danger call, though, so Kham assumed that the spotters must have recognized the visitors as friends. More visitors—the last thing Kham wanted. Jord heard the call, too; he came barreling down the stairs and skidded into the main room, nearly crashing as he scampered for the window.

"Jord, go on back to your ma."

"Aw, dad. I just wanna see who it is," Jord complained as he slipped open the spyhole in the board covering the window, and glued his eye to the spot. "Geez, it's elves!"

Neko sat up sharply and exchanged glances with Kham. The catboy tensed, hand close to his side.

Reaching for a weapon, Kham thought, considering the same option. But his heavy stuff was upstairs and all he had were a few blades and a popgun. These elves had better be friends. "Jord, go see your ma. Now!"

The kid jumped at Kham's shout and beat feet. Kham went to the entry. Just as he was reaching for the handle, the door opened and a tall elf in black leathers and chrome studs barged in. The white shag of his hair bobbed as he turned his head in a survey of the room.

"Greetings, Sir Tusk. You are well, I trust."

"I don't remember inviting ya in, Dodger."

" 'Twas surely an oversight for such a well-mannered ork as yourself."

"The Dodger?"

The elf turned to see who spoke his name so tentatively, and his eyes widened briefly in surprise. "You're a long way from home, Sir Cat."

Kham looked from one to the other. "Ya know each odder?"

Neko simply said, *"Hai,"* but the elf was more elaborate, as usual. "In truth, we have done some small business in the past, working our way through a tangled web of deceit in order to make the world a safer place. Though we disported in different dance halls, we moved to the same music."

Also as usual, the elf hid what he meant to say in flowery, oblique phrases, but Kham thought he caught the drift. "Da dogboy's big run?"

Dodger turned to him, his eyes wide in mock surprise. "I am amazed at the speed with which you leap to the conclusion, Sir Tusk. More amazed, however, that you are correct. Have you used the proceeds of your last run to have a brain implanted? Nay, nay, no need to answer, for I spoke too quickly. Surely, had your brain capacity increased, you would not have taken your recent excursion into the country."

"I ain't in no mood for your mouth, elf."

"Your manner is surly as ever, Sir Tusk, but perhaps you are correct that this is not the time for you and *I* to talk. This is not a social call. Perhaps some other day when things are not so busy."

The elf inclined his head, then swept a bow of greeting in the direction of the kitchen. Kham turned to see a group of juvenile and adolescent orks crowded in the archway. The kids must have come in the back way to gawk at the stranger. Kham shouted at them and they scattered, some back into the kitchen, some forming a ragged pack that tore across the main room past Neko, who wisely remained still as the kids flowed around him, then went screaming upstairs. In response to Dodger's remark, Neko bowed and started to leave.

Kham held up a hand. "Maybe ya oughta stay, catboy. Seeing as how ya know da elf and all." Neko smiled and stopped. As Kham had thought, the catboy's curiosity was stronger than his manners. It might be interesting to see the prissy elf squirm, to make him work at his fancy talk and try to phrase things so Kham would understand and the kid wouldn't. Then again, watching the elf while the kid was around might tell Kham something about their relationship. There had been a lot about the dogboy's run that Kham had not understood. "So, elf, ya wanta talk, talk. Don't let da catboy bother ya. He practically lives here anyway."

Dodger smiled, wide and cheerful, without a hint of discomfort. Kham was annoyed.

"As you wish, Sir Tusk. Your kindness is overwhelming. I had not thought you to be so considerate of a busy decker's time."

The elf actually seemed pleased that Neko was going to be present. Kham sneaked a look at Neko and found that the kid had dropped his poker face and actually looked as baffled as Kham felt. Not liking the twist things were taking, Kham growled, "Like I said, talk."

" 'Tis not I, but another, who wishes to speak to you, Sir Tusk. He awaits your invitation."

"And who might dis odder guy be?"

"You ask for a name? Alas, I am distressed to see you return to your old ignorant ways. Names? I thought the fair Lady Tsung had taught you better."

That was a clue to what was going on. "So Sally ain't involved den?"

Dodger sighed. "Alas, no. Her beauteous features grace some other venue and enrich some other shadows."

"So dis is some kinda biz offer."

"Biz, as you say, but biz that *was*, rather than biz that shall be."

"Drek, elf! Will ya knock it off and talk plain like real people?"

"As I said, it is not I who wishes to speak to you." To Kham's frown, the elf prompted, "An invitation is awaited, Sir Tusk."

"So get him in here. He's invited already."

"Ah, such grace." Dodger bowed to the open doorway, sweeping a hand wide in invitation.

10

The red-haired elf entering Kham's house didn't need a name after all. Kham recognized him from the vid. He was Sean Laverty, a member of the Tir Tairngire Council of Princes. Laverty's presence could only mean trouble—nothing else would bring such an important person to the slums of Orktown for a meet with a runner. Even if it was just biz, that biz would be trouble, too.

Laverty nodded greeting to Kham, then to Neko. "I apologize for my unannounced arrival, Kham. I thought it best."

Kham groaned inwardly, hoping he wasn't making any noise. It *was* trouble. "No problem," he said, hoping he'd be right.

"I wish it were so. I'm afraid that your involvement in a recent bit of shadow business has put you in danger."

"We didn't go anywhere near da Tir," Kham said defensively.

"No one is saying you did," Laverty said with a smile that vanished as quickly as it appeared. "Do you know who your principals were?"

"Dey didn't give dere names."

Laverty gave him a look that said Kham had not answered the question, then he shruged philosophically, and continued. "One of the principals in the recent operation is a bit draconian in his ideas. Wishing to keep the matter a total secret, he did not use any talent normally associated with him."

"So dey used us instead, ya mean," Kham interrupted.

"Indeed. I believe his original concept was that new tools would be unknown tools. No fuss. Loose ends perhaps, but unimportant ones without connections to other, shall we say, powers interested in the doings of this person."

"Ya come to da wrong ork, elf. I ain't ratting on nobody named Johnson. If dey're unhappy wid me now, dey'll be *really* unhappy if I rat on 'em."

Laverty looked thoughtful for a moment. "Do you believe that I stand in opposition to your recent employer? Or that I seek what they sought for my own use?"

Either or both was possible. Kham shrugged to show his indifference to Laverty's reasons. "Whatever. Dey sure was being secretive. Musta had dere reasons."

"Good reasons, indeed," Laverty agreed solemnly. "But let me assure you that although they intended me to remain ignorant of their actions, I was not the one whom they feared."

Kham didn't like the sound of that. "Awright, so ya ain't against dem or looking ta cop dere haul. So whattaya doin' here? I heard yer a philanthropist, but I ain't never heard of ya doing much fer orks."

"You cannot know all that I do," Laverty said warningly. "For the moment, believe that I am concerned for your best interests. Certain sources have suggested to me that one of your principals has decided that his tools have become a liability."

"Are you suggesting that he wishes us dead?" Neko asked.

Kham shook his head. "If he wanted us dead, he wouldn'a boddered paying us. Dey'd have done us all out in da woods."

" 'Twould not be unlikely that they feared your combined firepower, Sir Tusk. In the woods, you were all alert and looking for trouble. Your group would have been a more formidable threat."

Neko gave a quick nod of agreement. "Then this disgruntled employer seeks to eliminate us individually in an effort to hide his deed."

Scratching his head, Kham said, "If yer on da level, why should we worry? Yer being here makes dat pointless. Someone already knows about what we did—you do. If dis elf's worried about us talking, he's gonna be worried about you, too. If we're in danger, so are you."

"No. He can be sure that I will not inform those he fears. He cannot be sure of you or the others. Though you intend to be honorable, you may inadvertently become an informer. He will not be content to rely on your intent to keep confidentiality.''

''So yer warning us. Why?'' Kham asked. ''What are ya getting outta dis?''

''Hai. Your motives bear on your trustworthiness,'' Neko stated. ''Do you seek to set us against our former employer?''

''No,'' Laverty answered, waving his hand in a dismissive gesture. ''I only seek your lives.''

''A popular commodity today,'' said a new voice from the door. Forestalling several attempts to reach for weapons, the voice added. ''Anybody who moves dies now.''

Under his breath Dodger whispered, ''But we all go later.''

Kham, Neko, and the elves remained where they were, but their eyes took in the half-dozen newcomers. The hoods they wore were like the ones of the Humanis policlubbers, but these raiders were too well-equipped to be those hatemongers. Not only did they have matched equipment, but they moved with the precision of well-trained mercenaries. Spaced well for overlapping fields of fire, the four spread along the front wall were covering the room and the stairs, while the two by the door had a clear line into the kitchen. Professionals. They must be the repairmen Laverty had come to warn them about. Kham knew the score. The six raiders had guns trained on them, suggesting that they were ready to do just what their leader had threatened. Those guys wouldn't fool around; any cowboy kind of move and their guns would make history of Kham and his guests.

The speaker rapped out orders to his band and four of his raiders started up the stairs. Kham knew that a bunch of the kids were up there, despite Lissa's attempts to get them outside, but he didn't know who else was up there sleeping in. For a moment he thought that they might take the two left on the ground floor with them, then another four came through the door, closing it behind them. They covered the area of the first four, giving Kham no chance for action. Cautiously the new four advanced across the main room, leaving the leader and another man near the door.

A scream from the kitchen caught everyone off-guard. The leader looked disturbed and surprised simultaneously. Kham took his chance and smashed the man across the side of the head. He heard the raider's neck bones snap. Grabbing the body as it fell, he heaved it up, letting it take the slugs from the second man's weapon. Most of them, anyway: fire burned lines across Kham's biceps and rib cage while invisible hands plucked at his fatigues. Howling with the pain, he threw the body into the raiders, knocking them aside like tenpins.

Heat flared at his back and he risked a glance. Laverty was wreathed in an aura of fire, with strange, dull silver splotches hanging in the air around him. An automatic weapon opened up from the kitchen, where a new—what was he? number eleven?—gunman stood. His ineffectual fire showed Kham that the silver splotches were slugs that had halted and melted in midair.

The kitchen gunman went down in a burst from someone in the main room. Kham didn't bother to see who fired; he was obviously a friend. Diving for the weapon of the man he had killed, Kham used his momentum on hitting the floor to roll away fast as he snatched the gun.

The three raiders still in the room started firing in concert. Fortunately, they seemed to be ignoring Kham, concentrating their fire on Laverty. Taking down the mage first was standard strategy, but the elf wasn't making it easy for them. He stood still within his protective flames, light flickering over his head like a video transmission breaking up. Then the fourth joined in and the elf's magic couldn't handle it. He spun, spraying blood, and crumpled to the floor.

Kham crawled to the edge of the couch he was using for cover and pumped bullets at the raiders. Two went down, but the other two grabbed cover of their own. Something whirled over his head and as he jerked down, he saw a raider coming back down the stairs behind him. The woman had removed her hood, which let Kham see her look of bewilderment as the shuriken embedded itself in her forehead. She slumped forward, but probably never having seen what killed her.

Gunfire sounded from upstairs. Too many floors up to be the four—no, three now—Kham had seen go up; they couldn't have climbed that fast. That meant that another squad of raiders had also hit from the roof. He should have expected that; these guys were pros. The gunman he had seen in the kitchen and the sounds of combat from the back of the building said that they had come in the back way, too.

Sheila appeared at the top of the stairs, wrestling with someone dressed in combat armor and climbing harness—one of the rooftop squad. Grappling, the two of them crashed through the banister and landed in a heap on the floor. Sheila was on top, but she didn't get up. There was no time to see if she was dead or merely stunned.

A raider staggered through the arch from the kitchen and Kham cut him down. Not smart of him to expose himself like that. Kham's eyes widened as Lissa's favorite carving knife fell from the man's back and clattered to the floor when he hit.

Kham was up instantly, roaring and charging across the main room. The surviving raiders popped up to fire at him, but he didn't care. Lissa needed him. Miraculously, he made it to the kitchen. Behind him he could hear short bursts from the small-caliber weapon that had taken down the first raider through the kitchen arch. Ahead of him he heard and saw a vicious melee, orks of all ages tangling in close combat with a handful of raiders.

A highly chromed razorguy stood throttling a purple-faced Teresa with one hand and batting away kids with his razor-tipped free hand. Kham took aim with his automatic, but the gun clicked empty, so he tossed it away and threw himself at the razorguy.

As Kham smashed into him, they both went down, Teresa falling bonelessly beside them. Biting down hard into the first part of the guy that came near his mouth, Kham felt his tusks grate on metal, slide until they found soft meat, then sink in. The raider howled and slashed at him. The guy's claws sliced across Kham's arm, shredding his shirt and drawing blood, but Kham didn't care. He slammed his own chromed fist into the man's face, shattering his jaw. Kham couldn't afford to stop; the guy was probably hyped in one way or another and if he could get the initiative, he'd cut Kham to ribbons. Kham swung again and again, feeling muscle and bone turn to pulp under his pounding.

At last the razorguy stopped struggling. Kham hit him one last time to be sure, then crouched over the body. Warily he watched for another opponent as he searched for Lissa and the kids amid the carnage. There were no more raiders in sight, and the only sounds were the sobs and moans of the wounded.

Dead raiders lay scattered about the kitchen. They didn't matter to Kham. All he cared about was that orks lay dead. Far too many. Kham saw Komiko crouched protectively over her dead children, tears streaming down her face. But he knew she would not grieve for them long: her entrails lay spread and trampled on the floor beside her. Her killer had paid for his failure to kill her outright; he lay at her feet, his throat torn out.

Two bloodied ork bodies, one still breathing, lay in front of the pantry door, a trio of dead raiders entangled with them. Kham kicked the raider corpses out of the way and eased the grievously wounded Guido to a position that let him breathe easier. The kid tried to talk.

"Don't," Kham told him. "Take it easy."

The kid ignored him. "Good fight. Cyg okay?"

Cyg lay dead before Guido's eyes and Kham knew the kid wasn't seeing anything anymore. "She's fine. Ya did good."

"Thanks, Dad."

Kham almost corrected him, then thought better of it.

"Hi, Mom," was the last thing Guido said.

As Kham laid the dead warrior down and closed his eyes, he heard muffled whispers through the pantry door. Ork voices, worried but alive. With great relief, he opened the door and saw Lissa and his children huddled inside with the other survivors; Guido and Cyg had bought them their lives. Lissa threw herself into his arms and he hugged her close. But only for a moment.

"Keep everybody here till I tell ya it's clear," he said, snatching up one of the raiders' guns and handing it to her. Tully appropriated one for himself. "Stay quiet."

He closed them into the pantry again and grabbed a dead man's weapon for himself. Satisfied that his family was safe for the moment, Kham returned to the main room. Ratstomper called from the stairs, "You okay down here?"

Kham didn't know how to answer that question, so he asked his own. "Any more up dere?"

"Got 'em all."

Main room, kitchen, upstairs: all clear. It was over, then. "Take care of da wounded."

"They ain't got any."

"I meant ours, drekhead."

Ratstomper ran back up the stairs. Kham looked around the main room. Neko was nowhere to be seen, but Dodger was helping a pale and shaky Laverty to his feet. The decker was solicitous, even forgetting to talk in his hokey cant. Laverty's smile was forced as he assured his friend that he would be well. Kham doubted it, until he saw that what would have been lethal wounds for an ordinary person were already healing. The strange broken-video flicker over Laverty's head continued.

"Ya okay?" Kham asked.

"I'll live," Laverty replied. "This has been a costly exercise in humanity."

"Dese slags from dat bad boy you was warning us about?"

"Have you other enemies who would mount such a raid?"

"Nah. Least don't tink so. Maybe dey was after elves?"

"If they were, I would have known. Also, they would have come better prepared for my magic."

"Looked like dey was almost prepared enough."

"Not quite enough." Laverty eased out of Dodger's supporting arm. "I must go now."

"Dere may be more outside."

Laverty closed his eyes for a moment, then said, "No. It's safe. However, the upper floors of this structure are in flames. You had best get the survivors out of here, Kham."

"Then let us leave," Dodger urged.

Laverty nodded slowly, and accepted Dodger's help as he limped toward the door.

"Ya got a car or sumpin' nearby?"

LAUBENSTEIN '92

"Something, Sir Tusk."

"Watch dat elf, chummer," Kham said to Laverty. "He don't drive real good."

"Dodger will do fine," Laverty assured him.

A weak voice rose from the pile of bodies near the door.

"Dodger?"

The elf stiffened at the sound of his name. Slowly he looked down at the wounded raider. The guy was an old man, running on cyberware and booster drugs, but the blood that covered him said he wouldn't be running anymore.

"I used to know a kid called Dodger. We used to run together."

"Hello, Zip."

"Hunh. Zip. Yeah that's me. That's what they used to call me. Ain't Zip anymore." He coughed, and there was blood in the phlegm that dribbled down his chin. "Ain't much of anything anymore."

"He's dying," Laverty whispered to Dodger.

Dodger looked at Laverty, then at the wounded raider. In a voice even softer than Laverty's, he whispered, "Goodbye, Zip." Then he hustled Laverty out the door.

Kham moved over to the raider. If he was still alive, maybe he would talk. Throwing off the corpse that lay across the man's legs, Kham then heaved him into a sitting position. The wounded raider groaned under the mistreatment. Kham had no sympathy. This guy didn't deserve any.

"Who sent ya?"

The man's head sagged, so Kham grabbed him by the jaw, tilted his head back up, and repeated the question. The man coughed, a sick sound. Slowly he opened his eyes and looked at Kham.

"That *was* him, wasn't it? The boost makes you see

things sometimes. Things that ain't there. Dead and gone. It *was* him, though. I'm not crazy.''

''Nah, you ain't crazy. You're dead. Why not do sometin' good 'fore ya go, and tell me who sent ya?''

''What's the point?''

Neko appeared at Kham's left and addressed the old man. ''Perhaps you would do it for your old friend Dodger? You were chummers, weren't you? You could say that it was for old times' sake, that you were doing a chummer a good turn.''

The raider's attempt at a laugh was mangled by his coughing. ''Chummers. Yeah. Real good chummers,'' he said dreamily. Kham could see that the man was slipping. Without warning the raider reached up and grabbed the lapel of Kham's fatigue jacket, his grip insistent, though weak. ''Stick with your own kind, chummer. It's the wave of the future.''

The raider went slack, his pain-etched features relaxing. The wrinkles were still there, lines that showed years of travail, years that were now over.

''Kham, the building is burning. We must leave.''

Kham looked up. ''Drek! Get everybody out!''

''Where shall we go, Kham?''

''Frag, catboy, I don't know. Hide out somewhere.''

''Lady Tsung's?''

''Fragging hell, not now. We got trouble.''

''I am aware of that. I thought she was your friend. Would she not help?''

''I ain't dragging dis mess ta her doorstep. Look, ya know Cog, right? Well, one of his places is over on Maple Valley and Francis Lane. Can ya find dat?''

Neko nodded. Kham suspected that the catboy had no idea about the location, but that he would find it. Whichever. It didn't matter. What mattered was that they lie low. Maybe if they were out of sight, the fragging elves behind the attack would forget about them. That was the way it worked in the shadows.

"Perhaps we can meet later. Lay plans to deal with our hunter."

Smoke was starting to drift down the stairs, heralding the arrival of Ratstomper and the wounded from upstairs. Kham sent Ratstomper to get Kham's family and the rest, then turned to Neko. "Look, catboy. I got no interest in a war. Go see Cog and he'll take care 'a ya. Okay? Get lost."

Neko stood up straight, then made a stiff bow. Kham turned his back on the kid's damned Japanese formality. There were things he needed to get before he left. He ran for the stairs.

"*Sayonara*, Kham-*san.*"

Kham glanced back, but only for an instant. Through the smoke and flames he could not see if the catboy was still standing where he'd left him, or if he was doing the smart thing and saving his own hide. He hoped it was the latter; the kid was annoying at times and a little spooky at others, but he was mostly okay. Kham grabbed for the banister, but the flame-eaten wood came off in his hand. No more time to worry about the catboy. Time to start worrying about himself.

11

Lissa cried all night, and so did Shandra and Jord. Tully made like a man, but he still held tight to his father as long as he was awake. It wasn't till the boy was asleep that the tears began to flow. Kham neither cried nor slept. When the last of his family had drifted off to sleep, he went to the window and looked out.

From the upper floor of the abandoned tenement to which they had fled, he could see the hall, or rather the flames that clawed the sky. They lit the sky to the west, brighter than the approaching dawn did the eastern horizon. The plex firemen had finally arrived three hours ago, but it was only after the conflagration had spread to the neighboring structures. But this was the Barrens, and Orktown at that. Those brave civic heroes didn't bother to fight the blaze; they merely worked to confine it to a single block. Not much would be left of the block; the fire was well beyond what the local volunteer fire teams could handle.

Kham watched it burn, seeing his life and all he had built go up in smoke.

Sheila was dead. Like John Parker, she'd been one of his first runners. He'd lost count of the times they'd saved each other's butts in a hot run. She wouldn't be at his back anymore.

Ellie and Tump, the kids on watch, had been killed before they could sound a warning. Their deaths had been quick and clean, very professional, but they were dead nonetheless. Ellie had been barely ten and just coming into her full growth.

Cyg was gone, too. And Guido had joined his dad. Teresa. Komiko. Jed. Bill. Jiro. Charlie . . .

What was the point?

They were all dead.

Gone.

His nose suddenly picked up a faint scent, and he whuffed a couple of times to be sure. The creaky floor would have betrayed anyone entering the room, and the scent was nearby. That left only one spot. He craned his head around and looked up at the roof.

Above him a small, slender shadow crouched on the coping.

"Whatcha doing up dere, catboy?"

"We need to talk, Kham-*san.*"

"Den get down here so we ain't making a spectacle fer anybody."

Neko began to fuss with something at his belt, and Kham stepped back into the room, away from the window, to make room. The next moment Neko swung through the window with a faint rustle of fabric, landing softly on his feet. A deft flick of his wrist sent a ripple along the line from which he had swung, dislodging the hook he had attached to the coping. Kham barely saw it as it whipped back into a small box the catboy carried, but he heard the whine of the automatic line reel.

"The cyber mercs are dead," Neko said without preamble.

That made sense. If the bad guy was as dangerous as Laverty implied and if he wanted the orks gone, he'd want all the runners gone, all at once. That would be the best way, because it wouldn't give them any time to work against him. Still, it could be just coincidence that both the raid on the hall and the deaths of the cyberguys had happened on the same night.

"Howddya know it was dem?"

"How many pairs of twinned razorguys are operating in this plex?"

"Just dem, I guess."

"Seems likely. Therefore, it must be their bodies spoken of in the evening trid news."

Coincidence didn't seem likely any more. Any enemy that could arrange simultaneous hits across the plex was a powerful one. "What about Greerson?"

Neko's reply was hesitant, almost as if he were embarrassed. "I don't know. Cog thinks he left town."

"But he might be dead," said Ratstomper. She had

come in from the other room. The rest of the survivors—all red-eyed from smoke, crying, and lack of sleep—were crowded in the doorway. New crying burst out as soon as Ratstomper spoke.

"Shut up, drekhead. You're panicking da kids."

"I ain't worried about them, I'm worried about me. If the halfer's dead too, we're all that's left." Ratstomper's voice was shrill with fear. She'd never been one of the tougher ones. "They'll come after us!"

"I said shut up!" Kham cuffed her and Ratstomper stumbled back into the wall. She snuffled a few times and one tear rolled down her left cheek, but at least now she was quiet. The group's morale was too fragile to let her go on stoking their fears. "We don't know if da halfer's dead or not. We don't even know if it was da elves hit our place. And we don't know who did da chrome twins."

"It is likely that Greerson is dead," Neko said. "It fits with the red-haired elf's warning."

Kham's head was spinning. He didn't know what to do. He was losing control here, and he couldn't just knock the catboy into line. Especially because he was right. Kham was frustrated and angry, and it made his words hot and bitter. "So how come we're still around, den? If dese elves is so almighty tough and smart, how come dey didn't get us? We're only orks wid guns. What've we got dat'll stop elf mages?"

Kham's rage seemed to have absolutely no effect on Neko. He responded calmly, as if he were addressing a bunch of suits in a corp conference room somewhere. "I believe the red-haired elf was correct when he said that our enemy didn't expect him to be present when the raiders hit the hall. The raiders were all mundane, a suitable force to take out a place full of orks, but insufficient to deal with magical support. It was only because of the magical distraction provided by Dodger's friend that we were able to achieve surprise and turn the tables on them."

"Yer awful sweet on dat red elf."

"I believe he was trying to help us."

Even if he was, Kham knew that the elf was doing it for his own purposes, whatever they were. "He had his reasons."

"Of that I am sure," Neko agreed. "But whatever they are, they worked to our benefit. We must accept that."

"So whatcha suggestin'? That we run ta him fer help?"

"*Iie.* I do not believe that it would be forthcoming."

Kham narrowed his eyes and squinted at the catboy. The kid was ahead of him tonight; he already had a plan. "Den what ya got have in mind?"

"Cog is willing to help."

Kham knew about that kind of help. "For a fee."

"Of course."

The wry expression on Neko's face said that he knew about that kind of help, too. And why shouldn't he? For all that he looked like a kid, he'd been running the shadows. Kham knew how fast that made one aware of the realities of life. Still, there were unanswered—drek, unasked—questions here. Suspiciously, Kham asked, "He offered?"

"Would you expect an offer from Cog?"

Kham snarled. "Don' answer my question wid a question, catboy."

Again ignoring Kham's threatening tone, Neko smiled and said, "I made some suggestions."

"And ya came up wit sumpin' Cog would agree ta?"

"Correct."

"Awright, awright. Ya got me interested. What's yer plan?"

''Cog can arrange to make it look like the hit at your house was completely successful, and meanwhile we drop deeper into the shadows until it all blows over. We will need another hideout, of course. You and your people are too well-known here, and you have no supplies. You would have to go out, and you would be seen, and recognized. Someone would talk.''

Kham was only too aware of how cheaply some of his neighbors would sell them out. ''Find a hole and pull it in after us, huh?''

''Was that not your desire?''

''Yeah. I guess I did say dat was da ting ta do.'' Laying low was the usual way to avoid unwanted attention. But so many of his chummers had died. And his family had lost their home. Who was going to pay for that? Street justice demanded that he hit back, which was exactly what he'd have done if another gang had hit his gang. But he was a shadowrunner now, not a gang leader. The rules were different.

They'd already paid a high enough price to further the unknown ambitions of those mysterious elves. Lying low might be a cowardly response for a gang leader, but Kham didn't want revenge to cost them any more lives. He was no longer just a ganger. He had a family and a lot of other folks who depended on him. He'd already failed some of them. That failure made him mad, really mad, but he had to think about the living. If only he could believe that the danger would really end if they dropped out of sight for a while.

''How much is it goin' ta cost?'' Kham said.

12

Glasgian understood the reason for the starkness of the chamber, the barrenness of the walls, and the dry dustiness of the earthen floor, but he didn't like it. All was as Urdli had commanded, but Glasgian found the place too stark, too . . . primitive. His Scaratelli shoes had already picked up a film of dust.

In the wan ruby glow from the carved crystal Glasgian's fair skin looked ruddy, disgustingly like a norm's. Urdli's dark skin didn't show the effects as much, but it did take on an unhealthy sheen. Not that the other elf was ill, for he wasn't. A sick, or even dying, Urdli was a prospect that Glasgian found not unpleasant, just untimely. Urdli was vital to ferreting out the secrets of the stone, for he had a mastery of that substance that none in the Sixth World could match. Once that mastery had been employed and the secrets won, there would be no more need to cooperate with the insufferable Australian.

"You are early," Urdli said, turning from his work.

Despite Glasgian's most careful precautions, Urdli had been aware of his presence. Silently, Glasgian renewed his oath to discover the nuances necessary to mask himself from the Australian's senses. He walked up to Urdli and looked over his shoulder. Glasgian grimaced in disgust at the animal parts and carved stones arranged in odd patterns around the eviscerated lizard at the dark elf's feet. There was blood on Urdli's fingers. Likely he had gutted the lizard with his bare hands. Disgusting.

With forced politeness, Glasgian asked, ''Have you made progress?''

''Yes.''

''Well?''

''There are still details that remain unclear.''

''When will we know?''

Finally Urdli turned his eyes from the objects before him and stared up at Glasgian. The dark elf's face was all disapproval. ''You are impatient.''

Glasgian bristled inwardly at his partner's insulting attitude. Urdli was his elder, but he was still just a vagabond from Australia. Glasgian Oakforest was a prince, and the son of a prince, born of a line that stretched back to the beginnings of elvenkind. The Australian, fossilized in his old ways, had no justification for showing disapproval of Glasgian. What business had a vagabond disapproving of a prince?

''And you are old and slow,'' Prince Glasgian said, not hiding his indignation.

''I move with due caution, *makkaherinit*.''

Again Glasgian felt stung by the insult, but this was not the time to show his anger. He forced calm on himself. He knew that Urdli was goading him, deliberately taunting him, and he was determined not to give the dark elf any satisfaction. Harnessing his will, Glasgian controlled his temper. Later, they would see, but for now he'd turn the talk to other matters.

''The runners are taken care of.''

''You have moved against them already?''

''Of course. We cannot afford for word of our involvement in this matter to get out.''

''Then they are all dead?''

''No, not all. The dwarf escaped before my agents could reach him, but the others are dead. The cyberized norms died in street violence and the orks in a building fire. The Japanese norm, too. For some odd reason, he was with the orks at the time of the fire. I had thought his kind had more refined aesthetics. Do you think he was defective in some way? It was difficult to read him."

"He was a mere norm, of little importance. Less now, if he is dead. However, if you would apply yourself to the problem at hand, we might be quicker to achieve the results you so passionately desire. Have you studied my notes?"

"You should apply *yourself* to working, rather than to misguided attempts at correcting my education. Of course I have studied your notes. Didn't you receive my comments?"

"No."

"I sent a messenger."

"I did not wish to be disturbed."

"And *I* gave him orders to deliver my package to you. He will be punished."

"Unnecessary."

"That is not for you to decide. He failed to obey my orders and deserves punishment."

Urdli smiled coldly. "You misunderstand. I do not disagree that such failure warrants punishment, young prince. I merely say that your servant need not receive it from your hands."

"You took it upon yourself to—"

"A matter of prepared defenses," Urdli said, cutting off Glasgian's rage. "By the time I realized that he was yours, it was too late. Do you desire compensation?"

He did. Oh yes, he did, but he would not be satisfied with what the old law specified. "I will waive compensation." *Until I can collect it myself,* he added silently.

Urdli seemed satisfied "I have confirmed our earlier conclusions with regard to location. The crystal was indeed placed at the key junction of the triangle of the mana lines. More importantly, the stone is active.

Given time, we will be able to pinpoint the treasure it guards."

Glasgian was pleased. "If we had the location now, we could strike tonight."

"In undue haste." Urdli's expression was bland, but Glasgian could sense the sneer.

"Timely action," Glasgian said defensively

"You have a faulty sense of timing."

"I only desire what you yourself desire. Is it wrong to wish to see the thing done?"

"No. It is quite understandable, but yours is a child's reaction," Urdli said.

"I am not a child!"

"Consider to whom you speak, *makkaherinit-ha.*"

Glasgian heard the warning in Urdli's tone and decided that he would be wise to heed it. This was not the time for a split, which, he suddenly realized, might be exactly what the Australian was trying to provoke. Urdli had needed Glasgian's resources to take the first steps, and even now profited from Glasgian's facilities to perform his researches into the crystal's secrets. Perhaps Urdli had already achieved even greater success than he was admitting and was considering sundering their partnership to claim the stone for himself. Until the secrets were pried from the stone and shared, Glasgian was at a disadvantage; Urdli's magical experience was vital to unraveling the mysteries of the crystal. If a rift occurred now and Urdli retained control of the stone, Glasgian would be cut off forever from all that could be gained by using the crystal. That was something not to be contemplated. If their partnership must break up, it would happen only when it was to Glasgian's advantage; perhaps later, after they had shared the crystal's secrets.

"Ozidanit makkalos, telegitish t'imiri ti'teheron," he said, adding a bow to his apology and request for forbearance in the old formal way. "Forgive me, el-

der. I am overcome by the necessity of what we are about. I only wish success for our gambit."

"Then perhaps you will be willing to work for it."

"Yes, I will work for it."

"Then sit here in front of me." The spot Urdli indicated was spattered with the lizard's blood. Glasgian lowered himself and sat cross-legged. His suit would be ruined, but that was a small matter. Like many things, it could be replaced.

Urdli led him into trance and he followed. For hours they worked at the stone's mysteries, picking at the knots of power and slowly unraveling them. And through it all, Glasgian studied Urdli, learning.

13

Kham wandered the corridors of the subterranean district known as the Ork Underground. His tired eyes roved over the battered storefronts that had opened on the surface level in the nineteenth century, but which had been overtaken when Seattle rebuilt itself on top of them. During the previous century, the tunnels had been a tourist attraction for a time, and unfounded rumors of the extent of the underground had prompted Seattle's outcasts to seek refuge there in the bad times. Those frightened people had at first come only to hide, but many had stayed to live, digging more tunnels and making homes under the city, away from the light and the troubles. The enlarged Underground district was once again a tourist attraction—as long as the tourist was brave enough to enter a world populated almost exclusively by orks and trolls.

Turning down a broad tunnel, Kham left the old Underground and walked through the Mall, the broadest of the ways in the new Underground. The Mall was noisy all around him as orks hawked their crafts and wares. Because it was still daylight topside, some tourists still wandered in these corridors. Come see the odd orks and their subterranean city! Quaintness beyond belief!

He turned down a side way and the crowds grew less. Not many tourists along this route. Down here, away from the Mall, one rarely saw norms. The locals were a mix of metatypes, mostly orks and trolls, but also other metahumans who were too ugly to suit a norm's standards. Down here, the fittings were rustier, the dwellings more haphazard, but Kham felt more comfortable in these parts. He saw none of the garish murals or contorted statuary created for the gawking tourists. The shops catered to basic needs; they didn't bother with the trashy carvings, cheap trinkets, and brightly colored souvenirs that were the stock of the Mall's stores. It was just a neighborhood down here—always nightwise, dank, and smelly, but just a neighborhood. An ork neighborhood.

That was a small comfort. Rabo and The Weeze might be right that the Underground was a good place to hide, but Kham didn't like the idea. It was too full of old memories. The safety it offered outweighed that, however, and so he had agreed with the logic of bringing his family and the other survivors here, where there were more orks than anywhere else in the plex. Among thousands of orks they would be harder to find. Still, Kham wished that they didn't have to hide here. Some place—any place—else would have been better. So why couldn't he think of a safer place?

Until he did, this was where they would stay until the heat was off, until enough time had passed for whatever the elves were doing to be done. Normally, time was a disadvantage to a shadowrunner, always running out when you needed more. Now time was on Kham's side. As it passed, so too would pass the importance of silencing him and the others. Given enough time, the elves wouldn't care about them anymore.

Underground or not, none of it would have meant a thing had Neko not arranged it all with Cog. Kham didn't know how the fixer had managed to pull it off, and Kham didn't really want to know. Cog had succeeded in faking their deaths, but the fix had some unwanted side effects. The vids had picked up the story of the fire in the Barrens. Normally the media didn't give a frag about orks. After all, what was a bit of violence in the Barrens but filler news on a slow night? Somehow, though, the reporter snoops had learned that the bones of a young norm—one who didn't seem to belong to either faction involved in the violence—had been found in the rubble. Their stories were full of unpleasant speculation about strange ork practices, and it wasn't long before Humanis policlubbers—probably real ones this time—were voicing charges of torture and cannibalism against the orks.

In the Underground that kind of news was received with the derision it deserved. Sure, orks had an attitude toward norms: everybody who had to take the drek norms dished out to orks had an attitude about them. Sure, orks sometimes had some fun with a norm too stupid to stay where he belonged: those norms got what they deserved for trespassing. That was the kind of stuff that happened, the way life worked. Certainly, it was the way life worked down here. Down here, norm metatypes weren't wanted, and intrusions were often met with violence. But it was normal, honest violence. Nobody ever *ate* anyone. That was for beasts, and orks were people, even if Humanis policlubbers and their ilk didn't believe it.

Stupid norms.

Kham hoped that the elves—all of them and not just the badboy elf—were going to be stupid too, hoped they'd buy Cog's make-believe, but he doubted it. That's why Kham had brought the crew down here. If they weren't safe here, they wouldn't be safe anywhere. He had to believe everything was going to work out all right.

Still, for all its wisdom, hiding didn't feel right. Maybe it was just some kind of left-over gang reflex. Maybe it wasn't. Shadowrunners knew the risks, and they took them anyway, but families were supposed to be left out of it. This badguy elf had taken the shadow business and brought it into Kham's personal life. That wasn't the way things were done. Kham wanted to bust the elf's head and let some light into that dark, twisted mind, but taking any action against that elf, whoever he was, meant working the shadows. Sure, he had an advantage—assuming the elf bought Cog's fix—but once Kham and the guys started running, sooner or later somebody would twig to the fact that they weren't dead, and the fragging elf would know. That elf had already proved how dangerous he was; he might hit the families again. Down here, the families were safe. Maybe later, when everything had quieted down, he'd look into things. Maybe then he'd see what he could do to teach the elf the rules.

Hearing a familiar beat of footfalls accompanied by a jingle from behind him, Kham turned to see Ratstomper pounding down the way. She was flushed and out of breath but managed a shout when she saw him turn toward her. For an ork, she was in lousy shape.

"Catboy's bought himself trouble," she gasped out.

That wasn't surprising. "Why ya telling me?"

"Said we wuz supposed to watch out for him."

That was surprising, since Ratstomper didn't like the little Jap much. Her coming to Kham meant she was paying attention to biz, and the team. Maybe there was hope for her. "Topsiders?"

"Scuzboys. Green Band."

"Show me where," Kham ordered, giving her a shove to get her moving even after she'd started to turn. The scuzboys of the Green Band were among the tougher gang types in the Underground. They had connections with the power that ruled what passed for the Underground's government, and they took their connections as license to do what they pleased. If Neko had crossed them, he might be down one of his nine lives before anybody, Kham included, could help him.

* * *

Kham took the corner and found a trio of scuzboys trussing up a limp Neko. Two orks lay bleeding on the pavement, attesting to the catboy's struggle. If they were seriously hurt, Neko was in real trouble. The Green Band didn't take kindly to anybody hurting their members; they took revenge, usually in the form of body parts.

"Yo, Adam. Got company," one of the scuzboys said to the big one, who was likely their warlord.

None of the boys looked happy at being interrupted. They dropped Neko, who groaned when he hit the ground. At least he was alive. On second thought, Kham wasn't sure that was such a good thing. There were three of these scuzboys, and Adam, the biggest, was almost his own size. All Kham had for back-up was Ratstomper. Some back-up. Kham waved Ratstomper forward and wide to the left. She might at least distract one of them.

The scuzboys spread out, too, facing Ratstomper with their smallest. They weren't as stupid as Kham had hoped. The alley was tight, leaving little room to maneuver. The scuzboys hadn't drawn blades, but one of them was swinging a chain. Their turf, their rules:

LAUBENSTEIN '92

this was going to be head-butting only, no stickers and no guns. Kham dipped his hands into his pockets and slipped on his knucks. The scuzboys might be adolescents, but he was facing at least two of them and would need the edge.

The stalking stopped when a hunched shape scuttled from the darkness, whirling and rattling into the open space between the combatants. The newcomer had the tusks and mismatched eyes of an ork, but she was short and slim. Her tattered garments were festooned with rags, bits of bone, and shiny objects dangling from tassels and thongs. Silvered rat skulls hung from her belt and swung in layers of necklaces around her scrawny neck. Her streaky, snarly gray hair nearly hid her face when she swirled to a stop, her arms outflung in a dramatic pose.

"Scatter!" Ratstomper squealed as she dropped to her knees. "I didn't know these were your boys. If I had, I wouldn't have said anything! Honest! Don't blast me!"

The rat shaman ignored Ratstomper's plea and moved past her. Scatter seemed to skitter as she moved, deceptively fast, and planted herself in front of Kham. Before he could react, her head jutted up into his face and her beady eyes stared into his.

"So you're Kham." It was not a question. "Didn't anyone ever tell you that you can't go home again?"

"Haven't gone home."

Scatter laughed, a squealing, chittering sound. "I know that. But now you're thinking you might. I know you are. You're thinking you'll have to because of your *unusual*"—the rat shaman tittered the word—"attachment to this breeder." She scurried over to Neko and reached out a hand to stroke the cheek of the bound catboy, but his fierce glare froze her. Slowly she withdrew her hand. She snapped her head around, her lips curling up into a toothy smile as she said to

Kham, "Perhaps you were in a rush to join the others. Breeders need to learn their place. Oh, yes. Perhaps you're here to help, like a good ork."

Kham found her babbling unsettling, but he couldn't afford to let it show. The scuzboys were staring at her like she was their mama, and he noticed that each of them wore a silvered rat skull on a chain around his neck. They were hers, all right. Kham tried to be cool. "Don't know what you're talking about. I heard a chummer was having some trouble."

"You say he's your chummer, you the one gonna have some trouble," Adam said. "We give you the same treatment we gonna give him. But we gonna let you watch what we do to him so you'll know what we gonna do to you."

The scuzboy started forward and Kham dropped into a ready stance. Scatter slipped back between them and the scuzboy jerked back. Kham thought he saw a flicker of fear in the scuzboy's eyes when he looked at the rat shaman.

"No," Scatter said. "This is not a gutter matter. Take the breeder down to City Hall."

"Aw, no!" Adam protested. "He hurt Cholly and Akira!"

Scatter straightened, drawing herself to her full diminutive stature. Her hunched-forward head didn't turn. Though she continued to stare at Kham, there was no doubt she addressed the scuzboy. "A complaint. I thought I heard a complaint."

"No, Scatter," the scuzboy said quickly. "I ain't complaining. We'll do like you say. Right, guys?"

His companions nodded in agreement, and the scuzboys backed away a few steps before turning and hurrying to the now-struggling catboy. The smallest scuzboy lifted a paw to cuff Neko into submission, but was forestalled by a shrill cry from the rat shaman. "And no more damage to him!"

Kham saw Neko smile before planting a kick into the midriff of the one who had been about to cuff him. The ork yelped.

"Unless he resists," Scatter added.

Neko stopped resisting and submitted to being roughly helped to his feet. *Wise,* Kham thought as they led the catboy away. Scatter tugging on his arm, Kham followed. Ratstomper was nowhere to be seen.

* * *

The series of chambers called "city hall" was hardly what a topsider would recognize as government offices, but in the Underground they served. The reinforced walls and occasional weapon emplacement made it look like an armed camp. Knots of heavily armed orks congregated here and there, staring openly at the small procession, but the only time the ragtag parade was stopped was before a pair of large, ironbound doors. The squad of trolls stationed there were obviously familiar with Scatter and the scuzboys, but they showed the shaman none of the deference the orks did. She almost lost her temper before they agreed to let her pass alone. It was only a few minutes before she returned and led the procession into a huge chamber lit poorly by scattered fixtures. At the far end of the room was a stepped platform, surmounted by a large chair that rose like a king's throne.

The chair was occupied.

As they marched the length of the hall, the man on the throne rose, but he did not face them. Instead he stared off to one side. Kham glanced in that direction and saw a group of women tending a gaggle of young orks. Across the hall was another group of armed orks. Both clumps were out of earshot of the throne, but they would be able to see everything that went on.

The big ork on the platform was more hunched than usual for his metatype, but the effect was one of coiled power rather than of bowed weakness. A cloak trimmed with human and metahuman scalps hung over those shoulders and concealed his body, but there could be no doubt that the hidden body was powerful. His head was large and his bald pate covered with warts. As they halted, he regarded them sidewise with one narrowed green eye for a minute before turning full-face to them. His other eye—blue, larger, and set at least a centimeter higher than the green one—opened as he turned. When he spoke, his voice was deep, resonant, and had the ring of authority.

"Why are you here?"

A grinning Scatter turned to Kham, but he decided that he wouldn't give her any satisfaction. Hoping his voice would stay steady, he said, "Hello, Harry."

"Hello, Kham," the ork with the mismatched eyes said softly.

The big scuzboy exchanged confused and worried glances with his fellows. "You know this topsider, Harry?"

"Yes, Adam, I know him. He's my grandson."

14

The scuzboys left in short order as soon as they untied Neko. The Green Band might have connections with Harry, but scuzboys knew families came before gangs. They wouldn't be getting their piece of Neko. At least not for a while.

Scatter was less polite. Without invitation, she followed as Harry led them to a small private chamber behind the throne, settling down on the floor by Harry's side after he took a seat in a battered but well-upholstered chair. Everyone remained quiet while an old ork woman brought in a tray of refreshments.

Kham recognized her and his stomach clenched. When she offered him the tray, he was careful not to look at her face. Any other time the selection of treats would have been appetizing, but just now even his old favorite, fried cockroaches, made his stomach turn. The old woman moved on, allowing Neko to make a selection. Kham stood awkwardly before the chair, keeping his eyes on Harry and waiting for the old man to speak first. Harry downed a few of the treats and accepted a cup from the old woman before he spoke.

Gesturing toward Neko with his cup, Harry said, "This is *your* friend, Kham. Are you going to vouch for him?"

Kham nodded slowly. "Yeah, I guess so."

"You remember what that means down here?"

"Yeah."

"Does your friend know?"

"I'll tell him."

Harry said nothing for a while, and Kham began to wonder if he was waiting for Kham to explain the situation to Neko. If he was, he'd have a long wait. A lot of what Kham would tell the catboy about local customs wouldn't be politic to say here in Harry's office. Fortunately, Neko held back his usual fragging curiosity and kept quiet. Maybe there was something to be said for Japanese manners after all. Finally Harry spoke again.

"You came back, but you didn't come to see us."

That was so obvious Kham didn't bother to answer. What was he going to say, anyway? Harry's stare made him nervous.

"Something is bothering you, Kham, and it's not just whether this norm's gonna play by the rules. You wanta talk about it?"

Kham shuffled his feet, feeling his usual embarrassment before Harry. The old ork always made Kham feel like a pup. The foot-shuffling trick was something he thought had been left behind when he'd left the Underground. Angry at himself for falling back into it, he forced himself to stand still. Squaring his shoulders, he said, "Maybe. Don't wanta interrupt anyting, dough. Ya got lotsa stuff ta do. Maybe some odder time when ya ain't so busy."

Harry gave him a hard look, then drained his cup. "I may not go topside," he said, balancing the empty vessel on the arm of his chair, "but I've got ears up there. It was your hall that burned. The 'bodies' of you and your crew that were found. I don't have to work hard to guess that this breeder is the 'young norm' whose body was found in your hall."

"If ya know everyting, ya don't need me ta tell ya about it."

"You're wrong, Kham." Harry leaned forward. "I *do* need you to talk to me. If you're bringing trouble down here, I need to know everything you know about it."

"The fix is in. Ain't gonna be no heat."

"You're sure?"

Kham shrugged an answer.

Harry frowned for a moment then turned to Neko. "Say, kid. . . ."

"Neko," the catboy impudently prompted.

Harry frowned, caught off-guard.

"Call me Neko."

"Awright, kid, have it your way. Down here I can afford to be polite. This is my place, you know, and here the orks are in charge. Your kind doesn't belong here."

"I believe that I have been so informed," Neko said, pointedly rubbing at a developing bruise on his face. "I have been introduced to your hospitality."

"Oh, don't *we* sound annoyed." Harry chuckled,

then called for more drink. The old woman brought him a refill and took a place on the side away from Scatter, settling down by Harry's chair and resting her head against the arm. Harry took a draught and said, "Well, I've had experience with your kind's hospitality, too."

Neko placidly stared at the darkness behind Harry.

Scatter spoke up. "He thinks of himself as different from other norms."

Harry squinted at the rat shaman. "Does he now? Maybe he thinks he's not only different, but better."

"They usually do," Scatter said bitterly.

Harry harrumphed and redirected his gaze to Neko. "How old am I, kid Neko?"

Neko looked at him and shook his head slightly. "I do not know that much about orks."

"Guess."

Neko glanced to Kham in a silent appeal for help. Kham looked away, unwilling to get involved. If Neko thought Kham was abandoning him, tough. The catboy would get over it. The lack of support obviously didn't faze Neko, for the catboy spoke to Harry at once.

"You look younger than some of the orks I have seen here. That woman, for example," Neko said, nodding at the one who had served them. "You do not look that much older than Kham, but I know you are, therefore I am confused. Your familiarity with Scatter suggests that you might be of an age with her. Forty years perhaps?"

"Ain't surprised you can't tell." Harry reached a hand down to stroke the gray hair of the woman at his side. "This woman is Sarah, my daughter and Kham's mother. Hard to believe, ain't it? Gray hair, bent back, palsy—used up by the world and bent by the weight of time. Like most orks her age, she's burnt out, a cin-

LAUBENSTEIN • 92

der.'' Harry paused. ''She's not even thirty-five years old.''

Neko stared at Sarah. The old woman looked back with rheumy eyes and smiled, showing the gaps in her yellowed teeth. Kham had to turn away from his mother. He wanted to remember her the way she had been. Looking at her now made that too hard; she was just too old.

''Appalling, isn't it?'' Harry asked Neko.

''Age comes to everyone,'' Neko said quietly. ''But if you are her father, why are you not more aged than she?''

Harry laughed. ''Me? Me, I'm special. I wasn't always an ork; but then I guess I always *was,* or I wouldn't be now. That didn't make much sense, did it? I may not be burned out, but I ain't young either, and sometimes I get a bit confused. I'm not immortal, after all. And, like you said, sooner or later we all do have to pay the piper. Let me try again.

''I started my life as a norm like you, back before the turn of the century. I was down in Rainier when Saint Helens and Mount Rainier blew. The skies were gray with smoke for weeks. That was the first I heard of the magic that was coming into the world. Didn't much like it. Liked it even less when the Injuns used their magic to steal the land back from honest folk that had lived on it for generations. I remember the shantytowns around Seattle, saw them fill up with every bit of human refuse that could be crammed in, and watched the wall go up around the plex. I don't know who was worse then, the tribal guards with their holier-than-thou attitude, or the UCAS troops, enforcing the repatriation laws, always looking over their shoulders at the Injuns and playing yesmassa. They all treated us like cattle. I thought it was the worst thing that could happen to a person.

''I was wrong.

"If you think that living through the hell of those shantytowns will change a person, you're right. But let me tell you, it ain't nothing like what people'll do to you if you don't look like them anymore. If they can point at you and say, 'Look, that's not human.' You see, come '21 and the goblinization, I went ork. It wasn't a lot of fun. Pain, pain like you can't imagine, and you locked up inside while your body changes. Ever feel your muscles crawl or your bones squirm?"

Harry paused, as if waiting for Neko to answer. Kham knew better. No one ever answered Harry when he told the story. Somehow you just knew he wasn't expecting you to answer, he just wanted you to think about what he was saying. Neko stayed quiet, so Harry went on.

"I learned what hate really was back then. Hate changes people, kid, changes them a lot. People I thought I knew, people I thought were *good* people, did some pretty awful things. There was nothing to do but hit back. At least that's what I thought then. So I hit back, and went on hitting back for a long time. Sure, I did some things I ain't proud of, but I survived. Just like I've survived everything since then. And I got stronger. It was like some guy once said, if it don't kill you, it'll make you stronger. About eight months after I went ork, Sarah was born. She didn't have her fine tusks then, but you could still see what she was. Her mother wouldn't have anything to do with her, so I took her and left. I think Sarah's mother got one of those special divorces. I don't really know, and I don't care. Why should I? She didn't.

"Sarah and I went through some hard times, but we survived." He looked down and smiled at her, and she beamed back at him. Kham was sickened. The intelligent, vibrant woman who had raised him wasn't there anymore. Her expression was what one might imagine from a faithful mutt. Harry didn't seem to notice.

"The Underground didn't always belong to us," Harry said. "But it's ours now. We turned our backs on a world that didn't want us, and we made our own community down here. It was hard at first. Real hard, but we made it work. Most of the halfers that came down here with us couldn't take it, and they eventually left the tunnels all to us. World got easier for them topside once the strangeness eased off a bit; they still look almost human, if you didn't mind looking down at them. And I know a lot of norms who don't mind looking down on folks.

"We started a new life down here. I found a place and folks who appreciated what I could do. Made a name for myself. And all the time, Sarah was growing up. I was proud when she married and had kids. I thought she was a little young for it, but that was Fifth World thinking. We were in the Sixth World, now, and early on it was plain that orks come into their maturity much sooner than other people. Physically, anyway." He glanced at Kham and winked. Kham glared back. "Then I started to see that Sarah was getting older. Her hair was gray before mine. At first I thought she might be a freak, being the daughter of one, but she wasn't. She was just an ork. The others of her generation were just like her, old before their time. It wasn't fair. Orks were shunned and pushed into the bad places, and we were dying sooner. Just not fair.

"When you're ork, you find out that life ain't fair. You learn that there are some things you just can't fight, like people's hate. You just have to find another way. But age, and time? How do you fight them? Strength can't do it, because age knows how to steal that away when you're not looking. Brains? No luck there either. Orks may not be as dumb as most breeders think, but our best and brightest ain't got an answer to growing old. The breeder labboys haven't done any better. The reaper still waits for us all; he just has an express lane for orks. So orks get old fast, and then they die. Is that fair?''

Harry's spread hands made it clear that he expected an answer this time. Neko replied promptly. ''It appears to be nature, sir.''

''Yeah, and no one's ever accused nature of being fair.'' Harry laughed bitterly. ''Look at elves. They're children of this new age of magic, just like orks. But they're slim and pretty, like in the fairy tales. Tell me, kid. You ever seen an old elf?''

''No, Harry-*san.*''

''I don't think you ever will.''

Kham thought about Dodger. Kham had aged, yet the elf still looked just as he had when they had first met five years ago. Even Sally had aged, for all that she was still a beautiful norm. There were new lines around her eyes, harbingers of what was to come. But the elf, the elf looked like a teenager. Kham thought about what the raider leader had said, the one Dodger had called Zip. That old man had known Dodger. Zip had claimed that, as a kid himself, he had run the streets with an elf kid named Dodger. And the guy had recognized Dodger's face.

''It just ain't fair,'' Harry said.

''Perhaps elves age differently,'' Neko suggested. ''You have told me that orks do, and I have known dwarfs who look much older than their chronological age.''

''Sure, the halfers get *looking* old fast. Got beards down to their belly buttons by the time they're twenty, but they don't change after that. Like the damned elves, they stay the same.''

''I meant to suggest that once those metatypes reach physical maturity, perhaps they simply stay physically the same until old age sets in. I read about something like that once. A case where senescence set in and a person showed all the signs of age in only a brief time and died shortly thereafter."

"Fantasy stuff," Harry snorted.

"Are you suggesting that elves are immortal?"

Harry was slow to answer and, when he did, his voice didn't carry its usual conviction. "Me? Naw. I ain't no scientist, but I know nothing natural can live forever."

"Then you suggest that they have access to some magical way of prolonging life? Perhaps Scatter knows something of that possibility."

Uncharacteristically, the rat shaman had been staying out of the conversation. Now, even with attention focused on her, she kept her head bowed. "I have nothing to say on the subject."

Harry went on, unperturbed by his shaman's reticence. "Don't know about magic. Maybe the elves have got some special magic, maybe not. I don't know. Maybe it's just the way they are."

Kham thought about Zip's remarks and about what he had seen of Laverty. The elf had healed unnaturally fast. Was that a side-effect of life-prolonging magic? If so, it didn't belong to all elves, at least not to that degree. He'd seen Dodger wounded, and knew that the decker didn't heal magically as Laverty had. Maybe this immortality had to be . . . arranged. Like with magic crystals dug out of the ground in the Salish-Shidhe forest.

"Harry," Kham said, "if ya was an elf and ya had a magic way ta live forever, ya wouldn't want anybody else knowing, would ya?"

" 'Course not."

"And ya wouldn't want anybody knowing how ya did it."

"Makes sense. Leastways, it would to an elf. Those fraggers are too stuck up to be useful to people."

''And if ya lived forever, it would give ya kinda different perspective on life, wouldn't it?''

''I expect it would,'' Harry said thoughtfully.

''And on death too. Ya could afford ta wait fer things, let time wipe away anyting ya didn't like.''

''Makes sense.''

''But if ya was a young pup, and ya hadn't gotten yer dose of dis fancy magic stuff, ya might still be impatient, kinda anxious about tings.''

''What's your point, Kham?''

Kham cleared his throat. He wasn't exactly sure what his point was, the thoughts were coming fast and he was having trouble sorting them out. ''We been done over by an elf, an anxious one, and warned by anodder who said dat he didn't want ta see us killed. Dis odder elf never did say why he was warning us. Maybe he didn't like killing, like he said, but maybe dat meant sumpin' else. Maybe he meant he didn't like killing, but he didn't mind watching folks die naturally. Maybe dis odder elf was willing ta wait and let time take care of his problems, especially since we didn't really know anyting about what we'd gotten inta anyway. Don't take a whiz kid ta know dat killing people always makes waves, starts odder people asking questions. Questions could make more trouble fer dese elves. But dis elf dat came after us, he's a young guy, impatient, like he was too worried ta let time do his work fer him.''

Harry said, ''You wouldn't know any impatient folk, would you, Kham?''

Kham started to snap a reply and stifled it. He didn't want to open old arguments, so he just said, ''Maybe dat's how I know one of dem elves was young.''

''Takes one to know one,'' Harry said, still goading.

''Yeah, like dat,'' Kham agreed. The possibilities of what was going on made the old contentions seem unimportant. ''Dat crystal we dug out fer da elves might be da way dey do it. Dere immortality, I mean. If we had it, we might be able ta use it. We can get magicians ta figure it out."

Scatter perked up. She stared avidly at Kham, but didn't offer any suggestions.

"Just what are you thinking about, Kham?" Harry asked.

Kham looked at Sarah and said nothing.

Harry saw where Kham was looking and shook his head. "She's already old, Kham. Even if the crystal can do what you think, I doubt it has the power to reverse aging."

"But Lissa wouldn't end up like her," Kham said softly.

"You're dreaming, Kham." Harry took a sip from his cup. "Think about what you're suggesting. To get that thing, you'd have to go up against some powerful magicians."

"Fought magicians before."

"With magical help," Harry pointed out.

"I'll get help," Kham said defiantly.

"Where?"

"I got friends."

"Who think you're dead."

"I'll tell 'em different."

"Kham, this ain't a battle for orks. It's magic stuff; you don't have the resources. Besides you don't got any proof this idea of yours is right."

"But it might be," Scatter said.

It might. If Kham could win the secret of the elf's apparent immortality, Lissa would never have to get old. His kids could grow strong and stay strong. They wouldn't have to die at an age when norms were just hitting their prime. And it wouldn't be just for them. He wasn't a greedy pig like those elves. He'd share it. Yeah, he wasn't being selfish. He'd be doing this for all orks, making every ork's world better.

Yeah, sure.

Maybe he was just fooling himself, chasing after a pipe dream, and looking for a way to go out in glory and never have to worry about anything ever again. Fighting somebody with the resources of those elves was suicidal. Maybe he was running away. Again.

"Maybe I just gotta fight dis one, win or lose."

Harry looked into his cup and said, "It's your decision, but if you do decide to fight, you need to know who you're fighting."

Harry's words cut straight to Kham's fears.

"I don't think you ought to get involved in this," Harry said. "But if you're gonna, be smart about it. A shrewd general learns everything he can about his opponent. He discovers the enemy's weaknesses and takes advantage of them. He *plans* to take advantage of them."

Kham knew all that. "And if he ain't got any weaknesses?"

"Then you've picked the wrong enemy. You can't win if you don't survive the battle."

A valid point. Some orks said the only way to die was fighting, but they were young and stupid. Weren't they?

"That depends on what you are fighting for," Neko said, breaking into the conversation.

Harry stared at the catboy in annoyance, then his expression relaxed and he rubbed absentmindedly at his tusk. "Doesn't seem like much of a win if you can't celebrate."

"Perhaps," Neko said. "It certainly isn't 'a win' if your body survives, but your spirit is lost in the battle."

"Your spirit? You mean like your soul?" Harry snorted. "You're worrying about something that doesn't have much value in this world, kid."

"Doesn't it?"

Souls. Kham thought about a submarine full of bugs, and a wendigo named Janice. The dogboy had talked a lot about souls before he'd sent them off to that sub. The whole thing was supposed to have been some kind of battle to save humanity against some magic monster, but there had been a hidden meaning to what the dogboy had said. Stuff about souls, specifically about Janice's soul; they were supposed to have been fighting for that, too. Had she won or lost her battle? She certainly hadn't been at the party after the run.

Verner had also been one to talk about doing things for other people. Kham hadn't thought much about the dogboy's words at the time, but now everything was different. For the first time, Kham saw that he could do something that might really make a difference. Maybe he really did want to get this immortality stuff for everybody. He felt scared. Not because he might not make a difference, but because *he* might.

Kham wasn't used to thinking like this.

15

The conference with Harry went on for some time before it ended, drifting from philosophical discussion to practical approaches for working a run against powerful opponents. The question of whether the run would take place was still open when they left, but Neko knew that Kham had made up his mind even if the big ork still did not know it himself. During the walk back to their flop, Kham's monosyllabic answers to questions told Neko that further discussion would have to wait.

As Harry had said, however, the first order of business was knowing your enemy. Neko intensely disliked the idea that some unknown elf had tried to kill him. He intended to find out what was going on, and he wasn't going to wait while Kham tried to make up his mind whether or not to do something.

A direct reconnaissance against their recent employers was currently out of the question. It would expose Cog's deception and that could lead to further attacks against them. That left the indirect approach, which was more satisfying to Neko anyway. If he couldn't go after the opposition, he could go after someone who knew who the opposition was.

But the first order of business was determining what the matter was all about. Kham believed that he and his orks, and Neko as well, had become targets due to the elven desire to conceal the secret of their youth; but the evidence suggested that the elves had more than simple youth. Neko, too, had seen the raider named Zip identify Dodger as a childhood friend. It was entirely possible that in this magical Sixth World the elves had some kind of "immortality factor."

Clearly, all elves were not equal. Dodger's interaction with Zip suggested that the elf had the factor, or at least a part of it. And Dodger's solicitude toward the red-haired magician he had brought to Kham's hall suggested that the decker's companion was the older of the two. The mage's occult healing, a trait not shared with Dodger, might only be due to one being a mundane and the other a mage, or it might be a reflection of a superior immortality factor. Kham's thought that elves might need to acquire the immortality factor could explain the difference. Such a need would explain the avidity with which their recent employers sought the strange crystal. One—perhaps both, but certainly the younger—would, understandably, want to ensure his piece of immortality. Such motivation seemed plausible, but Neko couldn't be sure until he verified this immortality factor and knew the identity of their enemy.

Having determined to uncover the enemy through those who knew something of the enemy's doings, he considered the elves who had come to Kham's hall. Who was this Red Mage? For that matter, who was the Dodger, really? Answering those questions might confirm whether or not this immortality factor existed at all. Certainly the relationship between the two was interesting, suggestive, in fact. Dodger's deference toward the Red Mage seemed the attitude of a student to a *sensei*, the sort of respect reserved for one older, wiser, and more skilled than oneself. A most curious arrangement, considering that a decker's concerns were totally removed from those of a mage. Father and son, perhaps? An intriguing thought. Neko promised himself that he would investigate the issue, once more pressing matters were taken care of. Identities first, relationships later.

The Red Mage had shown himself at least somewhat sympathetic to the plight of Neko and the orks; he had come to warn them of their danger. Kham had suggested that the mage might be exercising a "wait and let them die off naturally" strategy, but Neko couldn't buy it—too many loose ends there, too many ways for it to go wrong. Besides, there had been no hint of danger prior to the Red Mage's warning. If the Red Mage was involved in their enemy's cover-up, his visit had undermined the strategy. Who would not be curious about why someone would want him dead?

No. The Red Mage may have been acting for unknown personal reasons, but Neko was sure he was not allied with their enemy. At least not in this matter. It was more likely the mage opposed something the enemy sought to do. But for all his potential good will, the Red Mage would hardly take direct questions readily. Any information they wanted from him would have to be ferreted out.

At least the mage's defenses would not be arrayed against them, not specifically, that is. The Red Mage had implied that he had other enemies and that he would be guarding against them. The other elves—or only one of them, if the Red Mage was to be believed—had already shown themselves paranoid. Had they not sent their raiders to eliminate anyone who knew they had merely acquired the crystal? Their defenses would be active and aggressive. Even if they had been taken in by Cog's deception, they would likely be mounting special guard on matters touching the likely source of their paranoia: the crystal and its capabilities. Who would surrender the secret of immortality easily?

Obviously, some research was in order. Unwilling to wait for Kham, Neko resolved to start his own investigation. The worldwide computer network known as the Matrix offered the best one-stop shopping. Information was the key, and once gained, who knew what doors might be opened? The Red Mage had some sort of connection to those other elves. Had he not known that one of them would strike? The link was hardly that of sworn allies, otherwise there would have been no warning, however belated, of the attack. So how were they connected? Determining the nature of that link might reveal a line of attack against the hidden master of the raiders.

Equally obviously, Neko did not have the proper resources. He was not a decker, nor did he have enough nuyen to hire the world-class decker it would take to penetrate the Matrix security he expected to encounter. Most of the fee from the last run had gone into Cog's coffers, paying for their "deaths," and there was not enough left to hire reputable talent.

So Neko talked to Cog, cajoling and dickering until the fixer offered the services of a certain Matrix runner who operated under the name of Chromium. This person allegedly made runs for the thrill and a percentage of the take. Neko was not happy about relying on someone who would tackle dangerous work without a guarantee of recompense, but Cog vouched for both the skill and the reliability of Chromium.

With time and nuyen in short supply, Neko had agreed to set up a working arrangement. Still, wisdom precluded blind trust, and he decided to test the decker with a series of relatively simple data retrievals, standard dossiers on a variety of personages. Among the files requested were those on a shadowrunning decker named Dodger and one for an unnamed mage whose portrait Neko constructed with a bootleg police composite program. A day later the chips were delivered to the appointed drop-off. Neko hid the bulk of them away for safekeeping—one never knew when data would become important—and popped two of the chips into his telecomp, bringing up the two files he had actually wanted.

Since Dodger's was slim, only a few megabytes, Neko began with it. The first item was a note from Chromium claiming that this poor showing was better than Neko would get from anyone else. There was no hard data, just Chromium's speculations and conclusions. And it wasn't much that Neko didn't already know. Chromium identified Dodger as a wiz decker, mentioning his association with Sally Tsung. Chromium also connected him with a number of runs that had occurred last year. Some of those connections were correct, for Neko had been involved in one of those runs and knew that Dodger had too. Although Chromium didn't mention Neko's part in the matter, the hired decker speculated that the actions had been global in scope, and controlled by a single, unknown master. Observing the details of several incidents of which he had no knowledge, Neko could see how those runs would have fit into the war against Spider. He found himself impressed at Chromium's powers of deduction. But on Dodger himself, there was nothing hard and factual.

As Neko sat pondering the lack of information on Dodger, the screen flickered. Data evaporated from his screen as he watched. He punched keys, trying to save it, but line after line winked out. He tried all the tricks he knew and failed to get it back. A system check showed the data had been erased from the chips. A few other files had been affected as well, but the only one that disappeared completely was Dodger's. If this was some trick by Chromium to ensure payment . . .

He tried the file for the Red Mage, half-expecting it to disappear before he could finish with it. He soon forgot his apprehensions when he saw the newsfile clippings that opened the dossier. One after another showed a handsome, red-haired elf identified as Sean Laverty. Neko studied the selection of datapics to satisfy himself that this Laverty and the red-haired elf who had visited Kham's hall were one and the same, finding little reason to doubt it. The visitor might have been a simulacrum or magically disguised, but Neko doubted that. Having seen their employers' disguises fail under stress, he was sure that any masking spell would have faltered when Laverty was injured. Now he understood why Kham had lost his surly manner when Dodger's friend had stepped through the door of the hall. Perhaps it also explained Dodger's deference. Sean Laverty was a member of the Tir Tairngire ruling council.

This was a man with clout. Laverty was not one of the more prominent members like Prince Aithne or Ehran the Scribe, but any Council of Princes member was a powerful political force in the Tir and, by extension, anywhere the Tir had influence. Seattle was only one of those *anywheres*. The metroplex served as a principal port for products of the elven nation, and the trade meant a great deal of revenue for Seattle. If what Neko had heard on the streets was correct, the governor was still more than happy to do whatever the elves wanted in order to ensure that the recent trade deal remained viable. There were even whispers that elves from the Tir secretly ran Seattle.

As the shock of discovery wore off, Neko noted another face in the pictures. The person was not prominently featured, nor was he identified, but Neko recognized him. It was the fair-haired elf he had privately named the Light One.

Accessing the public database, Neko ran his own impromptu check. He reasoned that anyone close enough to the Tir Tairngire council to be pictured with its members must be a public figure. Unless, of course, he was only security or an aide. The Light One had been too well-dressed for either. On a whim, Neko also requested a correlation with a description and composite sketch of the Dark One. Signing off more of his dwindling credit, he put in a correlation request to match both faces with names and biographies, then went back to studying Laverty's dossier, letting the library system do its work.

A few hours later, he pulled up the results of his search. No correlation was available on the Dark One, confirming that the dark-skinned elf was not another member of the Tir council nor an officer of the Tir government. The Light One turned out to be Prince Glasgian Oakforest, the eldest son of Prince Aithne. Not a member of the council, but close enough to be trouble. Glasgian had been born in 2034, a mere eighteen years ago. He was young enough to fit Kham's description of an anxious, impatient youth. If Glasgian was the one about whom Laverty had warned them, they would not find it easy to thwart him. Of course, the still-unknown Dark One might be worse.

There was a lot more to learn, but without monetary resources, Neko would have to use ingenuity to do it.

* * *

The flop wasn't in the nicest part of town, but the neighborhood wasn't trashed. Some of the property owners still struggled to maintain nice lawns and gardens and to keep their houses well-painted. Neko saw only a few abandoned vehicles among the cars parked along the street. Unfamiliar with the area, he couldn't tell if the neighborhood was on its way up or down. He didn't really care; he was here to do some biz.

The power junction box near the corner suggested that his destination would be well-supplied with heavy-duty lines, which was standard for any house where a decker was operating. Did all the other buildings harbor deckers as well? Or did the inhabitants have other, different needs for extra facilities? Maybe this box was here only for Chromium's convenience? All questions, but minor ones and not really pertinent just now.

There were too many factors operating in this case, too many possible avenues for exploration, and not enough money left to keep sending a decker out again and again, following up each hint of something interesting. If he were a decker himself, he could track down those leads, cutting the time involved and saving money. But then, if he were a decker himself, he would be running the Matrix right now, not walking along this street. Unable to do the work himself and unable to afford the back-and-forth play usually involved in hiring out the work, he had arranged a compromise: today he would work directly with the decker Chromium. Being present while the decker worked would let him direct the decker's skills in the appropriate direction much more quickly.

Halfway down the block he found the sign that announced the Wayward Home Residential Apartments. He turned onto the walk and moved noiselessly up it and across the porch. The screen door was closed, but the inner door was open. He glanced through, satisfying himself that the hall was empty before entering.

Upstairs, he found the door marked Number Seven and knocked twice, then three times, as arranged. He tried the knob and found the door unlocked, also as arranged. He entered and secured it behind him.

Number Seven was a suite comprising a main room, a kitchenette, and at least one more room beyond a closed door. The main room was sparsely furnished, holding only a couch, a rickety dining set of table and three chairs, a freestanding bookshelf, and a single upholstered lounge chair. On the floor by the lounge chair sat a personal computer, its monitor crowned with a cybernetic helmet sitting upon a coiled datacord. The cord connected the helmet to a box jury-rigged to the back of the computer, from which another cord ran to the back wall and through a tiny hole to some unknown connection. The cord went through the wall, of course, because it would have been easier to drill than the painted metal sheathing of the inner door. No hinges showed on that door, but a triple set of locks did. The arrangement was secure enough to let the decker escape should anyone try to force his way through.

"Good afternoon, Neko," a pleasant but androgynous voice said from the monitor. "Your sidecar's ready."

Neko turned and found the screen still dark, but he spoke to the device anyway. "Good afternoon, Chromium."

"Hey, if we're riding together, you may as well call me Jenny. That Chromium stuff is just for the shifty suits."

"Very well then, Jenny." Chromium might be a

name she used with the suits, but she still didn't trust him enough to meet him face to face. She was just being prudent. He didn't mind; most deckers weren't much to look at anyway. "Is everything ready?"

"Hot-wired and revved. Lay your bottom on the seat, pop on the top, and we'll fly."

"A moment, please."

He prowled around the room, placing sensors in advantageous positions. The helmet would blind him to the room, and the sounds transmitted through it might overwhelm his natural hearing. Since he did not wish to be surprised, the sensors were necessary to warn him of any intrusion. Jenny would be watching his precautions through a concealed video pickup, but that didn't matter. She would have to understand that he also had to exercise prudence. Satisfied that he would have notice of anyone entering the room, he settled into the chair and lifted the helmet.

It was light for its size, all plastic and composite material. The smooth outer shell covered a tangle of tiny wires and circuitry chips. Before trying it on Neko adjusted the inner headband, but then he had to take it off again and adjust it once more before it sat properly on his head. He felt the pinpricks of the neurosensor rods and saw the green LED register proper contact. Light leaked up from beneath the eyeshield, causing the innards of the helmet to glimmer.

"Ready," he announced, then was swirled away into blackness, to be blown at hurricane speed through a ring of lights and blasted into a galaxy of stars. Below him, the Matrix unfolded in all its neon glory. His viewpoint hung suspended over a nighttime city, the like of which had never been seen on the earth. Giant icons in a bewildering variety of shapes and colors marked the cyberspace locations of the megacorps, and towered over the lesser images representing the computer systems of smaller companies. Flitting pulses of light whipped across the dark space, cars of data on benighted datapath roads. His ears roared with the rushing wind of the silence.

"Want to see what you look like?"

Curious as always, Neko replied, "Can you do that?"

"Sure. I'll switch the feed to your screen over to the image monitor."

The sparkling glory of the Matrix winked out, replaced by a plain gray field. In the middle of the endless gray stood a curvaceous chrome biker girl in shiny black leathers. A chrome cat sat on her right shoulder like a modern-age familiar.

"You like?"

"Appropriate," Neko murmured.

The Matrix returned, and Neko's viewpoint now included the biker girl's spun-silver hair. He tried looking down to see his own chrome paws, but found that he could not. His viewpoint was slaved to that of the decker. Her hair remained as a visual reminder that he was there only as an observer.

"Where to?" Jenny asked.

"Let's start with double-checking some of the earlier data."

"Don't trust me?"

"It's not that. There are some ramifications in the Laverty files that I'd like to investigate."

"Chilled enough. Let's fly."

They did, soaring above the Seattle Matrix construct. With a dizzying shift in perspective, they dove, pulling out to whip along a datapath. They screamed along for barely a second before the Matrix winked off and then on again. As they rose up from the datapath, Neko could see that the Matrix landscape had changed. The Aztechnology pyramid, so prominent a moment before, was nowhere to be seen. Some of the others were still there, but seemed changed in size.

New icons had appeared, among them a cluster of crystalline structures that looked like glittering snowflakes.

"They look like ice."

"And ice they are," Jenny confirmed. "IC-type ice, intrusion countermeasures. The kind of ice that'll burn you if you touch it the wrong way."

"But it's so beautiful."

"Sure is."

"We're moving toward them."

"That's were you wanted to go. Second one to the right is Laverty's."

"Then these are the council's data systems."

"Fast boy."

They slid around the edges of the first iceflake and dropped down toward the second. Their point of view continued down, sliding around the major axes and gliding past the interwoven sub-branches, until the multifaceted arms of the structure stretched over them. Neko expected to slip into shadow until he remembered that the only shadows in the Matrix were the ones that had been designed into someone's interface. They halted before one of the lowest arms. It was plain compared to most they had passed.

"Laverty's public office system," Jenny said.

Then they were inside. It seemed like they were standing inside a glacier, but no earthly glacier had ever been composed of lattice walls. A pair of black-gloved hands appeared before Neko. The hands stripped off their gloves and flexed long, tapered fingers of chrome.

"Pick and choose, Neko. The files look clean."

"Let's start with a correlation of multiple locations for public activities by anyone named Laverty."

"You ain't got the bucks and I ain't got the time for that."

"Can you confine it to the last hundred years and

weed out anyone with no connection to the old United States or the Tir?''

''Sure. That narrows it down some, but it's still big.''

Neko frowned. ''*So ka.* Then start with Sean Laverty himself. Where does he spend most of his public time? Only pull locations he's visited more than once in a year or where he has a business interest.''

''Null perspiration.''

A scrolling list of locations superimposed itself over Neko's view of the crystalline lattice. With only a few exceptions, all of Laverty's public appearances were in Australia, England, Ireland, the former United States of America, and the former Dominion of Canada.

''What about the business interests?''

''Doesn't have any direct connections,'' Jenny said. ''Supports a lot of charity organizations, though.''

''Same places?''

After a moment, Jenny said, ''Yeah.''

''What kinds of charities?''

''See and learn, curious cat.''

Flashes of news reports replaced the Matrix imagery. They flew by too fast to absorb, but Neko got a sense of Laverty's involvements. Disaster relief, medical charities, work with the underprivileged, relief for the SINless. It all had a curious ring. The man had seemed too wise to the ways of the shadows to be a squeaky-clean philanthropist.

''Jenny?'' The images stopped. ''This Xavier Foundation shows up a lot. Let's look into that.''

''It's guarded.''

Instantly suspicious, Neko asked, ''Black ice?''

''Naw, just shades of gray.''

''Then let's start with the public stuff.''

''Okay. I'll patch through to the public base.''

She was as good as her word, and soon Neko was able to scan whatever he wanted to see in the public records of the Foundation. And what he saw was most interesting. The organization had been founded in the late twentieth century by a man of unknown age, but described as being in his twenties. That man would be in his eighties today. He was something of a recluse, understandable for one described as the heir to an unspecified fortune. There was one picture, taken in connection with the opening of a hospital in Portland, Oregon, sometime around the turn of the century. Though originally a photograph, the image had long since been rendered into a datapic. The most curious thing was that this young man, also named Laverty, looked exactly like the red-haired elf Neko had met. No older, no younger. Of course, the man in the picture didn't have pointed ears; or rather, those ears didn't show, being covered by beautifully coifed hair. The resemblance was too close to be father and son, unless the son had had reconstructive surgery. An unlikely possibility.

Answers always led to more questions. Neko smiled. That was how he liked it. Before the Awakening, this Laverty had run an operation that had sponsored many "special children."

"Jenny, I think we have to look deeper into this operation."

"You think you got something?"

"Let's see, shall we?"

"I think I like you, Neko. You're almost nosy enough to be a decker."

"Curiosity can be a curse. It can take you where you'd rather not be."

Jenny laughed. "Sure, but if it's all tame, there ain't no fun."

They rose through the crystalline lattice and raced along icicles of dazzling beauty. Despite Jenny's forebodings, for several moments it seemed that nothing was in their way. Then the bubbles frozen in the icicles around them began to flow, converging toward them.

"Uh-oh," Jenny muttered.

"What is it?"

"We've been spotted."

Neko's perspective shifted dizzily. "What's happening? What are you doing?"

"Running for cover. I had to load a lot of cutters for this run, so I'm not packing any heavy fighting programs."

The perspective shift halted with jarring suddenness.

"Drek!" The frustration in Jenny's voice was clear even through the voice modulator.

"Hello, Jenny."

Neko heard the words in his head but saw no source. He craned his head, trying to force the interface to shift perspective. He wanted to see who was addressing them. Slowly Jenny shifted her orientation, meeting with the intruding interface.

They were faced by an ebon boy in a glittering cloak of silver sparks. The icon was smaller than Neko expected. Had it been real, the figure would have been almost his size.

"Sorry, Jenny," the ebon boy said. "Even your boss' connections don't get you in here. Goodbye."

The boy waved a hand and a jolt like a roundhouse punch jarred Neko. The screen went dark. From the other room, a crash signaled that Jenny had been affected as well. Neko ripped off the helmet and ran to the door. He knew he couldn't breach it, so he started to work on the locks. Behind him, the computer spoke with Jenny's voice.

"It's okay. Just a little bit of dump shock."

"What happened?"

"We got kicked out."

"Another decker?"

"Yup."

"Can we go back?"

"We could, but we won't. At least not me. You can try somebody else, but I don't think they'll get anywhere against the Dodger."

Neko wasn't sure he had heard correctly. "That was Dodger?"

"In the electrons."

Neko was shocked, but not really surprised. He'd known Dodger was a decker and that Dodger was connected to Laverty. Who better to defend Laverty's secrets? The guardian decker's swift response to invasion suggested the importance of what was being protected. "He's that good?"

"The Dodger *used* to be good. Now he's special."

Special? Indeed he might be. Special enough to be one of Laverty's "special children"? Laverty seemed to have been born in a time when elves were not yet supposed to exist. Was the same true for Dodger? Zip's testimony said so.

Elves older than magic. That went counter to the accepted theories about the awakening of magic and the beginning of the Sixth World. Clearly, the elves had secrets. It could well be that one of those secrets was immortality. Kham could be right about the crystal and what it represented.

Stealing that secret from the elves would be a coup, and using the secret would be an even greater one. The runners who achieved it would be immortal—not just among the shadows. They would live long after their deaths in the tales that inspired those who came after. Sure, it would be dangerous, but Neko knew he would not miss this run for his life.

Neko wondered what his old master would think.

16

Agnes Tsossie, the security manager of Andalusian Light Industries, cowered before Glasgian like the human worm she was. She was right to fear his anger; she had not properly discharged her duty. For the moment, however, he would not express that anger. He would wait until he was satisfied that he knew the reasons for her failure, and had confirmed that the situation offered no threat to his plans. Until then, she remained a useful tool for his use. If she performed well in cleaning up the mess, he might even let her live. After all, it was her first failure.

Surveying the damage in the corridor, he took in the bullet holes, the explosion scar, the smoke stains, and the rusty blotches. A small battle, but a battle nonetheless. A battle that should never have taken place. "You have an explanation, I trust," he said, without deigning to look at her.

For a moment she said nothing. Gathering her courage, he assumed. She was competent in her field, and though he had never told her what had happened to her predecessor, she would know. When she did speak, her voice was marvelously well-controlled.

"As you have seen, sir, they broke in along the north perimeter, bypassing our alarms. Judging by the debris, their equipment was very sophisticated, well beyond what one would expect for a random group of shadowrunners. The conclusion must be that they were a corporate strike team. Our budget for defensive systems precludes complete security against those kinds of resources. We were unable to take any prisoners, so, unfortunately, I cannot confirm for you who the raid's sponsor was."

Glasgian waved his hand dismissively. "I don't care about the details or about your excuses. What I want to know is how they knew to strike at all."

From the corner of his eye, Glasgian watched her smooth her hair back in a nervous gesture. "I cannot answer that without knowing their objective. Without prisoners to question, that piece of data will remain unknown."

He turned and stared at her, letting his disdain show. "They came in from the north, did they not? Less than a hundred meters from the north wing of the light assembly building. They were headed toward Basement Level Four, were they not?"

Tsossie was not a pretty woman and her frown made her less so. "Possibly. They never reached it, though, so we can't be sure that it was their target. We have so many potential targets in the facility."

She knew where they were headed as surely as he did. He could see it in her eyes. "Basement Level Four."

She shook her head in brazen and open disapproval of his categorical statement. "I know you have ordered increased security in that area, sir, but your concerns are not known to outsiders. They would not know you place a high value on whatever is down there. Your desire to keep your new project secure seems to be prodding you to unwarranted conclusions."

Such cheek! He opened his mouth to put her in her place, but she didn't give him the chance.

"We may have had a perimeter breach, but none of the raiders escaped; therefore we have lost nothing. Your projects, including that in BL4, are still secure. I will not deny that a threat exists, but I am prepared to see that security remains good. I could do a better job, however, if I knew what I was guarding. I could be more confident in evaluating the threats we might be facing or in mounting more effective countermeasures."

Indeed, she might. But she might also use the knowledge to her own advantage; if she hadn't done so already. Being a mere human, she sought her own advantage, no matter how fleeting it might be. Perhaps she had been involved in the raid herself, tipping off the unknown sponsors to Glasgian's treasure. If so, she was a fool. Sooner or later, he would find out and, if she was guilty of treachery, she would regret it for the rest of her short life. Petty, fleeting advantages. Such ephemera were attractive to norms, he supposed, because their lives were so short.

"As to more effective countermeasures, I shall handle that. I will arrange for additional magical security. You have no problem with that, I trust?"

"None, sir."

Perhaps. Perhaps not. "I will have Madame Guiscadeaux report to you in the morning. She is a student of mine and I have implicit faith in her skill and loyalty. You will treat her as you would me."

"Yes, sir."

"And as to your level of knowledge, you have all that you need to know," he told her. "Unfortunately I do not. I must know who sent them."

"I cannot tell you that at this time. We have the lab technicians analyzing the raiders' equipment, but the preliminary reports are not encouraging. They were professionals."

"I did not expect them to carry identification cards."

"Of course not, sir. No one would. But corporate raiders are often equipped with products of their own corporation or its trading partners. Easy access, I suppose. These were carrying products of more than one megacorporate family; an attempt to appear as independent shadowrunners. We found nothing that was reliably incriminating, although a preponderance of the circuits in their equipment have manufacturing marks belonging to Miltron. I cannot place enough confidence in that report to target Miltron for reprisals.''

Miltron? The name was unfamiliar, but that was not surprising. No one could remember all the companies on the globe. Tracking the megacorporations was hard enough. One couldn't always know all of their subsidiaries, trading partners, and suppliers. If she saw fit to mention the name, she would know about the company. He decided to let her enlighten him. ''Miltron?''

''A small multinational trading in security magic and tech. Their equipment would be an obvious choice for penetrating our facility. Therefore the presence of such equipment is no sure indicator that Miltron itself is involved.''

''Bring me a file on them.''

''Yes, sir.'' Tsossie walked away and entered a room halfway down the corridor. Glasgian contemplated the damaged corridor. Extermination of the raiders had disturbed its serenity. In a few minutes, Tsossie returned and said, ''If you will follow me, sir. I have a terminal ready for you.''

Glasgian followed her. The terminal was indeed ready and he scanned the data. It was incomplete. ''There is no data on the owners of this company.''

''I can call up a listing of companies involved in the holding corporation that controls Miltron, but beyond that layer of corporations, the web expands. The ultimate holdings are unclear, and I thought it best not to weight mere possibilities with the appearance of certainty.''

''Show me.''

She edged past him to access the terminal. In a few seconds a list of company names appeared on the screen. She stepped back diffidently. For a moment he looked at her instead of at the screen and she stiffened under his scrutiny. She had always shown such efficiency, often answering his questions before he asked them. Not having the list of Miltron's owners ready was uncharacteristic. Perhaps she was hiding something; he would put a watchdog on her. On the other hand, perhaps she was just being cautious. He had not yet punished her; having failed once, she might simply fear a second, more personally disastrous failure. He gave off his scrutiny of her and pondered the names. "Dig deeper."

"It will take time."

"Do it. However, do not take too much time." If his enemies knew of what he and Urdli had hidden in Basement Level Four, he needed to know. So far they had managed to keep secret the location of their prize, or so he had believed until last night's raid. One of the names on the screen caught his attention, suggesting a possibility that had not occurred to him.

"One of the parent companies, Southern Cross Pharmaceuticals, is of especial interest to me."

"Why, sir?"

Tsossie's voice held no hint of fear, but there was definite interest there. Had she taken SCP's coin? Even if she hadn't and wasn't trying to find out if he was on to her, she had no business questioning his reasons.

"Just do your job," he snapped.

"Yes, sir!"

"Go! Do it!"

She fled the room and he sat down in the chair placed before the terminal.

Could it be that this raid had not been directed by outsiders?

SCP, as its name suggested, was a concern operating in the southern hemisphere. Australia, to be specific. Could it be coincidence?

Glasgian recalled hearing of SCP's rise to prominence in the Australian business community. It had involved making an unexpected fortune in a mineral deal. Coincidence? Unlikely. For Urdli, the uncovering of vast mineral wealth would be a trivial exercise.

Urdli knew where the crystal was being kept, and he knew the security arrangements. Was the Australian making a play to cut Glasgian out? Perhaps Urdli believed that removing the crystal from Glasgian's control would slow him down to the snail's pace that Urdli demanded.

If so, that dark-skinned fossil had no idea how wrong he was.

Despite what Glasgian had told Urdli, his own analyses were proceeding well and he anticipated having the answers he wanted very soon. And once he had those answers, he would no longer need Urdli. He would be especially glad not to have to listen to Urdli's constant corrections and homilies, so like those he endured from his father.

Once Glasgian had wrested the secrets from the crystal, he would have the power he sought. And nothing was going to stop him from wielding that power, using it to blast away the shadow of his father and to take his rightful place among the rulers of the new order.

17

Kham didn't know how the catboy had managed to set up a meet with Dodger, but took it as a sign that Neko was learning his way around the Seattle shadows. The kid didn't have the same problem as Kham and his runners. Norms were far more common in Seattle, and Asians were no small portion of that population. Being able to blend in more easily topside, Neko could leave the Underground more safely. Even now, two weeks after the burning of the hall, Kham was anxious about going topside.

But the catboy had been insistent, claiming that this meet would help Kham make up his mind. So now they were waiting in a loft on the Redmond side of Bellevue, their bikes stashed back of a garage down the street. Kham didn't like leaving his Scorpion that way—anybody could walk into the alley, jump the engine, and ride off—but there hadn't been much choice, not even any local gangers to sell them protection. If Rabo or Ratstomper had come, they could have stayed to watch the bikes, but Kham thought things were still too hot for any of the others to come along topside. That meant nobody to watch the bike. There wasn't supposed to be a lot of crime, grand larceny included, in Bellevue, but then there wasn't supposed to be a lot of crime anywhere in Seattle, according to the governor. Just the thought of leaving the big Scorpion unguarded made Kham's bottom itch.

Dodger arrived and there were friendly greetings all around. Kham was surprised that the elf was actually polite. Surprised and suspicious. Maybe Neko hadn't set up the meet. Maybe this was the Dodger's meet, and the catboy was getting Kham involved in more elf drek. But Kham's suspicion eased a bit when the elf melted into one of the chairs and draped a black leather-clad leg over the arm. That was Dodger's casual pose, the one he used when he wanted to show he wasn't really interested in Sally's latest run. If the elf was fixing, he'd be more formal.

Neko cut the prelims, stared straight at the elf, and said, "You were born before the Awakening."

The statement caught Kham off guard, but Dodger

didn't even twitch. He just smiled blandly at Neko. "Preposterous, Sir Cat. Everyone knows that there were no elves before the Awakening."

"What everyone knows is rarely what is real, and there are certain special histories known to the special few, are there not?"

" 'Twould seem you seek to spin a fairy story of conspiracies and shady doings." Dodger yawned. "Pray, Sir Cat, make it brief. I bore so easily, especially when there are real-world deeds to be done."

"I have not brought you a story, Dodger. Just conclusions. I find you prime evidence for one particular conclusion that seems inescapable."

"And what, prithee, is that?"

"That elves are older than the magic."

"You leap so blithely, Sir Cat. I must admire your agility, though your wisdom escapes my sight. Your mystery is no mystery and your great conclusion erroneous. Elves are simply a magical expression of the genetic code of humanity. In the absence of mana, there are no elves."

"Yet you were born before 2011."

"You have obviously assembled some data to convince yourself of that." Dodger turned a bemused face to Kham. "Have you seen this patented drek, Sir Tusk?"

"Ain't." And he hadn't, but for the moment he was inclined to play along with Neko's game and follow the catboy's lead. "But if da catboy says he's got it, I tink he does. Ya gonna come clean, elf?"

"Clean? Clean? What would you know of that, Sir Tusk?"

Kham sucked in air and clenched his fists. He wanted to smash the fancy-talking elf in the face and shove some of those pearly teeth down his throat, but a feather-light touch on his shoulder restrained him.

Neko waited until Kham let go of the breath before speaking.

"You'll not distract us with taunts and insults, Dodger." Neko produced a datachip from somewhere about his person and flourished it. "We know your history."

"Do you?"

Neko smiled the way his namesake might over a captured mouse. "Major William Randall and his tragic wife, Angelica. Beverly Park. Zip and the Hooligans. The fire at Everett Community College. Ice Eyes Estios. Teresa."

Kham furrowed his brow at the list of names. He couldn't make sense of them or see any connections, but the elf obviously did; Dodger's eyes were narrowed into slits and his expression was hard and sour as an unripe fruit.

"Enow!" Dodger threw himself out of his chair and stalked across the room. He stopped at the wall and, after a moment, glared over his shoulder at Neko. "You are a most curious cat, Neko-*san*."

"No argument," the catboy said with a grin. "So satisfy that curiosity and tell us how can an elf be born before *any* elves are born?"

Dodger returned slowly to his chair and stood looking down at it as if struggling with whether he should sit or not. In the end, he did, though not so casually as when he first arrived. Speaking softly and slowly, he said, "I am a spike baby, born at a time and in a place where the mana was stronger for a while. Elven genes express when the mana level is high enough. At certain times, and in certain places, the level was high enough for the genes to activate. 'Tis not such a great mystery. There are others like me. The records of such temporary resurgences of magic exist."

"In dark corners," Neko said.

Dodger shrugged. "Perhaps 'tis as you say. I did

nothing to hide such facts. What matter is it? Those events are decades old; spike babies are a phenomena of no import, for we live in the Sixth World and elves are common now, their existence notable but not noteworthy. You act as if you hold some dark and terrible secret over me. Pray, what is the point of this tiresome exercise? Surely this is no bout of unbridled and pointless curiosity.''

Kham snorted. ''Might be. Ya never know with the catboy.''

''Poor bluff, Sir Tusk. I have seen from your face that you are innocent of much of your companion's doings, yet you have come with him. Hitherto you have always sought your own interests before those of others, and I have had no indication that your inclinations have altered. Thus, you are aligned with him in this invasion of privacy.

''We have run the shadows together, Sir Tusk. I turn to you to sidestep the inscrutability of your companion. What would you have of me? For the sake of our former fellowship, have done with this fencing. Strike home and be done!''

Kham wasn't sure how much of the elf's theatrical speech was real and how much show, but something in the appeal touched him as honest. The elf was really uncomfortable about the topic. Kham liked that. It was nice to see the elf squirming for a change.

''So, how old are ya?''

''I remember the broadcast about the fall of the Empire State Building in the New York City earthquake,'' Dodger said quietly.

''Drek! Dat was nearly fifty years ago. Ya look like a teenager.''

'' 'Tis the way elves are made.''

''Ya ever gonna get old?''

''Each day I grow older.''

''Drek, ya weaselly elf! Ya know what I mean.''

"Ease off, Kham," Neko said softly. "We have no need to insult Dodger, no matter how evasive he is. You understand that one cannot always speak plainly, don't you?" He turned to Dodger. "You are under constraints in this matter, are you not?"

"Believe as you must," the elf replied.

"Oh, I shall," Neko assured him. "Laverty is an elf like you."

"In truth, you have seen him. You know he is."

"I meant something more specific," Neko said coolly. "Laverty is older than you. Is he another spike baby?"

Dodger inclined his head in a sign of affirmation.

Neko poked again. "Surely the mana spikes would have been noticed if they had occurred before the general return of magic."

"If they had been common," Dodger agreed. "But they are, or I should say, were not. Spikes are transient phenomena, short-lived. They come into existence as the mana rises, and vanish as it falls. At those times magical effects certainly occurred. Some things not generally possible until the dawn of this new age did happen. Not often, and certainly not everywhere. And, indeed, 'tis true that some spike-resultant phenomena were noticed, and reported, but the events and beings were dismissed as the fantasies of tabloid journalism."

"Such a casual discussion of history suggests an intimate knowledge."

"Or merely an interest in older matters," Dodger remarked offhandedly.

"Perhaps. But your easy acceptance of mana spikes compels my belief in them and I think I would have no trouble confirming the previous existence of spikes. I find the concept fascinating. Their existence requires a flow of magic, because each spike would, perforce, have a rising and falling component. Each an up and a down that has happened more than once.''

''I said nothing of repetitive spikes.''

''No, but you did say there were many spikes. They need not occur in the same place or over some definite period of time to suggest a repetitive nature to the overall phenomenon of spikes. Tides rise and fall but reach different levels, and tides are very cyclic. Your description of spikes makes me think of tides, of a repetitive element to the presence of mana. Cycles, perhaps. Have you heard of Ehran the Scribe's cycle theory?''

Without a pause, Dodger said, ''I have said nothing of cycles.''

''You have referred to a return of magic and a resurgence of mana. More than once. Those words refer to repetition, and strongly imply a waxing and a waning.''

Dodger turned away to stare out the window. ''I am no expert on magic.''

''But you know one,'' Neko said, smiling at the elf's back.

''I am not conversant with cycles or magic, but I do know enough to warn you that digging into this matter is unhealthy.'' Dodger faced them. ''Leave it alone.''

''A threat?''

''A warning. Such activity will bring you to the attention of certain persons. . . .''

''Elves?''

''Persons, Sir Cat. Persons who will take your curiosity ill. The proverbs, even in your country, tell of the results of undue curiosity.''

Dodger might be trying to hide it, but Kham guessed that the decker's ''persons'' were indeed elves, elves who were already hiding certain other secrets, elves who went around digging up fragging big crystals covered with carvings. Well, those elves didn't have to know that he and the catboy were on to them until it was too late for them to do anything about it. But right now, the attention of elves, any elves, was undesirable. Knowledge about elves, however, was a valuable commodity, and the catboy was persistently pursuing that knowledge.

"Is Urdli one of these persons?" Neko asked nonchalantly.

Dodger started at the mention of the name that meant nothing to Kham. "How do you know that name?"

"Good research. Connections. A collection of coincidences that must, perforce, be more than coincidences. Let us say that I put together a glimpsed face, a certain ruthlessness, memories of such ruthlessness shown in certain operations involving an elf of color, your own connection to this matter, and your previous connections to another matter."

Head spinning, Kham was beginning to be glad the catboy was on his side.

Dodger sighed. "All this in the name of idle curiosity, Sir Cat?"

"Hardly idle."

"Yeah," Kham agreed. "We got our reasons."

" 'Tis likely. I hope they are good enough for the risks you run."

"Run risks before," Kham said. "It's what runners do."

" 'Tis true. Too true."

"How old is Urdli?" Neko asked.

Dodger stared at the catboy for a long time before deciding on his answer. " 'Twould be fair to say he is well beyond his youth."

Kham again wanted to smash the evasive elf in the face, but Neko's feather touch was back, calming him. Kham realized that the catboy was right. Violence wouldn't get a response from Dodger. The catboy knew what he was doing. Kham left him to it.

"So he is older, too. I had suspected as much. Is he older than Laverty?"

Dodger said confidently, "You shall find no records of his birth."

Neko leaned eagerly forward. "How old *is* he, Dodger?"

"As I have said, he is no youth. You'll get no other answer from me, for I know not the truth of the matter. Were I to lie to you in this, you would take it ill. And were I to tell the truth as I understand it, you would think me a liar."

"Very old, then," Neko said, and the silence enveloped the three of them.

Kham didn't know who this Urdli was, but he had a suspicion. The catboy had said "an elf of color," and Kham had only encountered one of those recently—the Dark One. Like all the other elves, he looked like a kid, but here was Dodger saying that this Urdli was an old man. Kham could see now that he had been right; the elves did have a secret of youth, perhaps even of immortality. This was why Neko had set up the meeting, to prove to Kham that he had been right, to show him that they had to do something. "He has it, doesn't he?"

"Has what?" Dodger asked innocently.

Kham knew better than to believe that act. "Our turn fer secrets," he said.

"You do not know where you tread."

"We know more dan ya tink, elf."

"Sir Tusk, knowledge will not save you if you blunder around in your usual fashion."

"Ain't gonna blunder."

"Pray it be so," Dodger said solemnly.

Neko smiled. "Have no fear," he told the elf. "Like my namesake, I shall tread lightly."

Dodger looked at him with sadness in his eyes. "If you must walk this path, Sir Cat, you had best tread lightly and teach your friends to do so as well. Otherwise you had best hope that having cat for a namesake endows you with as many lives."

18

"Where are we going?" the catboy shouted over the roar of the bikes' engines.

"Talk ta Laverty."

"How are we going to do that?"

"Ya said we could talk ta Dodger 'cause he was coming inta town wit Laverty, right?"

"*Hai*, for a government conference. We can't get into that. Besides, Glasgian might be there. If he saw us, he'd know we're not dead."

"Ain't gonna see Glasgian. Conference's a business deal wit da government, right? Well, da payroll boys don't do overtime, not da big boys anyway. So's it's gotta be over 'bout da time business is over. Which is 'bout now. We go wait and follow Laverty when he leaves."

"And if he leaves by air?"

Kham hadn't thought about that. "Ya got a better idea?" he snarled angrily.

"I don't see any need to speak to Laverty. We got our confirmation from Dodger. Much better we retrieve the analysis on the splinter you got from the crystal's frame."

"Go if ya want. I want ta hear what Laverty's got ta say."

Neko didn't reply, but he didn't leave either. They

found spots behind a vendor's truck a half-block down from the Jarvis Building. They waited, buying some food from the vendor so they wouldn't look too suspicious. Kham wolfed down the first of his dogs, while Neko was more fastidious in eating the seaweed-wrapped whatever-it-was that he bought. Kham was halfway through his second dog when he spotted a crowd of media types gathering on the steps of the building. He elbowed the catboy and pointed with his head.

A few minutes later a knot of elves exited the building and were instantly rushed by the media. One pair of elves sidestepped the mob and walked down the steps unmolested, a trick which Kham knew required real magic. It was no surprise that one of the pair was Laverty. A sleek black Euro Westwind stretch limousine waited for them at the curb. Laverty got into the back of the limousine, and the aide, after assuring himself that his boss was safely inside, climbed into the front seat on the passenger side. The doors closed and the limo pulled out into traffic.

Kham and Neko followed.

It took a couple of blocks to catch up, but once they had, Kham pulled his Scorpion out and edged up along the Westwind's port side. When he was even with the rear door, he reached out and tapped on the window. The darkened panel polarized transparent, then it slid down, putting Kham face to face with Laverty. The elf was alone in the back compartment and the screen to the front was up and still dark. The red-haired elf gazed calmly at Kham as though it were an everyday occurrence for his limousine to be accosted by an ork riding a Harley Scorpion. Somehow, Kham suspected that the elf had known he was coming.

"Ain't no way ta hold a conversation," Kham hollered over the noise of his hog.

"I had not planned a conversation." The elf didn't shout, but Kham heard him easily anyway.

"Make plans." Kham slid a hand down to the firm-point on his bike, where he had reinstalled the Uzi after the meet with Dodger. Laverty's eyes flicked to the weapon, then back to Kham's. There was no worry in Laverty's eyes, and that was spooky. But Kham should have known better. This elf had stood up to worse, even without an armored limousine. Kham and his Uzi were no threat to the mage.

"Want ta talk about da Xavier Foundation?"

Laverty's eyes narrowed for the briefest of instants. "A few moments only. Drop back a block and follow."

Kham did as he was told. He didn't have much choice. Confronting Laverty this way had been a gamble, but perhaps it was now paying off. Certainly, he had been unable to think of any other way of contacting a Tir Tairngire council member without alerting Glasgian.

The sleek, dark vehicle was easy enough to follow in traffic, especially on bikes. When other cars got between them and the limo, Kham and the catboy just slid through the jam on the road lines. There were curses and the occasional threat, but Kham revved his engines when cutting off those who offered the first, and gave the finger to the rest.

After about half an hour, the limo pulled into an alley in the outskirts of the downtown business district. It was well past business hours and the area was quiet. It was too early for the after-hours delivery people and only the first scavengers were coming out, to scurry and hunt in the brief time they had before the cops began their evening patrols. The limo stopped halfway through a turn into a parking garage, the nose of the car disappearing into the structure's darkness.

Laverty's window was transparent, and Kham watched him watching them as they approached.

Kham brought his bike to a halt, but didn't bother to put down the kickstand. He draped his hands over the high-rise handlebars, fingers dangling. The sweat-warmed grips were a warm and comforting presence under his meat wrist, and the pressure sensors from his artificial arm gave him the same positional information. Either hand could reach a firing stud for the Uzi. Kham waited until the catboy's bike rolled up beside him.

"Dodger says you're older den he is."

"And you believe him, don't you?"

"We know he was born before da Awakening."

"Do you?" Laverty evaluated them as he spoke. He must have found them convincing, because he went on, "I can see you believe it, too. All right, then, I will not deny it. Dodger must have told you about spike babies. What else would I be but just an older spike baby?"

"Many things," Neko said.

"We got a good idea about what your kind can do," Kham said.

"What about Urdli? Dodger says he's older still," Neko said.

"He told you that?"

Kham answered the elf with silence, and he was glad that the catboy played along. Let the elf make what he would of their silence. Laverty was playing information control, using innuendo and misdirection as a shield. Let him have a taste of it himself.

"Very well then. No matter what Dodger told you, and however you react to what I have to say, I can see that you will draw your own conclusions, regardless of the facts." Laverty sighed softly. "I am not the oldest of my metatype, certainly. There are and always have been places that are foci of magical energy. Even when the mana is strong, it is stronger in such places. At these places, special magics can sometimes be worked. Urdli is Australian, and Australia has many of these focal points. There are only a few left in Europe, places like Stonehenge and an old crypt in Aachen, but the Pacific Northwest has many, which is why Tir Tairngire is situated where it is, as I am sure you have guessed.''

''Australia and the Northwest are wild places, or at least moderately so. They are places where man has not entirely disturbed the natural state as extensively as, say, in Europe, where he has lived and polluted and worked the land for centuries,'' Neko said.

''As you say, the living world is the source of all mana, and mankind has not been kind to the natural world,'' Laverty answered solemnly.

''So dere was magic before da Awakening,'' Kham said.

Laverty spoke in a coy tone. ''The evidence does seem strong, doesn't it?''

''And there are cycles of magic, with this but the latest,'' Neko said.

''If you wish to believe in cycles, perhaps you should go talk to Ehran the Scribe. I'm sure he will be happy to expound on the subject. On the other hand, such effort may not be worth your while.''

Ehran? Was Urdli a street name for the Scribe elf? ''He's not da odder elf, is he?'' Kham asked suspiciously.

Laverty laughed as his window started to slide up. ''Your small friend knows better than that.'' The elf was still smiling as the panel winked to opacity and the car began to roll. The conversation was over.

Kham stared stupidly as the limo pulled the rest of the way into the garage and the roll-down grill slid into place, preventing them from following. What more could he have said or done? Would Laverty have helped if Kham had asked? He doubted it. For all his friendliness, the red-haired elf was still playing his own game, whatever it was. But Laverty's departure without threats or warnings suggested that he would not interfere should Kham and the others take up arms against the elf who had tried to kill them. Or the whole thing might just be an elven way to set them up.

"Now what?" Neko asked.

"Now we go see about dat fraggin' splinter."

* * *

"Good evening, gentlemen," the labcoat said when he met them at the back door of the facility. He looked something like a lab rat himself, all pointy nose and white hair and chinless face, but Cog had vouched for his abilities. Besides his price wasn't too bad. He led them inside and down a corridor that smelled of things Kham couldn't identify, but didn't like anyway. When they reached a room full of humming machines, computer workstations, and glass-fronted cabinets, the labcoat picked up a small glass vial with the remains of their sample and said, "I'd like to ask you a lot of questions about where you got this."

"Ya ain't gettin' paid ta ask questions, just ta answer 'em."

"No need to get testy. I understand the terms of our agreement. As soon as I can verify the transfer of the rest of the agreed-upon price, I'll answer your questions as best I can."

Kham thought there was something *off* about the labcoat. The guy was too edgy. Nevertheless, he agreed to the transfer, watching quietly while the scientist verified it. More credits gone. Kham hoped it was worth it. Letting his impatience show, he asked, "How old is it?"

The labcoat sat back in his chair and folded his hands in front of him. "Very."

"Dat all ya got ta say?" Kham was livid. "You're supposed ta be an expert."

"No violence!" The labcoat was sweating. "There are guards within call."

"Dey ain't gonna be fast enough," Kham said as he pulled his Uzi. "You're gonna do better or you're gonna get ventilated."

Neko spoke from beside him. "That will not help our position, Kham. There are a lot of guards."

"Fine by me."

"But not by me. Perhaps we should let this man tell us more. We certainly have paid for more. I am sure an expert of his caliber has more to tell us."

Kham grimaced, reluctantly holstering his weapon. "Suppose so."

The labcoat looked relieved, but his sweat had stained wide circles under the arms of his labcoat, and he stank. He tried putting a good face on it, though. "No supposition about my expertise, chummer. But I can't tell you what I don't know. This little sliver of yours is a puzzle."

"Elucidate," Neko suggested.

"Yeah," Kham agreed. "And tell us everything about it, too."

The labcoat smiled in a way that told Kham that he'd shown his ignorance and allowed the guy to feel superior again.

"Normally, we can place the age of wood by comparing the pattern of the growth rings with catalogued patterns from trees of known age, but your sample was too small for a dedrochronological analysis. The standard dating technique for organic material is a radiometric analysis using carbon 14. It is based on a comparison between the amount of carbon 14 remaining in the sample to the known ratio for living organisms, a fairly constant value. There are some variations in the ratio over time, so there are some correction factors to be applied, but in general, the method is quite accurate. The analysis was quite simple, but I didn't believe the results at first because the wood seemed so recent.''

''Just what didn't ya believe?''

''All of the carbon 14 has been converted to nitrogen 14.''

''So how old does dat make it?''

''I don't know.''

''Whaddya mean, ya don't know?''

''I can't tell. The carbon 14 method is only good to about fifty thousand years before the present era. In organic materials older than that, all the carbon 14 has been converted, just as in this case. So, without knowing the context or having no other material that might be datable by another method, I cannot tell you how old this wood is.'' He held up the small vial and ruefully frowned at it. ''Beyond saying that it is likely more than fifty thousand years old. Perhaps if you gave me more information? Some sample of the sediments in which it was found?''

Kham started to lose his temper again, but Neko touched his arm in a gesture that was becoming familiar. Kham clamped down his anger while the catboy reached out and took the vial from the labcoat.

''*Arigato,* doctor. We appreciate your efforts.''

They didn't talk about it until they had gone to ground at Club Penumbra. The noise, and the club staff, were their insulation, making them safe from listeners. Jim brought them beers. Kham downed his, but Neko just leaned over his glass and said, ''You realize what this means?''

''Yeah,'' Kham groused. ''We just blew too much nuyen on a wurtless labcoat. Dat stick of wood ain't any help.''

Neko chuckled. ''Not directly. But its existence is highly suggestive.''

"Of what?"

"Of the longevity of elves and their magic. That frame was built by human, or metahuman, hands more than fifty thousand years ago. The carving and the construction were too advanced for the primitive cultures of the time, even if there had been any in the Salish-Shidhe back then. The carvings on the frame were derivative of those on the crystal, further suggesting that the crystal itself and whoever carved it are older still."

"Ya tink da elves did it?"

"They knew where to find it."

"Yeah, so dey did." Pieces were beginning to line up, suspicions turning to certainty. If there were elves, there was magic, and if there were really old magic, the elves weren't telling the whole story. Maybe that Ehran the Scribe elf was the one telling the truth. Maybe there *were* cycles to the magic. It all swirled around into one shape, one thought that kept hanging there before Kham's eyes. Old magic meant old elves. Old elves that looked like kids. Immortality. "Dey got it, don't dey?"

"It seems so."

"Ya want it, catboy?"

Neko sat silently for a moment. "Personally? No."

That was not the answer Kham had expected, but the catboy sounded sincere. "Why not?"

"Personal reasons."

"Ya been a good chummer. I ain't gonna pry. But I gotta know sumpin' else. Ya gonna help?"

Neko raised an eyebrow. "That depends."

"Can't pay ya, leastways not yet."

"Then you are going after it."

Kham's throat was dry. He was scared. Going after the crystal meant going up against Glasgian and maybe the whole Tir council. He had a right to be scared. But the prize. Oh, the prize! "Gotta try."

Neko smiled tightly. "I have to admit to being curious about the result."

"Den you're in?"

"I'm in."

Harness the Talented

19

''There is a mage nearby.''

The certainty in Scatter's voice gave troublesome weight to the rat shaman's announcement. Kham looked around the sea of desks and workstations that surrounded him and his crew. He saw nothing; no sign that anyone had entered the room. The Weeze shook her head, signifying that she had spotted no one in the corridor. Over by the window, Neko was giving a similar all-clear. The Tacoma facility of Andalusian Light Industries wasn't all that big, but the tangle of buildings, garages, sheds, and warehouses offered more than enough places for even a mundane to hide, as they had proven in penetrating to this office structure.

''Anybody wit him?'' Kham asked, but the rat shaman ignored this question as she ignored most of his questions. Kham had to be philosophical about it; even if she answered, he wasn't sure he could trust her estimate. She had her own ideas about how to run things, as he had learned in their quarrelsome planning sessions for this run. Perhaps she was trying to force him into certain actions by playing information control, trusting that she could handle any problems. That would be trouble. Scatter had a lot more faith in her abilities, both as a magician and as a strategist, than Kham did, but he knew he could count on her to do her best, however little that was, as long as she needed their mundane firepower to save her hide.

Walking over to the workstation where their decker

Chigger was jacked in, Kham looked at the screen. The display of whirling geometrics and shifting computer images meant nothing to him. For all he knew, Chigger could be playing some kind of arcade game. Damn, he hated depending on deckers. They were less reliable than magicians, which was saying quite a bit, and none of it in their favor. He spent a brief moment wishing he had Dodger for the Matrix work; he knew Sally Tsung thought the elven decker was wiz. Then he remembered that the elf would probably be even less predictable than usual in this context.

He punched Chigger lightly in the shoulder. ''Come on, get inta da files.''

Chigger just rolled his head back and sighed.

''Hurry, Chigger!'' urged Ryan, the new kid. Ratstomper and The Weeze had recommended him, saying he might be green but he was good with locks. They had already used him to get into the building, but the kid wasn't going to be any use to them if he panicked. From the look of him, Ryan was on the edge of letting his fear take control. Kham hoped he'd calm down; they didn't need a panicker. Ryan continued to urge the decker to greater efforts, while nervously fingering the snarl of amulets and talismans around his neck.

It was bad enough they were doing this run with a first-timer kid. They didn't need one who had also lost his grip on reality. Ryan was dripping with the rat shaman's hoodoos, which in itself wasn't bad. Most of the kids in the Underground had them, though maybe not quite so many as Ryan. Those gewgaws would be worthless to him, magically anyway; Ryan was mundane. But whatever they did or didn't do, the kid believed they worked. Maybe the trinkets would keep him calm.

What did worry Kham was the amulets *his* guys had taken up. Like Ryan, Ratstomper and The Weeze were wearing the silvered rat skulls and tangled bits of bone that were Scatter's tokens. Even Rabo had one of the skulls. Kham had noticed the way Ratstomper had fawned on Scatter, back when the Green Band's scuz-boys were working Neko over. Now, The Weeze had taken to backing Scatter's suggestions. Even Rabo had agreed with one or two of the shaman's ideas. Bad signs, all. Scatter was gaining influence with his guys, and she was the only available magician for this run. What was the next step?

He checked on Scatter, thinking maybe she was doing something about the mage she claimed was nearby, but she was just sitting where she'd plopped herself down when they'd entered the room. Her legs crossed underneath her, she swayed slightly, occasionally humming to herself. Her eyes were rolled back in her head and the eyelids twitched irregularly, giving her a disturbingly uncanny look. She might be doing magic. Or she might just be wigged out on drugs.

You just never knew with shamans.

Ryan's exhortations were growing more frantic. So much for his faith in Scatter's magical protection. Kham hissed at him and told him to keep the noise down, but it was only a minute or two before the kid was back at it again. Despite Ryan's agitation, the only reply Chigger gave to all his urging was an occasional grunt.

Frowning, Kham turned to Rabo. "Ya said dis guy was good, Rabo."

"He is, Kham, he is. Must be a lot of ice."

"Well *we're* gonna get iced if he ain't outta dere soon wit what we need."

"He'll make it," Rabo insisted. "Trust me."

"It's yer butt, too."

Rabo thought about that for a second. "Come on, Chigger. Move your virtual butt."

Silence descended on the room, save for the intermittent flurries of tapping from Chigger's fingers flying across the keyboard of his cyberdeck. The seconds dragged into minutes; long, sweat-producing minutes. Kham nearly jumped when Scatter announced, "The mage has moved on."

They all breathed a collective sigh.

"We were lucky," Neko commented.

Scatter turned eyes of deep, dark mud on the catboy. "Nothing of the sort. My spirits protected us. They shielded us from the Andalusian wage mage, blinding her eyes and ears to our presence."

"Way to go, Scatter," Ryan said, giving her a double thumbs-up.

On the other hand, Kham thought, it could be that the mage just decided to go to the can. They had no way of knowing if Scatter had done anything at all. They still hadn't really gotten anywhere.

Then Chigger gave a moaning chuckle, the same queer victory signal he'd uttered when he'd secured copies of the IDs used by the company that serviced Andalusian's phone system. The decker dropped into the real world and said, "Got a loc."

"Don't keep it ta yourself. Pop it over ta Rabo's screen and get back ta grabbing anyting dey got on da crystal."

The decker mumbled something and resumed his tapping on the cyberdeck. His screen still churned with agitated shapes, but the monitor on which Rabo had been following his progress blanked for a second. The new image that appeared was a diagram of the facility. Kham recognized the layout of the buildings, so he knew that the red dot identified their current position. A red line zigzagged across the compound to a flashing pip that should be the area where the crystal was stored. It was two buildings over. Kham didn't like it; too many of the areas on the diagram were dark.

"What's dis drek? How come so much is blacked out."

"Must be a partitioned system," Rabo said. "Different parts of the facility are under different security protocols."

"Why didn't Chigger cut into the main program?"

"There may not be one. Depends on how paranoid the security chief is."

"We got anyting on how secure dat area is?"

Rabo ran the keyboard, causing a series of windows to pop up and vanish in rapid succession. The stuff went by too fast for Kham to make sense of the data. At last Rabo hit the Enter key with a flourish and said, "There. That's what we got."

Yellow dots appeared at scattered locations of the diagram, some brighter than others. The clusters at the gates and in the security headquarters building Kham took to represent guards. Surprisingly, there were only a few along the route Chigger had shown them; the decker had done his job right.

"Alarms?"

"Chigger'll ride cover."

"Good enough." It had better be. If the decker couldn't override the alarms as the rest of the team proceeded, they'd bring all of Andalusian's security down on their heads. "Now just where is dis place we're headed?"

"Main assembly building. Ground floor's mostly open space and automated assembly lines. They'll still be running, which means supervisors, but we'll miss all that if we follow Chigger's route. We'll be coming in along an access tunnel into Basement Level One. The rock's three levels down on Number Four."

"Underground. Yes. That is where we must go." Scatter chuckled. "The spirits speak of secrets hidden beneath the earth."

Geez, don't need this mumbo-jumbo drek. If only he

had been able to get a real magician. Kham tried to ignore her. "How come the security's so light?"

"Perhaps they are running the purloined letter gambit," Neko suggested.

Without Kham noticing, the catboy had joined them at the console. That meant nobody was watching the outside. Kham sent Ratstomper; he'd rather have the catboy's advice than 'Stomper's. Besides, with 'Stomper out of the conversation, Scatter wouldn't have quite so much support among his guys for this round. "Okay, catboy, what's dis letter stuff?"

"I meant that perhaps they conceal the importance of what they hide by not hiding it at all."

"No," Scatter said sharply. "There are magical defenses."

Kham didn't doubt that, even if he didn't believe Scatter had definitely determined their presence. "Ya gonna be able ta deal wit 'em?"

"My spirits are strong."

"Right."

They skimmed Chigger's data filchings for what they could use and laid plans to further penetrate the Andalusian facility. Kham started to feel a slim hope that they might actually pull it off. Half an hour later, they left Chigger to dig for files and ride Matrix overwatch, and Ryan to guard the decker while he worked. They made it down to the basement without a hitch, but a sentry at the entry to the tunnel required a bit of special attention from Neko. The catboy amazed Kham with the stealthiness of his stalking and the sureness of his strike. The guard never knew what hit him, but then Kham didn't either. One moment the uniformed man was standing there. The next minute he had crumpled to the ground. They stowed the fellow in a utility closet, and waited for Chigger to signal that he had overridden the lock. Then they headed down the tunnel.

The entry to the assembly building's basement had a manual lock as well as an electronic one. Chigger cut the latter, but he couldn't do anything about the former. Before Kham could regret having left Ryan with the decker, Neko stepped up and began working on the lock. His skill in opening it was another surprise from the catboy, leaving Kham to wonder why he had needed Ryan on the crew at all.

Lights and occasional noises from some of the rooms indicated that there were still active company folk on this level, so they moved through it as quietly as possible. That wasn't too hard. The late-night wage slaves were snugged by their consoles in isolated cocoons of light. They had no interest in the corridors, or anything beyond their little worlds of chair and workstation, for that matter. Besides, it was easy to sneak along on carpeted floors.

Once aboard the freight elevator, Kham pressed the button marked BL4 and they started down. Chigger overrode a signal from Level Three, ordering the car to proceed without responding to the suit or wage slave calling for an elevator on that floor. Reaching Level Four, they soon found new reason to be cautious. Most of the illumination panels were out and those that remained lit were functioning at reduced output.

''Economy measure,'' Ratstomper suggested tentatively, almost as if she didn't believe it herself.

Kham reached up and lifted the panel covering one of the darkened fixtures. Like its covering, the bulb was intact. In the first office they found, Rabo used the terminal to contact Chigger.

''Cut off,'' the decker told them. He didn't know who had done it, but he was sure that it wasn't an authorized reduction.

Kham cherished the thought that an employee might be responsible, until they found a guard sprawled at the first corridor junction, his neck broken from be-

LAUBENSTEIN '92

hind. The conclusion was inescapable; someone else had also made an unauthorized entry into the facility.

Two minutes later, in the fitful light of the darkened corridors, they saw who.

There were three of them. They were moving cautiously, too, and even more slowly than Kham's crew. They were rough boys—mercs or razorguys, judging by their looks. A professional team, too, judging by their stealth and the seamless coordination of the drill they used when passing doors and corridor junctions. The problem was that they were between Kham's guys and the rock and headed in the same direction.

They might have been shadowrunners, but Kham had never seen more than two runners who went for the same look. Though each of these guys was different from the others, their overall appearance showed a striking similarity. Kham thought about the twinned cyberguys they'd run with; maybe look-alike was the new style.

All of these rough boys were big—bigger even than Kham. They looked a little oddly proportioned; their heads seemed too small for their bodies, like caricatures of professional bodybuilders. They wore what looked like close-fitting helmets and their heads were protected from behind by a jutting ridge from their backpacks. Wire-thin aerials poked up past their sleek pates, and other wires protruded at irregular intervals along the sides of the backpacks. They were blatantly armored with extensive matte-finish chrome and they were dripping with weapons—from holstered pistols and knives to what looked like Ceres tribarrel machine guns. These guys were pure heavy metal from hell.

The last of the three rough boys stopped and turned slightly. His position under one of the lit ceiling panels gave Kham a good look at him. Much of what Kham had taken for armor were cybernetic replacement parts, but what struck the ork most was the guy's face. What he could see of it. The little flesh that wasn't plated over looked gray and shriveled. Tubes snaked from his nose and slithered over his shoulder to disappear into a junction on the backpack's ridge, and the light from above glinted coldly on the gleaming chrome orbs of his eyes.

"Who da hell are dese guys?"

"Not security," Neko whispered.

With awe in her reedy voice, The Weeze added, "They're carrying three times the ordnance we got."

Ordnance was ordnance, and a single bullet could kill you just as dead as twenty. These cyberized bozos were here and interfering in Kham's run; that was all that mattered to him. "Scatter, why didn't you spot 'em?"

"They were not there," the rat shaman said, pouting.

"Well, dey're here now. You saying dey teleported in, like from da *Enterprise?* Drek, wouldn't dat be sweet."

Scatter gave him a withering stare. "No teleport; they have no magic."

"You sure? Dey been hiding from you."

"No magic," Scatter insisted. There was a frantic note in her voice, which was also rising in volume. "None!"

"Geez," Kham hissed. "Keep it down, ya old bat."

"Lay off the shaman, Kham," Ratstomper whined. "She's already saved our butts plenty."

The crew quieted down, but it was too late. With slow, machine-like precision, the heavy metal intruder swiveled his head to stare into the darkness between the light fixtures where Kham and his runners were crouched.

20

Before they could react, the rough boy had them covered. His tribarrel hissed softly as the barrels spun at speed on their silenced bearings, but for some reason he didn't fire. Kham was relieved; this was no place for a firefight with opponents armored so heavily they looked almost made of metal. Since only one had tumbled to their presence, there was a chance that he and the guys could take these bozos down if their fire was fast and accurate enough. But Kham's guys would take losses. They'd blow the run, too. Kham knocked Ratstomper's hand away from her holster before she could get a grip on her gun.

The metal man, apparently satisfied that Kham's team offered no threat, snapped the snout of his weapon up into carry position and began to mumble to himself. Kham dared to breathe once more, but only until he realized that the tribarrel was built into the guy's arm. These guys were some kind of super soldiers. What the frag had he and the guys bumped into?

The metal man started toward them, moving quietly, for all his bulk. The scent he gave off was mostly machine oil, cordite, and plastic, but underneath it all, Kham caught a whiff of something rotten and decaying. The guy stopped a few meters away. A good leap might put Kham inside the sweep of the tribarrel. The idea was gutsy, but not bright. That kind of cowboy move might work against an ordinary opponent, but it would be suicide against the coiled-spring speed of this metal man.

"WHAT—" The sound of the guy's first word reverberated so loudly in the corridor that he stopped speaking immediately. He hummed to himself for a moment, then began again, his voice much softer. ''You are not Andalusian personnel. What are you doing here?''

Kham managed to find his voice; no one else in his group seemed ready to speak to this guy. Hostile wouldn't get them anywhere, so he tried to make his tone casual and friendly. He also hoped he sounded confident, but he doubted it. ''Could ask ya the same, chummer, 'cause ya sure ain't on da Andalusian staff.''

The hard line of the rough boy's mouth twitched down at the corners. ''I am not here to answer questions. I have the gun, you will answer my questions.''

''Eliminate them,'' the second one said. The other two had come ghosting up behind the first.

''Negative,'' said the third. ''Elimination entails unacceptable reduction of mission success-probability due to noise factor. Beta has already lowered probability by two percent with speech volumes.''

''What are these guys?'' Ratstomper wailed, voice cracking. ''Some kind of fragging robots?''

''Silence!'' commanded number three. Something in the manner of the other two suggested that this one was their leader. ''Interference in our mission will not be tolerated. If your talking sufficiently raises the probability of discovery, your elimination will no longer threaten our mission, and you will be eliminated.''

Ratstomper looked bewildered.

''Da chummer just told ya ta shut up, 'Stomper. Do it.'' Kham returned his attention to the metal men. ''We don't want no trouble wit you chummers. None of us is Andalusian, so we ain't got no feud. Ya do yer biz, we do ours, and everybody's happy.''

''You will remain here. You cannot be allowed to interfere with our mission.''

"Don't want ta."

"Beta, move them out of the corridor and remain with them."

A gesture with the tribarrel pointed out the chosen room, and Kham nodded to his guys that they should go along. Everybody moved quietly, pointedly keeping their hands away from their weapons. Kham carried his AK in his left hand, and held his right up at chest level, well away from the butt of either the holstered automatic or that of the magnum protruding from his belt.

Their captor waited until the door to the corridor was closed before turning on the room lights. The place was some kind of electronics lab, but Kham didn't know enough about such things to even guess at the uses of most of the equipment. He was sure that none of it would be useful as a weapon. Neko tried to put a counter between him and the metal guy, but a shake of the rough boy's head, emphasized by a pointing tribarrel, brought the catboy back around to the front. Neko gave Kham a shrug, then sat with his back against the counter and shut his eyes. Kham was damned if he didn't think the catboy was taking a nap.

Time dragged on. Though their captor never seemed jumpy, he was always alert, reacting to their slightest movements, but only bringing the tribarrel to bear when somebody's hand got too close to a weapon. One by one, the guys got tired of standing and sat down; all except for Scatter, who stared venomously at the metal guy.

After about twenty minutes, Kham felt the pulsed flashes of heat from the earpiece of his headset. It was the signal that Chigger wanted to communicate with them. He would have simply ignored the signal, but their captor turned cold chrome eyes on him.

"Explain the signal."

Somehow this guy knew that Kham was getting

a message. Denying it wouldn't help. "Car's over-parked."

"Unlikely. Try again, smart boy."

Kham considered keeping his mouth shut, but he wanted to know the reason for Chigger's call. If there was trouble, he doubted that Andalusian security would make fine distinctions between the two groups of intruders. "It's a call from our decker. He wants ta talk ta me."

The metal guy blinked once. Kham couldn't be sure about those featureless orbs, but he thought the metal guy's gaze was roving the room. Then the man pointed at a workstation and said, "Order your decker to input to this station."

"Why should I? What's in it fer us?"

"Your lives," the metal man replied with the ghost of a smile.

He was probably right. The Andalusians would have them if they ignored Chigger, and this rough boy would waste them if they ignored him. Some choice. Kham did as ordered.

"Whatcha got, Chigger?"

"Got an alert on the system. Routine now, but the trigger seems to be somewhere near you. You guys blow it?"

"Naw. We're just sitting around."

The metal man reached past Kham and switched off the voice input. "You will order your decker to penetrate the security system and set off false alerts."

"That'll wake up da whole place."

"It will reduce their security's effectiveness by spreading their effort. They will not know which alarm is real and which is false."

"Yeah, so?"

"It will hide our efforts."

"Ya mean *yer* efforts. We ain't in dis togedder."

"Kham," Neko said softly, eyes still closed, "if

Andalusian security concentrates their efforts here, we are in as great a danger as our large friends are. More, perhaps. I suggest you do as he says. Confusion is profit to the shadowrunner."

Only when you're in charge and know what's really going down, Kham thought. Still, there was a certain logic in the argument. Kham relayed the metal guy's orders to Chigger.

While Kham was convincing Chigger to do as the metal man said, the rough boy popped open a panel in his chest plate and pulled out a jack. Plugging into the console, he said, "You will also have him disable the alarms at the locations I transmit."

"I suppose it can't hurt." Us, anyway. Who knew what kind of IC Chigger'd run up against? Kham hoped it wouldn't be bad. "When ya got dat done, try dis," he said, telling Chigger what their captor wanted. Then he cut the connection, leaving Chigger to do what had to be done.

"We have achieved a significant increase in success probability. The random elements have provided a Matrix operative with access to portions of the inner facility system," their captor said. Though he was talking, he did not seem to be addressing them. Kham and his guys could hear him, too.

They waited some more.

Scatter twitched like she was seeing something. Then Kham heard distant gunfire: short, controlled bursts as the characteristic moan of a tribarrel answered a scattering of single shots. It didn't last long. Within less than a minute, the door to their jail slid open, heralding the return of the other two metal men. Seeing one carrying the crystal in a padded harness slung over his shoulder, Kham thought his eyes would bug out. Drek, the guy was as strong or stronger than a troll; it had taken three orks to manhandle that same rock into the elves' van.

Their guard nodded to his cronies like he was answering a question. He seemed to listen again, then said, "Acknowledged. You may leave," he said, turning to Kham. "We have no further interest in your activities. However, I suggest you flee. Andalusian security is active."

No fragging drek.

These bozos had stolen Kham's prize out from under his nose and now they were offering him and his guys a chance to provide yet another distraction to Andalusian security. Real fragging swell.

The metal men took off down the corridor. Released, Kham's team started digging out their weapons. They were itching to go, but he was worried the first one out the door would catch a burst from a tribarrel. Kham tried to grab Neko as the catboy bolted from the door. He missed the snatch, but it wasn't disastrous; the catboy pulled up short without going through, listening.

"They're around the corner already."

Drek, they were fast!

There was a rush for the door. As Scatter went by, she started to turn away from the direction the rest of the guys were running. Kham collared her. Their team didn't have the firepower of the metal men; they'd need an edge to get out of the facility alive. "Wit us, rat-lady," he said, pulling her along.

They backtracked through the facility, heading for where they'd left Ryan and Chigger. Much to Kham's surprise, and relief, they made it back without trouble. Gunfire from outside told him the guards had found the rough boys. Kham smiled at that; who was providing whom a diversion now? With his crew reunited, it was time to beat feet. He gave Scatter a shake.

"All right, rat shaman. If yer spirits are so hot, let's see 'em get us outta here."

"Put me down, oaf," the old woman snarled at him.

"Ya gonna help us or scamper like yer totem?" She struggled ineffectually in Kham's grip. "Ya got a better chance if we're along wit ya."

She stopped struggling and stared sullenly at him. "You could be right."

"I am."

"Put me down."

He did. She made a show of dusting herself off and making ineffectual passes through her snarled hair. Worthless preening, and a waste of time as well, but Kham knew she was only trying to impress her importance and dignity on him. Let her try; nothing she did could give her dignity in his eyes. Importance? Well, important was as important did. Rationally, he knew that there was another purpose in what she did; a magician needed to be calm and collected to do her magic. Not so calm as to think she could double-cross them, though. He showed his tusks and said, "Dere are enough of us ta get ya if ya try ta frag wit us. And even if we don't get ya, ya still gotta get past da guards. Ain't gonna be nobody ta shoot de Andies on yer tail if ya dump us. Dey got a mage, remember?"

"There is no need to threaten me. I have accepted your evaluation of the situation." She stuck her runny nose up in the air. "Now, be silent! I must speak with the spirits."

Scatter raised her arms above her head and rattled her collection of charms and talismans. Swaying, she danced a few steps and hummed. The dance speeded up and she began to chant.

"Oh mighty Donsedantay, hear me. Come, oh mighty spirit. Walk with us and shield us with your cloak. Guide us out from this place, guard us from those who would do us harm. Donsedantay, dweller in this place, hear me. Donsedantay, come to my call."

The old woman chanted on while Kham sweated. This was taking time, too much time. Why couldn't she just wave her hands and do the magic? That was the way Sally Tsung worked. Fragging shamans always had to make a show out of the thing. Besides, while this rat shaman was doing her song and dance, the Andalusian guards might be closing in on them this very minute. Certainly the Andies were sealing off the entrances to the complex.

There would be no getting out the way they got in. With a full alert on, the bribes Kham had paid wouldn't keep the guards bought. He couldn't afford to pay them not to see the people huddled in the back of their bogus Gaeatronics Telecommunications repair van. There would be fighting, and the van was just a van; he and the guys would never make it past the front gate without armor. They'd have to drop back to plan B: head for the wire, blow their way through, and disperse. And pray they got away.

''We have the protection of the mighty Donsedantay,'' Scatter announced.

For whatever that's worth, Kham thought. Yet something had changed; the air around them seemed charged with electricity. This wasn't like Sally's magic and that made Kham uncomfortable. Still, somehow, in some indefinable way, he felt safer. ''Dis better work.''

''Have faith, boy. The spirits are strong and they heed my call. I shall lead you to safety.'' Ryan, Ratstomper, and The Weeze looked relieved as she stepped into their midst. Even Rabo perked up. Scatter pointed to the door. ''We leave that way.''

The guys starting moving, Scatter leading from within their group. Neko gave Kham a shrug and a bemused smile before also falling into step. Kham noted the catboy held his little SCK submachine gun ready. Kham checked his AK and followed.

They left the building by a side door, after making

sure no Andalusian guards were in sight. Keeping to the shadows, they moved through the complex, avoiding the main thoroughfares, where occasionally they could see security vehicles prowling. Several times squads of Andies passed at various crossroads, often hesitating, but never turning toward them. Scatter's magic seemed to be holding. But Kham knew that somewhere out there was a mage, and he wasn't sure the rat shaman's magic would be enough to hide them from a magician's sight.

The sounds of combat tore his thoughts away from magic and mages. Kham heard first an explosion, then gunfire, coming from no more than a hundred meters away. From the sound, the firefight was going on ahead of them, probably somewhere on the next thoroughfare. Neko stole ahead to scout. He signaled for a cautious approach, so Kham joined him to see what was going on.

The Andies had engaged and injured one of the metal men. The wounded rough boy was crawling away from a crater in the pavement, trailing an oily black sludge from gaps in his shredded chrome leg. Sprawled in the middle of the road was an Andie clutching a rifle-mounted grenade launcher; he'd paid for the shot that had gotten the cyberguy. The Andies buddies were peppering the cripple with light-weapons fire, but they obviously didn't have any more heavy stuff. And none of them was taking the chance of running out to recover their downed chummer's weapon. Too bad, Kham thought. That was the only way they were going to be able to dust this guy. But then, the Andies would probably have reinforcements soon, and those newcomers would doubtless be loaded for bear.

Metal glittered in the darkness across the way, spooking Kham. He brought up the AK, but held fire when he saw what was coming toward him: the other two metal men. Instead of charging the runners, however, the two guys took the corner and raced down the thoroughfare with unnatural speed. Their tribarrels moaned in short, sobbing bursts and an Andie dropped with each burst. One of the metal men stopped by his fallen companion and helped the guy up while the other stood over them, placing bursts that kept the Andalusian guards under cover. Despite all the confusion of the weapons fire, Kham realized that these rough boys no longer had the crystal.

Drek! All that fuss and the bastards had lost the rock. Now that the elf was alerted that someone knew where he was keeping it, they'd never have another chance to get at it again. At least not one that Kham could mount. Every bullet being fired was another hole in the balloon of Kham's dream; they'd lost the gamble. The only good thing was that those fragging piles of walking hardware were attracting all the Andalusians' attention, giving him and the guys a chance to get away.

But before he could get his guys organized enough to take advantage of the Andies' preoccupation, screeching brakes announced a new arrival. A vehicle had arrived somewhere out of sight behind the guards' position. The reinforcements, no doubt. Moments later, a woman stepped around the corner of the building. Glowing with arcane energy, she gave off enough light for Kham to see the grim determination on her face. The Andie wagemage had finally made her appearance.

The metal man on overwatch gave her a burst, but the bullets howled away in whining ricochets. Smiling tightly, the mage waved her hands in a conjuring gesture, then straightened one arm in a casting motion. Lambent energy streamed from her fingers, coiling into a brilliant beam that shot through the air like a laser. The air around the trio of cyberguys began to glow, lighting them up as if they stood in the glare of a hundred arclights. The edges of the sphere of light wavered like pavement on a hot summer day; the forms of the metal men within the light were just flickering shadows. The wounded cyberguy howled as his injured leg started sparking, the flashes of light even brighter than the flaring magic around them. So hellishly intense was the light that Kham expected the rough boys to start smoldering and then wither away to ashes. For a moment nothing happened, as everyone watched the cyberguys engulfed in the wage mage's spell. Time seemed frozen. Then the glow surrounding the metal men faded some, then a bit more. Continuing to dwindle away, the light dissolved into the ruddy glow of dying embers, then winked out. Seemingly untouched, the cyberguys remained standing where they had been.

The mage looked worried.

As one, the metal men raised their tribarrels and opened up on the mage in a triple stream of fire. The tracers burned lines in the night no less brilliant than the mage's spell. The wage mage staggered back, her magic still shielding her, but Kham could tell that wouldn't last long. Turning, the mage tried to run for cover, but it was too late. A small rocket launched by the cyberguy leader impacted at the mage's feet, tossing her into the air. Her arcane shield faltered and three streams of tracers intersected in her, ripping her apart.

Under renewed fire from the Andalusian guards, the metal men started a slow retreat back toward the runners, indicating that the rough boys weren't planning to stay and finish off this batch of Andies. Kham and his guys couldn't afford to wait any longer. There was no telling where the cyberguys would head. Drek, they might even decide to take up residence in the alley the orks currently occupied. It was time to go now and make the best of it.

Kham led his guys out of the alley, urging them to run like hell across the road. To his surprise, they were not instantly riddled with bullets. One slug did strike the pavement near him, but Kham concluded that it was a stray or a ricochet when no others followed. Once everyone was safely under cover and sheltered from fire by the building, they stopped for a second to confirm that no one had been hit. Fortunately, all was well.

Looking around, Kham hoped desperately that he might discover some other option than running straight down the alley; the cyberguys might come this way just as easily as they might have stumbled into the place where the orks had been hiding on the other side of the road. About ten meters down, he spotted a turn-off from the alley, but it led north, probably right back to where the Andies were taking cover from the metal men. Other than that, the alley went on for a ways before dumping out into what looked like one of the complex's main thoroughfares, though Kham couldn't tell which one.

Then he noticed something. A truck, sitting hard by the side of the building near the turnoff that led north. It was pointed toward them, but its rear doors were open. Though bearing the Andalusian logo, something about the vehicle just didn't look right to Kham. "Hey, Rabo. Whaddya make 'a dat truck?"

The rigger squinted at the dark shape. He screwed up his face in concentration, then spoke with the assurance of a rigger who knows his hardware. "Marked Andalusian, but it's not standard Andie issue. Armored for sure. Carrying a load, too. Maybe it's the wheels those other bastards came in."

"See anybody in it?"

''Naw.'' Rabo went pale. ''You ain't thinking what I think you're thinking, are you?''

Rabo was quick and Neko was just as fast, adding. ''You want to walk home?''

''They'll kill us if they catch us heisting their wheels from underneath 'em.''

''Tink da Andies wanta give us hugs and kisses?''

''Time is wasting,'' Neko pointed out.

''Right.'' Dragging Scatter along in hopes it would keep her spirit's alleged protection around them, Kham led the way to the truck. Once they were closer, he could see that the cab was indeed empty. No one came out the rear to challenge them, either. ''Can ya handle her, Rabo?''

Rabo peered into the cab. ''She's rigged. If the system ain't guarded, we'll be rolling in two.''

''And if it is guarded?'' Chigger asked in a panic.

''Then I get fried,'' Rabo answered with a resigned shrug. ''And you get to try next.''

Chigger protested, ''I'm no rigger.''

''Truck's only going to roll for somebody with a jack. If it ain't me, it's you.''

''You're wasting time,'' Neko said.

Rabo turned on Neko. ''Look, catboy—''

''He's right,'' Kham said.

''Yeah,'' Rabo said sheepishly. Pulling the door open, he climbed in. He looked at the plug for a moment, his tongue slipping along his lips. Then, with practiced skill, he snugged it home into his datajack. Lights flickered on the console and Rabo slumped.

Not another one, Kham thought, but his fear was unfounded. Rabo stirred as the lights on the console steadied.

''She's mine,'' he said with a grin. ''All aboard.''

Kham hustled the crew around to the back doors, but stopped dead in his tracks when he saw what was inside. Sitting there in a padded cradle was the crystal.

This vehicle definitely belonged to the metal men. They must have loaded the rock, then gone back for their injured comrade. Such touching sentiment! Kham ran a hand down one side of the stone. They'd fragged Kham's run, and now he was going to return the favor. Serve the tin-plated bastards right.

The firefight between the metal men and the Andies was winding down, which meant they didn't have much time. After making sure everybody was aboard, Kham swung the doors closed. None too soon; a moaning tribarrel blasted shells against the door just as he snicked the latch shut.

"Roll it, Rabo!"

Kham was knocked from his feet as Rabo accelerated. They careened through the Andalusian facility, taking a few wrong turns before Rabo figured out where they were. At one point they plowed straight through a surprised squad of Andalusian guards, but the Andies didn't fire on them. They were too busy trying to deal with the metal men, who, in their single-minded pursuit of the truck, blasted through the corp guards as if they weren't there. The vehicle, however, was fast enough to outrun the hyperactive rough boys, and the orks howled their glee as the cyberguys dwindled away, firing all the while in impotent fury. Rabo crashed the truck through the outer gate, the purloined van's armor shrugging off the guards' fire. Safely through, Kham and his crew roared off into the night.

21

Kham could tell from the frown on Zasshu Chen's face that the dwarf wasn't happy to see them; he didn't need all the yelling and foot-stomping. It wasn't hard to understand Zasshu's ire, because the truck the runners had abandoned in the Andalusian facility was the dwarf's and it might be traced back to him. Even offering to replace Zasshu's lost truck with the one they had hijacked didn't make the dwarf any happier. He claimed that the bullet scars would make the truck too easy to spot, and the tech on board made it too hot. Once Zasshu had spent his fury and calmed down a bit, Kham persuaded him to accept promises of recompense once the runners realized a profit from their haul. Fortunately, Zasshu wasn't nosy enough that Kham had to explain what they had in the truck. The dwarf must have figured that dumping the truck's own tech on the black market would turn enough to cover his expenses.

But Zasshu wanted to minimize his own exposure, and Kham couldn't argue with that. The dwarf wanted them gone, and soon. It took some fast talking to get him to give the truck a quick spray of paint to hide the Andalusian markings, but in the end even the cautious dwarf had to agree that unless they had at least a little bit of camouflage, they probably wouldn't survive to pay him.

While Zasshu was taking care of the truck, Kham took the opportunity to use the dwarf's telecom. He punched in the code for the flop in the Underground. Lissa answered.

''Hoi.''

''Hoi, Lissa.''

''Kham?'' Her voice quivered a little, as it always did when she realized that he'd survived another run.

''Yeah, babe. We done it.''

''Are you coming home now?''

''Got some biz ta take care of first. Be home soon, babe, and when I get back we're gonna do some serious celebrating. Dis run's gonna set us up fer life.''

''But you're not coming home now?''

''I told ya. I got some biz ta take care of.''

''You're just going to get yourself killed.''

Maybe, but he wasn't going to tell her that. ''Ain't gonna be a problem.''

''Like it wasn't a *problem* for John Parker last time. Like your *problems* didn't come home with you. Kham, how can you keep doing this to us? To the kids? What are you thinking of? You're a father. You've got responsibilities.''

''I know dat. I'm doing dis one fer ya and da kids.''

''Don't blame your idiocy on us,'' she shouted, and then was off on one of her tirades.

He listened. What else could he do? She needed to vent her steam. He knew that Lissa was motivated by fear, that she dreaded the thought of her and the kids being left without his protection. He understood that. Once, he had thought she worried about him getting hurt, but he wasn't so sure anymore. A few years ago, things had been different. Or had they? Maybe he'd just been younger and stupider then. Whatever the truth of the matter, all of Lissa's concerns were valid, even if her words stung him.

When she ran out of steam, he said, ''I'll be careful.''

''You always say that, but somebody always comes back dead.''

''Dat's not true.''

"It's true too often."

Before she could start up again, he said, "Gotta go," and hit the button to sign off. That small lie ended the conversation, but it didn't solve anything. Lissa would still be there when this was all over, and he'd have to face her. She wouldn't be happy that he'd hung up on her.

He took a moment to gather his thoughts back to biz before he punched in Sally Tsung's number. The calm, pleasant voice on the other end told him that Sally wasn't in and asked if he wanted to leave a message. Nothing new there. Kham wasn't sure what sort of message to leave. He wanted Sally to look at the crystal and tell him all about it, but he didn't want to trust anything to the phone. So he just said that he had a proposal for biz and that Sally should meet him tomorrow just after sunset, at the usual place just off High Bridge Road. He figured she wouldn't balk at that choice for a meet; it was Ghost's territory and she'd feel safe there to meet with an ork she probably still thought was dead.

Out on the floor of Zasshu's place, they were stripping off the tape that had protected the truck's glass from the paint. It was time to go. Kham rousted the crew.

"Where's Chigger?"

"Buzzed," Rabo told him.

Kham digested that. The decker didn't know much about what was going on, unless he'd learned something in the Andalusian system that he hadn't passed on. But Rabo didn't seem concerned, and Chigger was his chummer. Kham decided to let it ride. Too bad Scatter hadn't gone with the decker; the shaman was back inside the truck, running avaricious fingers over the surface of the crystal.

"Surprised ya didn't buzz wit Chigger. Waiting fer a ride back to da Underground?"

The shaman looked at him with eyes that gleamed from beneath her brows. "Yes, yes. The Underground is the place for this."

"Well, it ain't going dere. Zasshu's right; dis armored van is a hot item, and I ain't about ta dump it in one of da Underground's garages. If it's spotted dere, its owner is gonna know just where ta look fer us, and dat's too close ta home."

"It can be protected in the Underground," Scatter said. "I can protect it."

"Maybe ya can, maybe ya can't. Widdout knowing who dis heap belongs ta, ya don't know what ya gotta hide it from. Whoever sent dose metal men has got resources, and lots of 'em. Until I know what we're dealing wit, I don't wanta call anybody's attention ta da Underground."

"I concur," Neko said. "But some sort of place must be found."

"This ain't it," Zasshu cut in. "You got yer paint, so you can get the fragging hell outta here till you can pay up."

Not wanting to upset the dwarf further, Kham hustled the crew back aboard the truck. "Yer bein' real understanding about dis, Zasshu."

The dwarf hawked and spat. "Ain't got much choice."

"I'll remember dis," Kham said as he climbed into the truck.

"If you don't, I will. And I know where you live."

* * *

"They spent the day rolling through Seattle, stopping only to fuel the truck, grab a bite, or take the chance to drop a load. It wasn't much fun, but neither Kham nor any of the others could think of a safe place to stash the truck.

It was late afternoon when they rolled into the Red-

LAUBENSTEIN·92

mond Barrens, moving down High Bridge Road into one of the more built-up, and consequently tougher, sections of the Barrens. Paradoxically, this part of Redmond was safer for orks because a good part of it was territory that belonged to Ghost-Who-Walks-Inside. Ghost was an Indian and had known his own share of blind intolerance, so he was more accepting than the bulk of the district's population, and his people mostly followed his lead. Still, the Injun didn't have control of the whole population. Who did? Kham sent Neko out to spot when they pulled up to wait for Sally. As the only norm in their crew, he was the best choice. No sense looking for trouble, even if they were in Ghost's territory.

Neko drifted back in. "A blond woman in fringed leather and a stocky Amerindian with beaded headband and a matched set of Uzis are coming down the street."

"Sounds like dem." Kham looked out at the gathering darkness. "On time, too."

"You don't need her," Scatter said.

The rat shaman had refused Kham's periodic offers to drop her off near one of the entrances to the Underground, apparently preferring to stay where she could touch the crystal. Kham didn't like, or trust, her possessive attitude toward the thing.

"Need who?" he said offhandedly.

"The Tsung witch."

He squinted at the shaman. "Howddya know who I'm waitin' fer?"

"I am a *shaman.*"

"Yeah, right." She was that, but she was a sneaky little bitch as well. He remembered her hanging about Zasshu's office while he made his calls. It was almost the only time he'd seen her away from the crystal since she'd first laid eyes on it. "Got good ears, do ya?"

Scatter ignored his remark. Instead she caressed the crystal and crooned, "It is old. Very, very old."

"Tell me sumpin' I don't know. Like how it works."

"That will take study," she said in a hushed whisper. "But I will learn."

Kham looked out the passthrough to the cab. Through the front window he saw two figures turn the corner onto the street where they were parked. Sally and Ghost. He left the truck and walked around to meet them.

Ghost nodded greeting, and Sally gave him her usual sardonic grin. "Hoi, Kham. Looking good for a hunk of dead, burned orkflesh. 'Zappening? Your call sounded like you had something hot."

Kham nodded. "Some hot magic." Kham led them around to the back of the van, noting that Ghost's eyes roved over the battle scars on the van. The Indian was a street samurai, more highly modified than Kham, but less obviously so. Ghost knew his way around a firefight, and Kham was sure the Indian could smell the new paint. Having checked out the truck, Ghost's eyes now examined the orks clustered at the truck's back doors.

"New boys," Ghost noted. "Tough fight?"

"Not dis one," Kham said.

The Indian nodded—he'd be making his own judgment on Kham's performance, as always—but he said nothing. Kham opened a path through the knot of his guys so Sally could get through. Sally looked into the body and said, "When did you take up understatement, Kham?"

"Told ya it was hot. Whatcha tink it is?"

She shook her head, frowning in puzzlement. "Static on the screen."

"I told you she would be no help," Scatter said from the darkness of the truck.

Sally turned cold eyes on the rat shaman. ''And who's this paragon of knowledge and *haute couture?*''

''Scatter,'' Kham said.

''Our shaman,'' Ryan added proudly.

''Shaman, hunh?'' Sally cocked her head. ''Rat, right?''

''Rat is my totem.'' Scatter's tone sounded a trifle defensive to Kham.

''Well, if you could have done what my chummer Kham needed done, I don't think he would have called me. Do you?''

Scatter hissed at her. ''I *will* unravel the crystal's secrets.''

''Sure you will, stinky. But for now, step out or step back. It's time for a pro to go to work.''

The rat shaman refused to budge, but Sally climbed into the truck anyway. She looked the crystal over, running her fingers along the carving, then she sat down crosslegged in the clear space near the doors. Pressing her hands together, she touched her index fingers to her forehead and closed her eyes. After a moment she lowered her hands to her lap. She stayed that way for long minutes.

The guys began to fidget, shifting around and speaking in low tones. Ghost just leaned against one of the doors, watching Neko watch Sally. At last Sally came out of her trance and shakily started to stand up. Ghost was beside her in a flash, catching her before she could lose her balance. She looked drained, and the smile she gave Kham was a faint reflection of her earlier one.

''You weren't kidding when you said you had hot magic, Kham. Do you have any idea what this is?''

''It's got someting to do with da way elves live a long time and stay looking like dey ain't never gonna grow up.'' He told her about the run into the Salish and the double-cross by Glasgian. He almost told her about Dodger, but held that back, using Laverty as his example of a long-lived elf.

''Oh, yeah,'' Sally said, turning thoughtful eyes back to the crystal. She was quiet for some time. ''It's powerful, all right. Maybe even powerful enough to be some kind of eternity magic, but there's something else about it.''

''What?''

''I can't get hold of the spells; they're different somehow from what I know. Primitive, but powerful.''

''Then *you* cannot tell how to use this power, either,'' Scatter said vindictively. ''You have no reason to scoff at me.''

Sally's response had none of the flip arrogance of her earlier banter with the shaman. ''I'll argue about reason to scoff, but I'll also admit that I can't tell how this thing does whatever it is it does.''

''Could ya figure it out?''

''Maybe. Given time, but that isn't something I've got right now. Besides, this poking-prying stuff has never been my long suit.''

''Ha!'' Scatter crowed triumphantly. ''I told you she was worthless, Kham. I will unravel the crystal's secrets for you. We shall share those secrets together.''

Sally gave the shaman a harsh look, then turned back to Kham. Her face was serious. ''I'd sell it before I trusted her, Kham.''

''Sell it?'' Kham hadn't thought of that. ''Ta who?''

''The highest bidder. Cog could handle it. A piece like that should fetch a fine price on the open market, and selling it has the added benefit of getting you out of the loop with this elf and the owner of the truck. They'll leave you alone if you get rid of this thing.''

''What if da bad guys buy it back?''

Sally shrugged. ''Then soothe your conscience with the money. You'll live, and you'll live rich.''

"You must not sell the crystal," Scatter insisted.

"And why not?" Sally asked.

Scatter scurried forward and pointed an accusing finger into her face. "You mages have no souls! You don't understand the true nature of the world! This crystal has a spirit, as do all things. Selling it for gain would pollute that spirit. It is your kind that is corrupting the magic. Defilers! Defilers, all! Now you would defile this mystery just because you do not understand it."

"What drek!" Sally batted away the shaman's hand, and Scatter retreated a step. Sally turned her back on the woman. "Kham, you'll only get yourself more trouble if you're going to listen to this pile of rags. You've been a good chummer. We've had a lot a fun, had a lot of good runs. But this is something I don't want a piece of. You keep it, and all I can do is wish you luck. Dump it and come up cool, then we can do biz. You know the number."

Sally started to walk away, and the orks parted to let her go. Kham couldn't think of anything to say. Sally had been his hope of unraveling this magic. Without her, how could he do that?

"Do not stay too long in one place," Ghost advised as he turned to follow Sally down the street.

Dumbfounded, Kham watched them go.

Neko herded the other runners back into the truck, then tugged at Kham's arm. Reluctantly, Kham climbed in and watched the catboy swing the doors closed. They rolled.

Kham had always valued Sally's advice. She'd said this stolen crystal was powerful. He knew it had to be, if it could do what he thought it could. Still, she didn't want any part of it, and that puzzled him. This magic could help norms as well as orks. More than once he'd heard her complain that she was getting too old for running. He had the answer to that sitting in this truck with him, but she didn't want a part of it. What did she know that he didn't?

She said to sell it. She said they could get a lot of nuyen for it. Well, selling it would get him out of his financial problems, and it would go a long way toward settling the score with that fragging elf Glasgian. If Glasgian didn't end up as the buyer, that is. But maybe even then, especially if Scatter was right that selling the crystal would mess up its magic.

But using that magic . . . what *that* might do! He would never be old, never worn out and wrecked like his mother. Lissa would never grow old either. And the kids. They would no longer be condemned to an ork's short life. They'd have a chance to learn and do and be. All he had to do was unlock the crystal's secret.

But how?

He didn't know what to do.

22

''Hey, Kham. One thing you *can't* do is sell these wheels to Zasshu.''

The raw eagerness in Rabo's voice brought Kham out of his funk. ''Why's dat?''

''They're too, too sweet. That halfer wouldn't appreciate even half of what this baby has got in her, real cutting edge once you look under the hood. I'll bet half the circuits are prime Miltron. Gotta be, with what this baby's packing. Sure ain't Ares tech. Ain't no ID's on the boards, but this rig has gotta be Miltron make. The mesh is just too smooth to be a slapdash. But that halfer just ain't got appreciation; he'd probably break her up for parts."

"Safer that way," The Weeze pointed out.

"You ain't got no soul, Weezer. This beauty deserves better than that."

"My butt says otherwise. This bucket could use better shocks," Ratstomper complained.

Rabo laughed her off. "You're just pissy 'cause you been sitting too long. The ride's fine up here."

But riding was something they couldn't do forever. "Don't get too comfortable up dere, Rabo. We gotta dump dis heap soon as da stone is safe."

"Aw, Kham, you don't understand what you're giving up. This baby's got armor, weapons, and lots of wrinkles I still ain't had time to figure out yet. Give me a week or two and I'll have her humming to my tune. You'll see. We got us a real street chariot here. Lone Star's Citymasters ain't gonna be a problem anymore."

The rigger's enthusiasm got old quickly. Couldn't Rabo see the problems that keeping the hijacked truck would cause? Kham decided to point out the most obvious of them. "Rabo, ya wanna be around when dose metal guys come ta repossess dis ting?"

"Who says they're gonna?" Rabo was uncowed. "They were rockin' and rollin' with the Andies last we seen them, and with no way 'a gettin' outta there without wheels or wings. We got their wheels, right? And they didn't have any wings."

"What if they did?" Ryan asked. "They were tough bastards."

"Drek, yeah," The Weeze agreed. "You see the way that one kept fighting even with his leg out? Howled like a gutted cat when that wage mage tried to fry him, but he was hosing down Andies soon as the light faded. Sure as flux leaves ya dripping drek. I wouldn't want to square off with one of those guys."

"Ain't gonna have to," Rabo insisted. "I'm telling you they're history. This baby's ours now."

Ryan's face twisted into a worried grimace. "How can you be sure they don't have friends? We don't know who they were working for."

"Yeah," Ratstomper echoed. Kham was beginning to think the two of them had become a team. "You don't think they was working for that other elf, do ya, Kham?"

"Drek! What you got for eyes, Stomper?" Rabo asked. "They weren't elves. Under all that chrome they were breeders."

"Go frag yourself, drekhead," Ratstomper snapped back. "Just 'cause they're breeders don't mean they weren't working for an elf. Ain't we worked for daisy-eaters ourselves? And we sure ain't no pointy-eared, flouncy elves."

That got the guys laughing, even Rabo. When things quieted down, The Weeze said, "You know, Stomper might be right. Maybe those two elves who went with us to the Salish had a falling out. Maybe we just got caught in the middle of a family spat."

"I don't think those cyberguys were working for an elf," Neko said quietly.

All the ork eyes in the back of the truck turned to him, including Kham's, who wanted to know how Neko had reached that conclusion. "Why not, cat-boy?"

"They didn't operate with any magic."

"No," Scatter said definitively. "They had no magic."

"Good point. Elves love dat stuff. Running a team witout it just ain't dere style. At least not fer Tir elves."

Ryan wasn't buying it. "So who says the ones after us was Tir elves?"

"One of 'em was," The Weeze said. "That Glasgian twerp."

"Maybe so," Ryan agreed reluctantly. "But the catboy said the other was Australian. *I* don't know how Aussie elves operate. Do *you*, wisearse?"

"If Urdli had wanted the crystal, he would have taken it himself," Neko asserted.

His tone was confident and the others nodded in agreement, but Kham found himself wondering. How could Neko be so sure? As Kham recalled, he had first heard Neko identify the Dark One as Urdli to Dodger, who had not batted an eye, like they both knew what the catboy was talking about. Neko hadn't told Kham or the guys anything more than that the elf was an Australian, but the catboy obviously knew more about the dark-skinned elf. The catboy liked his secrets too much to be a real chummer. That was fine by Kham unless those secrets might be important to their survival. But was this the best time to try to pry them out? Before Kham could frame his question, The Weeze was asking one of her own.

"Well, if it ain't a spat between Mister Dark and Mister Light, why were those heavy metalboys after the rock?"

"The conclusion is obvious. Someone else knows about the crystal," Neko replied.

"Another elf?" Ryan asked tremulously.

"What's with you? You got elves on the brain," Rabo said. "There's a lot more folks out there working angles besides elves."

Holding on to his idea, Ryan whined, "But how would anybody else know about the elf eternity magic?"

"*We* know," Kham pointed out.

"So who do *you* think it is?" Ryan asked, turning on him. "Rabo said this rig was Miltron hardware.

Those are some scary boys. I don't want to frag with that corp."

"Now, I didn't say it was for sure Miltron," Rabo protested.

"But it *could* be," Ryan insisted. "They make mil-spec stuff. Drek, maybe they *made* those cyberguys. If they did, they could make more. Drek, we're gonna get hosed."

"Calm down," Neko suggested. "Panic will not do us any good at all."

"Somebody's got to worry about it," Ryan said.

"We're all worried," Neko said quietly. "We're just not panicking."

Ryan cast frantic looks around the enclosed space. The other orks were almost as calm as the catboy. The kid looked to his shaman, but Scatter was absorbed in the crystal. Ryan turned to Kham. "What do you think, Kham. Is it Miltron?"

Kham shook his head. "Dunno."

"Well, what are we going to do?" The young ork looked about ready to freak, but Kham didn't have the answers to satisfy him. If Ryan couldn't handle not knowing who was out there looking for them, he wasn't cut out for shadowrunning. Best to find that out now, before the kid lost it during a run.

Ryan stared at him, chewing his lip. He fidgeted for a while, then said, "Harry would know what to do."

"Harry hates magic." Ratstomper turned to Scatter. "Present company excepted."

"Not excepted. Harry tolerates my presence because he understands my importance, not because he likes me or my magic. You are right, Ratstomper; Harry hates magic. He would not welcome you bringing this to him, but that does not mean we should not take the crystal to the Underground. We will be safer in the Underground. And perhaps Harry will have a solution to the problem. Certainly he has survived where younger, more stubborn orks have perished.''

Kham knew the dig was meant to undermine him in front of the others, something he couldn't allow. He whipped out an arm, caught a handful of Scatter's rags, and dragged her from her seat. Of necessity, she collapsed to her knees in front of him. ''Dis ain't Harry's run,'' he growled. ''Now, I know ya got good ears, ratface. And I know ya already heard me, but I'm gonna say it one more time anyway. We ain't taking da rock back ta da Underground. It's too dangerous.''

He let go and the rat shaman scrambled back to her seat. They rode in silence for several minutes, Kham aware of the glances shooting back and forth among the orks. He was also aware that the catboy avoided eye contact with any of them. The Weeze was the first to break the silence.

''Can't ride around forever, either.''

Neko stretched, drawing attention to himself. ''So we find a place to rest where we can hide the truck.''

''Where?'' Ratstomper slapped the bench seat. ''We been riding around for hours and nobody's come up with anything.''

''Kham, you know that I am not familiar with Seattle's shadow world, but when I was conversing with Cog, he suggested that Mickey's Garage on Welbourne was a congenial establishment.''

''No good,'' Rabo said. ''Mickey was hit by the Azzies the other night.''

''What? When?''

''While we were humping our butts around the Andie dump.''

''How da hell d'ya know dat?'' Kham snapped.

Rabo chuckled. ''I told you this baby was a sweetie. Her 'puter's got a little program that swipes realtime updates from Shadowland Headline News. But, you know, I been thinking about it, and I remembered an abandoned warehouse out near the reservoir in Puyallup. The scuzboys from Forever Tacoma been using it for tumbles with the Black Rains. It's nice and quiet when the boys and girls ain't playing.''

Ratstomper guffawed. ''Real sudden interest in finding a place to park, Rabo. Could it be your butt's been planted too long, too?''

''Maybe I just got sympathy for the weak-minded.''

Ratstomper started to retort, but Kham cut her off. ''Anybody got outstanding problems wit da Eff-Tees or da Rains?'' Nobody admitted to any, so Kham told Rabo, ''All right, den, dat's where we're going.''

Traffic made the trip long, though they encountered no trouble along the way. The Eff-Tees were in residence when they pulled up, so they had to negotiate. The big troll that was the gang's warlord took one look at Scatter and demanded she do some magic for them as the price of dossing down in the warehouse. ''I will do this for you,'' Scatter said to Kham, clearly implying the need for repayment. She disappeared with the gangers for an hour or so, then came back grinning with self-satisfaction and bearing an armload of bags from the local Voodoo Chili franchise.

Kham was too tired to care.

He shoveled in the stuff along with the rest of the guys, and watched them drop off one by one. The Eff-Tees were standing watch as part of the deal. Not the best security, but they'd do because nobody knew Kham and the guys were here. Before long, he too drifted off in a troubled sleep.

Some time later, he awoke. Something, a noise that didn't belong in the warehouse, had nudged him out of his dark dreams. Whatever he'd heard had stopped, but there were strange scents in the building. Befuddled by sleep, Kham couldn't place the vaguely familiar scents. Wary, he reached for his AK. Better armed than sorry.

A foot descended on his wrist, grinding it to the floor. The pain forced a snarl from him and he twisted over onto his side, but the effort only brought more pain as something swiped him across the temple. He fell back, the darkness lighting up with stars that weren't there. When he could focus again, Kham found himself staring at metal-armored legs. He looked up, a long, long way to the open maw of a tribarrel and further on to the tiny chrome-plated head beyond it.

It was one of the metal guys.

He'd seen their strength and knew that struggling wouldn't get him anywhere. He watched helplessly as a second metal man removed the AK. Once the weapon was out of Kham's reach, the first released him, gesturing for Kham to stand up.

There were only two of the cyberguys this time, but that was two too many, because once again they had the drop on Kham and the guys. In a matter of minutes all of them were clumped together under the metal men's guns. Kham noticed that the cyberguys kept most of their attention on Scatter, but he doubted the rough boys would have anything to worry about from the cringing rat shaman. He also didn't believe that the cyberguys' preoccupation would offer even a halfway decent chance to make a break. There was nothing to do but wait.

While one of their chrome-plated captors kept watch, the other went over to the control box on the front wall and opened one of the bay doors. A few seconds later a long silver limousine rolled in, followed by a trio of dark vans. Two of the four vehicles had to bump over the bay boundaries into the next one in order to fit; their companion vehicles and the orks' truck pretty much filled the first bay.

None of the vehicles carried any insignia, but the cleanliness and uniformity screamed corporate. The men and women who climbed out of the vans were as corporate as their vehicles: all wore identical, unmarked coveralls and flak vests and all carried identical weapons. As if those overchromed rough boys needed more goons as back-up. Kham gave his attention to the limo; that was where his future lay. The big shot inside would decide.

The car had halted with its front bumper nearly touching the gathered orks. Its interior was unknowable behind polarized glass. After a moment, however, its rear doors opened to reveal a dapper norm getting out from the near side. Kham had never seen this suit before, but there was no mistaking the uptown finery and the air of habitual and utter authority that clung to him. The suit smiled pleasantly at him, but Kham wasn't in the mood to smile back. He was looking at the guy getting out the car's other side, somebody who Kham suddenly realized wasn't lined up with the rest of his runners like he should have been. It was Neko the catboy, and still armed.

23

"Sticking wit your own, catboy?" Kham asked. Ratstomper growled in accompaniment to the question.

The suit answered before the catboy could open his mouth. "I suggest that you refrain from admonishing Mr. Noguchi. Your anger is misplaced. He is not my own, Kham. Pardon me if you find it overly familiar of me to address you by name without formal introduction, but you have done so much to aid my enterprise that I feel we should be friends. My name is Enterich, by the way."

"Mr. Enterich sponsored my trip here," Neko said.

"Ya been working for him, huh? Shoulda known no breeder would be a real chummer. Just biz, huh? That why ya led 'em ta us."

"I didn't—"

"Please do not view Mr. Noguchi as a Judas, Kham," Enterich said smoothly. "Though it is true that in pursuit of my principal's interests I arranged for his transport to this continent and saw that he was chosen for Glasgian and Urdli's run out to the Salish lands, I did not set him as a trap for you. Mr. Noguchi was placed as part of an insurance policy which, unfortunately, was necessary. Your involvement was, shall we say, unanticipated. Had not a certain impetuous personage sought to hide his deeds completely, you would have gone quietly on with your life without ever knowing that Mr. Noguchi and I had done business. As it was, our interests ran parallel for a time, but that time is over. Now it is time for our ways to part."

"So now ya take us out of da way."

Enterich raised his eyebrows. "Why would you think that? You have been more help than hindrance."

"Too bad."

Frowning, Enterich said, "Kham, I don't believe that you like me."

Bright boy. Kham spat onto the concrete floor. "Don't like elves dat hide dere faces."

Enterich's frown vanished, replaced by a faint, patronizing smile. His gold incisors sparkled. "An elf? Oh no, I'm not an elf."

"Didn't say ya were. Work fer one dough, doncha? Dat Aussie elf."

"Urdli? Hardly. If you knew Urdli as I do, you would know that he would never countenance working with me."

All right, so it wasn't the other elf. The catboy had

really known what he was talking about when he said that somebody else knew about the rock. "Den who'dya work for? Miltron?"

"Still guessing? You should be careful about that. Someone might think you've been looking too deeply into the toys you've had on loan. Much as I like you, Kham, it would be unwise to tell you. You might find such knowledge unhealthy. A family man like you has to think about the future."

As if their situation wasn't unhealthy already. Enterich's rough boys had been willing to kill Kham and his guys merely for endangering their mission. Talk was the biggest danger to secrets—and it was clear that Enterich had plenty of those, and wanted to keep this crystal business as one of them. Dead men don't tell no tales; neither do dead orks. "Don't look like me and da guys got much of a future."

"You misunderstand. Your escapade with the truck was annoying, especially since the transport was a valuable asset, but it has also had some benefits. Even now the young elven prince is looking in all the wrong places, searching for you and ignoring my operatives. It is a minor advantage, but one that has already proved useful, and so you have my gratitude. In return, I would like to assure you that if you bow out now, peacefully, I will not hold your earlier interference against you and your friends. As one who abhors unnecessary violence, I will even go so far as to ensure that the hellions will never bother you again."

"The what?"

"Ah, yes. You would not know." Smiling, Enterich indicated the metal men with a wave of his hand. "These gentlemen are hellions. Wondrous artifacts of technology, are they not? Elite volunteers—trained to perfection, heavily modified with state-of-the-art cyberware, then, of course, trained some more. Freed from most of the constraints of the flesh, they are tireless, swift, and powerful. The ultimate blend of man and machine, near-perfect soldiers. I have great hopes for them, once the bugs are worked out of the system. The mechanical components confer a remarkable resistance to magic, but the necessarily limited organic component is sometimes prone to irrationality. But we have safeguards for that.

"You must excuse me, I tend to wax overly enthusiastic over new baubles. I'm sure my problems with new technologies are of no interest to you."

Enterich sketched a little bow, as if in apology. Meanwhile, one of his corporate goons had left the group checking out the hijacked truck and had come over to hand Enterich a slim silver chip-holder that she said was from the computer aboard the truck. Enterich gazed thoughtfully at the thing for a moment, then turned back to Kham.

"Ah, you see. You have been even more helpful than I had originally realized. I am sure I will find these files your decker—Chigger, wasn't it?—removed from the Andalusian matrix to be of interest. However, at the moment I have other matters to attend to and wish to conclude our business. Do I have your word that you will drop all interest in what the truck carries?"

Thoughts of what he'd be giving up raced through Kham's brain. There was nothing he could do about it right now. "If I don't give ya my word?"

"That would be unfortunate. For you. As I was saying, the hellions lost their companion in the Andalusian raid. As they blame you and your runners for the death of their comrade in arms, I fear that they would like to pay you and yours back in kind."

"We didn't do nuttin' ta get dere chummer geeked."

"They believe your complicity sufficient, and wish to make a response. Their small minds are filled with loyalty to their friends; misguided loyalty at times, but strong nonetheless. The streak of irrationality, I suppose.''

Kham knew a threat when he heard one. And the fact that the catboy knew where his family was hiding meant that Enterich probably did, too. ''Don't see anyway ta stop ya.''

''A wise conclusion.'' Enterich held out one hand. ''I do not wish us to part enemies, Kham.''

Kham merely stared into the suit's face until the man dropped his hand. The Weeze muffled a snort.

''Very well,'' Enterich said, taking a credstick from his pocket and holding it out. ''A business arrangement, then?''

Kham ignored that, too.

Uttering a soft sigh, Enterich dropped the credstick. It clinked and clattered on the hard floor.

''There is a small compensation there, along with a number you can contact if Glasgian continues to annoy you or any of your runners. Like you, I do not wish to see him prosper.'' Enterich returned to his limo and climbed in. One hand on the door handle, he seemed to have another thought. ''You may believe that I have cheated you in this, but it is not so. The crystal is not precisely what you believe it to be, and though I cannot expect that you will take my word for it, you would be wise to do so. The crystal is not for you, or your kind, and you would do well to forget its existence. That would please me, and you would find that my good will can be helpful.''

How could Kham forget the crystal, especially in trade for nebulous promises of nonexistent corporate good will? No matter. He knew better than to reveal his evaluation of the worth of Enterich's compensation. ''Maybe I will.''

''If you do not, I think that my principal will be less lenient than I have been.''

The suit shut the door and the limo started up. A

squad of the uniformed goons boarded the truck, while the rest of them scurried back to their vans. All but one of the vans pulled out with the limo and the truck. The hellions waited, covering the departure of their boss. Then they too took off in the last van, the sound of the vehicle's engine echoing hollowly off the warehouse walls.

24

Once the hellions were gone, the orks were free to recover their weapons. Most of them did so at once, but Ratstomper turned to Neko instead.

"Your suit friend didn't say we couldn't take our frustrations out on you."

Heedless of his weapon, she charged the catboy. Fortunately for her, he didn't use it. He sidestepped, his hands touching her briefly and sending her crashing into one of the beams. Moaning, Ratstomper collapsed to the floor. The rest of the gang wasn't so reckless. Once they were armed, they spread out and surrounded the catboy. Kham's regulars were careful to keep out of each other's line of fire, but Kham had to adjust his own position to avoid hitting Ryan, who wasn't too bright. He knew he wouldn't hit the kid if he fired, but he couldn't count on Ryan being as good a shot.

The catboy was cool about it, not making any sudden moves. Kham almost wished that Neko would try to use his SCK. The submachine gun was perfect for such close quarters, even better than Kham's skeletal-stocked AK, but the catboy was too smart to try to shoot it out against so many guns. Or maybe too stupid; the guys would make a point of taking their time if they killed him with their bare hands.

"I did not betray you," Neko protested. "It was the truck."

"Trucks don't talk," Kham said.

"That one did. Enterich said it had a homing device."

Kham had to concede the possibility. But a homing device in the truck was one thing, the catboy's coziness with the suit was another. "What about it, Rabo? Ya find any squealers on dat rig?"

"Naw."

"Gonna hafta do better, catboy."

Behind Neko, Ratstomper pulled herself to her feet. Taking in the circle around the catboy, she bared her tusks in a smile. Then she pulled thirty centimeters of steel from the sheath at her hip, and tested the edge with her thumb. Kham had seen her use that knife with great precision in the past.

The catboy cocked his head slightly as she approached; Neko knew she was there, but he didn't move. She slashed with the knife, cutting the strap on his weapon and slicing through the outer layer of his windbreaker. Kham recognized the sound of steel slithering along ballistic armor-weave. The SCK clattered to the floor.

"You are making a mistake," Neko insisted.

"You're the one made a mistake," Ryan said.

"We're gonna see just how many ways there are to skin a catboy." Ratstomper chuckled evilly and flourished her knife.

Everyone held still for a moment. Then Neko spun and the knife went whirling away, nearly skewering The Weeze. The little Jap was crawling all over Ratstomper. The two of them went down, the ork squalling. Kham cursed and put up his AK; there was no clear shot while the two of them were tangled. He stepped in, ready to club the catboy with his weapon's butt.

The warehouse suddenly lit with a harsh flare of light and everyone, even the two combatants, froze. A mocking laugh drifted down to them from the catwalk servicing the overhead crane.

"My, my, my, squabbles among thieves. And I'd heard that shadowrunners were supposed to have more honor than common backstreet burglars."

His long coat emphasizing his height and lean angularity, Prince Glasgian Oakforest glared down at them. Rabo spun and lifted his weapon, but a flash of fire from Glasgian's hand struck the rigger's assault rifle, and he dropped it with a yelp. The weapon fell to the floor, glowing cherry red. Rabo jumped back in time to avoid the explosion as the ammunition cooked off. A fragment cut through Kham's pants leg and scored his thigh. He hissed at the pain, but held his ground; the wound was only minor. It didn't look like anybody else had caught any of the shrapnel.

"I have no time for your foolishness," Glasgian shouted down to them. "Where is my property?"

"Ain't got nuttin' dats yers," Kham told him.

Glasgian smiled wickedly. "Then you won't mind if I verify that."

"Look around all ya wan—"

Pain exploded in white-hot incandescence in Kham's head. Fiery fingers poked searing furrows through his brain as fragmented images of the hijacked truck, the crystal, and Enterich chased each other across the inside of his eyelids. He thought he screamed before the darkness overwhelmed him.

When he came to, he was flat on his back on the concrete, his head aching worse than it had after his last tumble at Grabber's place. Overhead, the elf was still there. A shuriken glinted dully in the wood of the catwalk and the elf clutched the side of his body, a trickle of blood leaking through his fingers. Glasgian was staring at something to Kham's left and holding one hand outstretched.

Wincing with the pain caused by the movement, Kham rolled his head around to see what the elf was focused on. The catboy was a foot off the ground, his hands beating at some invisible opponent. Neko was turning purple as if someone were strangling him.

The elf made a contemptuous, throw-away gesture and Neko dropped to the floor in a heap. Kham couldn't tell whether the catboy was still breathing or not.

"I thought it was dogs you lesser types took to be loyal, not cats." The elf looked down imperiously at the orks. "Enterich must not be allowed to keep the crystal. Though he is not long since departed, there is no time to gather forces. You will help me recover the crystal."

"You're fragging crazy," The Weeze said.

"Incompetents! You don't know what you have done!" The elf raised his head and growled his rage at the rafters. "Have you any idea of what you have been dealing with?"

Nobody answered him.

"How could I expect you to? The chain was long, and even *I* had a difficult time following it to its end. *He* was very clever, using subordinates with other connections. I first thought that I was being thwarted by my erstwhile colleague, but I should have known better. That Australian fossil would never move so quickly. Once we had dissected that cybernetic monstrosity *he* had created, I knew Miltron was behind the harassment. I had but to look for the company's sponsors, and there among the minor shareholders, hiding behind a facade of other firms, I found *him* coiled in ambush. I should have known that Miltron would have less savory sponsors than foggy-headed old men whose time had passed. Finding Enterich involved here converts suspicion to certainty.''

''So those goons *were* Miltron,'' Rabo mumbled.

''Miltron?'' Glasgian snorted. ''Of course they were Miltron. Miltron is but one of *his* many fronts, trog. Another puppet for the secret master. The Enterich with whom you spoke is an agent of Saeder-Krupp, ultimate master of the puppet Miltron.'' The elf shook his head in false pity. ''You still don't understand, do you?''

Provoked to anger himself, Kham snapped, ''Since we're so stupid, why doncha just tell us den?''

The elf glared at him and spoke slowly, enunciating each word as if speaking to an ignorant child. ''Saeder-Krupp belongs to the dragon Lofwyr.''

Kham felt a chill run down his spine. Drek! A dragon. No wonder this whole mess was so effing screwed up.

Glasgian slammed his fist against the railing. ''And you have given him what he wanted. All that comes from this shall be on your heads.''

''Wasn't us dat dug da ting up.''

''Do not try to displace the blame for this fiasco onto me. Had you all died when you were supposed to, none of this would have happened. You are responsible for the crystal falling into *his* hands. You must take the responsibility for that hideous mistake.

''*He* cannot be allowed to control the crystal. Even you must know that. We cannot leave that magic to a dragon. You must help me recover the crystal.''

Much as he hated to think it, Kham knew the fragging elf was right. Dragons never did anything straight, and Lofwyr, the dragon that had gone corporate, was known everywhere as a devious old worm. What would Lofwyr do with the magic of the crystal? Sure as hell wouldn't be anything to help orks. Kham didn't want to help this elf bastard, but neither would he be able to live with himself if he was responsible for letting the dragon bury—or worse, warp—the magic of the crystal.

25

Glasgian had a Hughes Airstar waiting on the roof for transport. Most of the passenger seats had been removed, rather sloppily, and a padded cradle installed in their place, no doubt to carry the crystal the elf wanted so desperately. There were enough seats for all of them, especially now that Scatter had disappeared. Kham didn't like the rat shaman, but he thought it unwise to make any noise over her disappearance. There remained a small possibility that she was hiding, staying undercover to back them up. He didn't think it likely, but he found himself hoping it was so. They had put themselves into the elf's hands in order to snatch the crystal back from the dragon. That done, the elf would want the stone for himself and Kham and the guys would very likely be in need of a rescue. Realistically, the cowardly shaman had probably noticed the arrival of the elf—or possibly even Enterich's crew, since he hadn't seen her when the Miltron goons rounded everybody up—and hightailed it for home.

The elf had high confidence in his abilities. The absence of a support crew was proof of that; he had come for Kham and the guys alone, even though the Airstar was big enough for a squad of goons. When Glasgian installed Rabo in the cockpit, Kham saw enough of the control panel to know the Airstar was well-armed despite its smooth, docile outer appearance. *Sort of like your typical elf,* he thought.

Knowing that Rabo could handle a chopper's armament, he was glad the Airstar was equipped for combat. Sure, they had their own weapons and Glasgian had implied that heavier stuff was available if needed, but they were going up against the hellions and the rest of the dragon's goons. They'd need really serious fire support. The elf's spells could provide that; Glasgian had implied that his magic was more than enough for the job at hand. But even if the elf was as tough as he thought, Kham had serious doubts about their chances of success should the dragon himself put in an appearance. Dragons were just plain bad for biz.

The elf sat up front with Rabo, leaving the buckets in the main bay to Kham, Neko, Ratstomper, and The Weeze. Glasgian also left the bulkhead door open, so that he could keep an eye on them. By the same token the open passageway let Kham listen to the radio traffic. He supposed that he shouldn't have been surprised when Glasgian told Rabo not to bother calling in to Seattle Air Traffic Control. This Airstar almost certainly had Tir Tairngire Council registry. That kind of clout would let them fly the Seattle sky with impunity.

The wasted reaches of the Puyallup Barrens were a snarl of streets, rubble, abandoned buildings, and stalled urban renewal. Since the Eff-Tee's playhouse was just about in the middle of the main disaster zone, Enterich's crew would still be working their way through the maze no matter where they were headed. The Airstar might occasionally have to detour around a block of tall buildings or some corporate industrial enclave, but it could make far better time than ground vehicles confined to what passed for roads. And if they didn't catch the dragon's goons before they left the Barrens, the helicopter still gave them an advantage: air traffic didn't get as congested as that on the ground. They'd catch up with the truck and its escort, if they could find them.

For the first few minutes they circled the warehouse, then, following Glasgian's vague directions, Rabo sent the bird hurtling through the evening sky. They changed course a few times, but they certainly weren't flying a random search pattern. Kham suspected that the elf was using some kind of magic to track the stone.

During a period when the elf was clearly hard at work figuring the direction, the video screen in the bulkhead between the cockpit and the cabin flickered to life. The image that appeared turned out to be a bird's-eye perspective of the ground below from a camera located in the nose, to judge by the antennae and probes projecting into the bottom of the frame. Tiny white letters scrolled across the lower screen. "Thought you might like a view." Kham smiled a little. Rabo was working his way through the controls. The rigger was not stupid and if he could find a way to make the chopper work for them, he would. That could give them an edge against Enterich's crew—or the elf.

They flew for almost half an hour, the elf's directions coming closer and closer together. Kham was caught off-guard when Rabo suddenly decelerated hard and banked the Airstar. The maneuver tossed the passengers around and Ryan actually got dumped on the deck. When they straightened out into a hover, Rabo apologized and, over the complaints, announced that they had found the caravan.

Kham hadn't seen it on the screen, but he did when Rabo brought the chopper around a tall building and hovered over a street leading to a main thoroughfare. One by one, the vehicles he had seen in the warehouse passed through the intersection. All except the limo. In the lead was the armored truck with the crystal, the other Miltron vans following at varying distances. Had they gotten into their spotting position too late to see

Enterich's limousine pass through the intersection or had the suit taken another route?

Enterich might not actually be part of the convoy; he'd said he had other business. Maybe he'd gone elsewhere to attend to it. Kham hoped so. Though he hadn't noticed any weapon on the suit, the man had given off an indefinable aura of danger. Even if Enterich wasn't personally armed, Kham couldn't believe that his car was not. If Enterich was really elsewhere, the tactical situation was better, improved by the absence of one of the opponent's maneuver elements. There was one less angle to watch.

Kham heaved himself up and leaned into the cockpit. "All right, elf. We found 'em before dey got home, like ya wanted. Now what? Dey're on a busy street."

"Now you will see how easy this will be. First, an illusion, a fantasy of ordinariness to lull our real prey. It will be the first step in isolating them from their protectors."

For several minutes, the elf stared avidly out the cockpit windscreen while the Airstar crept after the caravan on silenced rotors. Kham had seen similar looks of concentration on Sally Tsung's face when she was doing magic, but he didn't see anything happening. He even checked the video monitor to see if the machine was picking up something his eyes were missing.

"Don't see nuttin'. How ya gonna keep dem hellions off our back?"

Glasgian sneered. "The spell is only the *first* step, brute. It will require another to cut them from the herd. Now return to your seat and let me concentrate."

Kham did as he was told; but he did it slowly, trying to make it look like it was his idea, in case the guys hadn't heard the elf. Rabo had heard, but he was okay;

they'd done enough biz together to know that sometimes you had to let the other guy think he was in charge. Usually when the other guy *was* in charge.

About the time Kham took his seat, the last of the vans swerved a little, brake lights flashing on. For a moment, Kham thought the driver had tried to avoid crashing into a vehicle that had cut him off, but there was nothing there, just normal traffic—and more and more space opening up between the van and the rest of his convoy. Kham could imagine the van's horn blaring and the driver cursing. Anyone with a dragon for a boss would not welcome a disruption of his schedule. The van accelerated, quickly reaching its previous traveling speed, then exceeding it. Perhaps the driver thought his companions in the truck were accelerating as well. Whatever the case, the van was soon exceeding the safe speed for the traffic flow, weaving in and out of the traffic, passing the other vans. Suddenly, the driver cut to his right, directly into the space between the lead van and the armored truck. The chopper was sound-proofed too well for Kham to hear the sounds of the crash, but he saw it all too clearly. The swerving vehicle was rammed by its companion, and its side crumpled. The other bounced off, its rear end skewing around and bashing into another car. Beneath the Airstar the street turned into a sea of red lights and sparking flashes from colliding vehicles. In moments, the avenue was hopelessly snarled. All three of the vans were involved.

Half a block ahead, and increasing the distance all the time, the armored truck drove on. Glasgian tapped Rabo on the arm, then pointed. The Airstar tilted forward and flew after the departing vehicle.

The Weeze was watching the video screen as avidly as Kham. "Drek, those goons ain't even looking back. Didn't they hear the crash?"

Glasgian leaned around to look into the cabin, an

expression of superiority on his face. "They see only what I intend them to see and hear only what I wish them to hear, which is normal traffic and their companions following faithfully." Glasgian sounded very satisfied with himself. "Soon they will see the turns I wish them to make as the only ones open to them, and when the time is right, they will see nothing at all."

Gradually the truck moved away from the main arteries, out of the evening traffic. They followed, crossing out of the downtown district and back into Tacoma. Kham guessed that Glasgian was herding the driver of the truck toward the Andalusian compound. Not a real bright move; Enterich was likely watching the place and might have reinforcements on hand. But the elf wasn't as foolish as Kham feared; the truck was still well away from the compound when he struck.

The truck began to drift, as though the driver had dozed off, which maybe he had. A car in the oncoming lane bumped up onto the curb to avoid the wandering truck, narrowly avoiding a collision. That driver escaped, but Enterich's people were less lucky. Wandering back to the other side of the road, the truck made it to the next intersection before drifting further and careening into the curb. The force of the strike was enough to send the vehicle over to one side so that when it hit a parked car, it rode up and over, overbalancing. The side of the truck smashed down onto the pavement and the vehicle skidded along, gravel and sparks flying, until it slammed into a light post. The light flickered and died, dropping that section of the road into gloom.

At Glasgian's frantic urgings, Rabo brought the chopper down to a quick and bumpy landing in a nearby rubble-strewn lot. Glasgian slid open the Airstar's main door and jumped out, calling for the orks to follow him. Kham thought about using the opportunity to take care of the elf, but even after all Glasgian had done, Kham couldn't bring himself to shoot the bastard in the back. Besides, they might need him if the dragon showed. Or sooner; some of Enterich's goons had survived the crash and were groggily hauling themselves out of the wreckage.

One of the survivors pulled a pistol and fired at the charging elf. Her aim wasn't too good, but her shot had effect anyway. The bullet took Ryan in the gut as he stepped out of the Airstar. The stupid kid had opened up his armor vest for the chopper ride and hadn't sealed it before debarking. He sat down hard and looked stupidly at his bleeding gut. The catboy took a round, too, and tumbled backward, bloodlessly; his armor saved him.

Ratstomper screamed and opened up on full auto, nearly nailing Glasgian. The elf dove to one side, taking cover in a doorway. Things got confused real quick, as another goon started firing and the orks shot back. It was short and sharp, and the outcome wasn't any real surprise. The goons were still rattled from the crash, and Kham, Rabo, and The Weeze had done this sort of thing plenty of times before. They moved smoothly, spreading out and keeping up a good volume of fire. Even with Ratstomper mostly wasting scenery, the firefight went thirty seconds, max, before it was all over. There were no more survivors of the wreck.

Ratstomper ran to Ryan as soon as she could, dragged him off the street, and leaned him up against an abandoned car. The rest of the guys gathered around. The kid was their only serious casualty. Not bad, considering the open area in which the firefight had taken place, but not good enough for Kham.

"Rabo," he bawled. "Bring the first aid kit from the chopper."

The rigger was fast, but that didn't matter; the kid's wounds were too serious. Kham could see that even

LAUBENSTEIN '92

though they had done all they could for him, it was not enough. The orks gathered around, watching helplessly as the life bled out of their comrade. With Ryan already unconscious, Kham was spared having to decide whether or not to end the kid's pain. He knew what most of his guys wanted in a situation like this, but there had never been time to ask the kid.

A triumphant laugh sounded from the direction of the overturned truck. Glasgian's laugh. Kham turned to look and saw brilliant rays of emerald light leaking from the sprung doors. The light grew in intensity, and Kham had a sudden suspicion.

"Cover!" he yelled.

The guys ducked low, trusting his reaction. He hoped the bulk of the abandoned car would shield them. He also hoped he was being overly cautious and would look stupid soon.

It was not to be.

With a rending shriek the armor panels of the truck bulged and burst apart like an overstretched balloon. Angry hornets of metal buzzed through the air, spanging off everything in a thirty-meter radius. Glasgian, standing on the padded collar and clinging to the crystal still strapped into that collar, rose from the ruins of the truck. He glowed with power.

The elf laughed as he rose higher into the sky. Experimentally, Kham fired off a shot and was not surprised when it had no effect. The elf never even stopped laughing.

"Guess he's got his own ride home," Neko said dryly.

Tracer rounds stitched up the pavement and into the remains of the truck. Its fuel ignited and burst into flames. Huddled behind the abandoned car, the crew was safe for the moment, but those tracers and the moan accompanying them were familiar: the hellions had found them. How, Kham didn't know; it didn't matter. Once more they were facing long odds with the dice loaded against them.

He looked into the sky. The retreating elf was a mere speck, leaving them to face the hellions alone. And Glasgian probably knew he was doing it, too. There was no point in cursing the bastard; Kham had known the elf might do just such a thing when he'd agreed to help the weedeater recover the crystal from the dragon's goons. Kham had believed that the need to keep the magic away from the dragon made taking the chance necessary. He'd hoped to be able to keep the crystal from the elf as well. He should have known better. Another good ork life spent, with nothing to show for it.

Bullets chewed at the metal that shielded them. Ratstomper looked up from the body she cradled in her arms. "What do we do now, Kham?"

He wished he knew. There didn't seem to be a lot of options. The Airstar's armament could take out the hellions, but they were too far from the chopper; Rabo would get wasted trying to make it across the street. Without the chopper, their own firepower wasn't going to be enough against the hellions.

"It's not worth dying for an empty truck," Neko pointed out.

Kham wondered if it would have been worth dying if the truck were still full of what they had come after. This eternity magic, if that's what it was, was getting awfully expensive.

"Enterich said he'd call the hellions off," Kham began.

"If we stayed out of it," Ratstomper reminded him needlessly.

"Suit's your chummer, catboy. He good for his word?"

"Again, he's not my chummer. As for his word, we would seem to have broken the pact ourselves. However, we would have little chance if we fight. Perhaps they will be lenient if we can claim that the elf forced us.''

''If they let us talk,'' Ratstomper said gloomily.

There was a lull in the firing, and Kham could hear a car approaching.

''Only one way to find out,'' he said, but before he could act, Neko had jumped up, tossed away his submachine gun, and stepped around the car's fender. The catboy walked forward, hands in the air. ''News,'' he shouted. ''We have news for Enterich.''

Kham half-expected to see the little Jap kid sliced and diced by the hungry red tracers, but it didn't happen. A car rolled out of the gathering darkness. Its doors had been ripped off to accommodate the huge cyberguys: one hellion was crammed into the driver's seat and the other clung to the passenger side, his tribarrel pointing in their direction. The car squealed as if protesting mistreatment as it slowed to a halt. Unsurprisingly, the tribarrel never wavered from its target.

Kham tossed his own weapon away and stood, shouting, ''Don't shoot. We got news for your boss.''

For a long, sweaty moment, he thought they weren't going to buy it. Then, the muzzles of the tribarrel dropped, and the hellion made what sounded like an exasperated sigh. The hellions emerged from the car, its springs sighing in relief at the removal of their burdensome weight. One hellion monitored the disarming of the orks while the other checked over the wreckage of the truck. If they cared whether their colleagues were wounded or dead, they never gave a sign. Satisfied that the crystal was gone, they herded the orks and Neko into the Airstar. Once more they took to the air in the commandeered chopper, but this time Rabo wasn't driving.

26

"It is unfortunate that you did not heed my advice," Mr. Enterich said, his voice sad, but his face expressionless. The suit stared at them from the video screen for several minutes without saying anything else. Enterich was only an image on a screen, but still Kham felt discomfited by the man's eyes. Their look of disapproval was too much like what he usually saw in Harry's eyes, the slight hint of distaste too much like that in Lissa's.

What did they all want of him anyway? He tried to do what he thought was right. Was it his fault there was always another player with a bigger stake or better cards? He was just a street ork. What more could they expect?

Enterich shook his head slightly. "I had hoped that this matter was closed."

One by one, the suit questioned them closely about their brief alliance with Glasgian. He started with Neko and was working his way through the team to Kham.

While The Weeze was giving her version, Kham looked around the room where they were being kept. The walls were bare and featureless, bland in the dull fluorescent light from the overhead panels. The way it was fitted out with chairs and low tables made it seem like a doctor's waiting room; there were even stacks of magazines on the tables. Bored with the constant repetition, Rabo had found a tech journal to stick his nose into. The hellions hadn't let them see where they'd been taken. They'd blanked out the Airstar's windows for the ride, then hustled the team out into a darkened hangar and through darkened halls. Kham and his runners could have been anywhere, but everything was all straight and real clean, so it had to be corporate property.

The catboy was the only one who seemed relaxed, like maybe he'd been here before. Maybe he had; especially if his real loyalties did lie with Enterich and his dragon master. Still, Neko had been disarmed and incarcerated in the cabin of the Airstar with them, lending some credence to his protests that he was not one of Enterich's agents. Of course that might all be part of the scam to make it seem that Neko was an independent, just like the questioning.

In his turn, Kham gave the same story of Glasgian's arrival as everyone else had, but he put a special emphasis on the elf's insistence that they not leave the crystal in Enterich's possession. As Kham was confirming for the fifth time that Glasgian had said Enterich worked for Saeder-Krupp, the picture on the video screen changed. The suit's image was reduced, remaining only in a small inset box in the upper-left corner. The rest of the screen was black. But only for a moment. A new image appeared, a golden dragon's head. The screen was two meters tall and the head more than filled it, the dragon's horns projecting up and out of the image area. Though there was nothing in the picture that could give scale to the image, Kham had the impression that the image was smaller than life-sized. This beast was big, even for its kind.

"I am Lofwyr."

The shock of the dragon's speech buzzed in Kham's head. It hadn't moved its lips or opened its mouth, but it had spoken; he had no doubt of that. The feeling in his head was almost like the one he got when the wagemage they'd blasted on the last run with Sally had gotten into Kham's head, but it was different, too. He didn't understand how the dragon was communicating, but it didn't matter. It was, and he was hearing it.

So were the others. Ratstomper and The Weeze were staring round-eyed at the screen, and the catboy had come out of his lazing slump and was sitting on the edge of his seat. To Kham's surprise, Rabo was still absorbed in his magazine. Hadn't he heard the dragon announce himself? Kham elbowed the rigger, who looked up and did a double-take when he saw the video screen.

"Drek! When did that drop in?"

The dragon ignored his remark. *"I have listened to your stories and have heard enough. Time, even as it is measured by your kind, is short. This elf, Glasgian, is dabbling in matters that he does not understand, and the magic he is playing with will cause dire consequences. If he manages to complete his plans, I will not be able to contain the situation."*

The dragon stopped speaking, seemingly waiting. Nobody else reacted, so Kham screwed up his courage. "Dat sounds like a pitch. Yer boy said he wanted us outta it."

From his little box, Enterich said, "As should be obvious, the situation has changed."

"I didn't wanta deal wit ya before I knew who ya worked fer," Kham objected. "I prefer dealing wit elves. At least dey're human."

"They would not agree with you." Lofwyr produced a rumble that might have been dragonish laughter. As the rumble died away, Enterich added, "The elves believe other metahumans to be lesser races than themselves; they dream of the old days when magic ruled, and wish to establish a world order in which their superiority is acknowledged."

"Elves *über üntermenschen,*" Neko said *sotto voce.*

"Essentially," Enterich said. The suit went on to

sling more mud at elves in general, but Kham tuned him out; it wasn't anything he hadn't heard before.

"Where'd ya pick up German, catboy?" he whispered to Neko.

"Old American war movies," Neko replied casually.

Enterich concluded with, "If Glasgian is not stopped immediately, he will disrupt delicate balances. Assuredly, he believes that the change will benefit him and his kind, but there is no guarantee that he is correct. Whatever the ultimate outcome, your kind will not fare well."

"You will believe what I tell you, if you are wise," Lofwyr said. *"Act, or end as a slave, as your race was in ancient times."*

Neko leaned forward. "So there were orks then, too. There really are cycles."

"How could it be otherwise? Life is a cycle. Magic, born of life, must be one with it. Only a dangerous fool would think otherwise."

"I knew it." Neko grinned. To Kham he said, "I told you."

"Consider da source," Kham grumbled back at him. To the dragon he said, "Maybe dere was orks and elves a long time ago. And maybe orks was slaves ta da daisy-eaters. But dis is America and we don't got no slaves here anymore. Even if dere was, tings are different now. Dere's a lot more orks dan dere are pointy-eared slave master wannabees. We orks ain't gonna bow down ta no elves."

"Numbers are no match for their ancient knowledge. And though you breed as quickly as you like, soon the elves will have you in their hands."

"Well, if we ain't worth anyting, what ya want us fer?

"It is not my choice."

"Well, it sure as hell ain't ours. We know about dealing wit dragons."

"Do you really?" There was something sardonic in the dragon's tone. *"It does not matter, though. You are already involved."*

"You are responsible for the elf recovering the crystal," Enterich added.

"I suggest, great Lofwyr," Neko said deferentially, "that had your minions been more . . . competent, they would have retained the crystal. We added little or nothing to the elf's attempt to regain the crystal. No more than any muscle might have done."

Kham was afraid the catboy's smart remark would anger the dragon, but the beast rumbled its amusement. *"Crown the wise, harness the talented, and cherish the lucky."*

What was that supposed to mean? Something in the timbre of Lofwyr's words suggested that the dragon was repeating an often-heard phrase, like a proverb or a bit of street wisdom. Kham had never heard the words before and they didn't make much sense to him. He exchanged glances with the catboy. Neko obviously didn't understand what the dragon meant, either.

"You agreed to help the elf when you thought my agents had stolen something of elven magic. You believed that no dragon should have access to what the crystal represented. I tell you now that you were wrong. Sadly wrong.

"Know this. It is the elves who have stolen something of dragon magic; a turn of events that was never meant to be. It is an outrage that an ephemeral mammal has bonded with the crystal, and I will not countenance it. You shall be my instruments. You led him to the crystal, now you will take it from him and return it to me."

The dragon's "voice" shook Kham with its intensity, making him quite sure that their only choices were cooperation or death. The usual. But now that the dragon had taken a personal interest, Kham didn't see any way to avoid the second choice. Either they said no and died now or said yes and died later, either fighting Glasgian or silenced later by the dragon. "We don't even know where he went."

Enterich responded pedantically. "The files you took from Glasgian's Andalusian operation reveal an interest in a certain triangular section of real estate in the southeastern Salish territory. Interestingly enough, the autopilot of his Airstar contains a flight plan that would allow him to travel to the central portion of that same area. I suggest that the conclusion is obvious."

"It might be a red herring," Neko said.

"A scarlet fish," Lofwyr grumbled. *"Ah yes. A ruse."*

"Yeah," Kham agreed. "It might be just a fake."

"It is not." There was absolute certainty in Lofwyr's response.

"Ya got your bad boy hellions and tons of goons, whatcha need us for?"

"You are responsible for the elf having possession of the crystal."

"*He* said we were responsible for *you* having it."

"He was lying."

"And you're not, hunh?" Kham blurted out, then realized that his words were a direct challenge to the dragon's honesty. He'd heard that the beasts had a strange sense of honor. If Kham had given insult, he'd just bought himself a problem and the dragon's wanting him to go after the elf wouldn't save him.

Strange lights swirled in the dragon's eyes, and Kham held his breath.

"Ah, I have always preferred the blunt honesty of your race to the duplicity of the elves."

Emboldened, Kham said, "Ya like blunt, I'll be blunt. I don't see no reason why we should help ya."

"You have been offered your lives."

"I seen what dat elf can do. I seen what yer hellions can do. Even yer norm goons ain't slouches. Ryan learned dat real good. Seems ta me, if we get caught in the middle again, we ain't gonna come out of it alive."

The dragon was silent for a while. Up in his little box, Enterich watched them impassively. Ratstomper started to fidget. Finally, Lofwyr spoke again.

"I could compel you, but that would lower your efficiency and dispel your luck. Instead, I will appeal to your philanthropy.

"Glasgian seeks a war, a war that will devastate this planet. Even your kind must have some concern for the world on which you live. Glasgian's war could well result in the end of life, certainly the end of life as you know it.

"You have children, Kham. As do you, Weeze and Rabo. Consider the kind of world Glasgian's war will bring. If he wins, the elves will dance on the bones of the dead and be served by those they deem fit to live only as their slaves. If he loses, the devastation will still be extensive. In what kind of world would you have your offspring dwell?

"If you do not act to stop Glasgian, this war will come. If you act, it may *be averted. You all consider yourselves to have free will, and so I give you the chance to exercise your choice.*

"Stand by and watch the world, your world, go up in flames.

"Or act."

The dragon's words rang in Kham's head, tolling with sincerity. No one wanted their kids to live in a world destroyed by war. The world had seen what man's wars could do; the might of the modern war machine was terrible. How much worse would a war with magic be? Or one in which dragons fought? He felt sure that it could only be worse, far worse.

But was his fear of possible war, his conviction that it would come if they didn't act, truth? Or was it a side effect of the compulsion that Lofwyr had suggested he could create?

More than ever, Kham wanted to see the elf pulled down. Glasgian had taught him that he could never trust an elf, and everyone on the street knew that you could never deal with a dragon and come out ahead. Sometimes, you had to do what had to be done, even if it meant you came out on the short end; that's what Harry had told him. But Harry had also said, with equal conviction, that you always look out for yourself first. So what was it going to be?

"You ain't sending us after da elf alone, are ya?"

Enterich replied. "The hellions will accompany you."

"Watchdogs?" Neko inquired. "To eliminate us when the jobs done?"

"I do not countenance waste."

Kham looked his guys over. From their expressions, they were as torn as he. Rabo said, "If the wizworm's right about a war, we gotta do it. I've seen war, Kham. I don't want my kids to. It ain't no gang rumble, or even a hot run."

Turning to the catboy, Kham asked him, "What about you?"

"I will aid the dragon in this."

"Still on da payroll?"

"Still trying to convince you otherwise. This is a necessary thing."

"So ya believe the wizworm."

"He is convincing."

"Yeah, I guess he is."

Truth or compulsion?

"Cherish the lucky," the dragon repeated enigmatically.

Kham still didn't understand the reference, but he felt the satisfaction Lofwyr exuded. The dragon was getting what he wanted, and in a way so was Kham. By agreeing to the dragon's demands, he and his guys would get out of the wizworm's paws. They'd still have to face the elf and deal with the hellions, but a long shot was better than no chance at all.

27

Once more they were in the air, in pursuit of the magical crystal and its current possessor. Neko looked around the aircraft at the strangers in whose company he traveled. This was not a new experience, of course, but an uncomfortable one when facing danger. Battle was best faced with trusted comrades, and what little comradeship left between him and the orks had evaporated under accusations that he was Enterich's agent. As for the hellions, the only thing that had ever existed between him and them was antagonism. The warriors carried by the Airstar were a strange crew, united in their grimness but so disparate in all other things.

In the cockpit, Rabo was happy to again be at the controls of a fine machine, his mood much improved since the hellions had allowed him to pilot the craft after leaving Enterich's facility. One of the cybernetically enhanced toughs, Alpha, remained with him, probably to prevent him from using the craft's computer to backtrack their course. Enterich seemed determined to cloak his lair in mystery. A fine challenge to find it, should they survive this run.

The other hellion, Beta, sat with a stillness unnatural in a living being. He simply watched them all, taking no part in the fitful, short conversations.

The Weeze checked and rechecked her weapons, paying particular attention to the Colt M22A2 assault rifle the hellions had given her from the stock aboard the Airstar. It wasn't clear whether she distrusted it because it came from Glasgian's stock or because the hellions had given it to her, but her suspicion was obvious, her behavior strangely compulsive.

Kham sat staring at the blackness of the opaqued window. Neko didn't know if the big ork was looking at his own reflection or staring off at some inner landscape. Perhaps he pondered the future of which Lofwyr had spoken, or the dragon's curious proverb concerning the wise, the talented, and the lucky. Whatever thoughts occupied the big ork's mind, they isolated him from the rest of the Airstar's passengers.

Ratstomper sat by herself, unusual for her. But then she had withdrawn since Ryan's death. That was just as well; she was the one who had first turned a weapon on Neko when they had thought he was in Enterich's employ. If she still believed that, she might try again, but not until the danger was over. She was a victim of her emotions, but Kham hoped she was not so foolhardy as to start a fight under the hellions' eyes. Those metal monsters might not care to distinguish between the initiator and the victim of any fight between her and Neko.

For his own part, Neko found no need to talk. What was there to say? Soon they would be facing a hostile, powerful elf and whatever allies he might call up. Already they had made what skeletal plans they could. Without more information, further discussion would not gain them anything. They were in the hands of fate, set to win or lose according to their karma. Lofwyr seemed to think them lucky. Could a dragon detect such things? If so, and if Lofwyr had detected what he called luck in them, they might survive this night. After all, what was luck but good karma?

Unlike the compulsive Weezer, Neko did not feel the need to check his weapons. He'd done it after making his choice from among those in the Airstar's arsenal. The Colt assault rifle sitting across his knees was heavier than he normally liked to carry, but more suitable to the task at hand. He had found no deficiencies in the weapon or its ammunition, such as The Weeze seemed to be searching for. Why should there be? Lofwyr wanted Glasgian stopped; he would not send them into battle armed with inoperative or malfunctioning weapons. If Lofwyr wanted the team to die in the battle, he could leave the task to his hellions. The dragon's watchdogs were better-armed and better-armored, the most likely survivors of the battle. They would be able to silence any extraneous persons who managed to escape from the elf.

But the answers to all such questions and speculations were in the future, and to ponder them now was fruitless unless one could do constructive planning. With all the variables, that wasn't possible at the moment. Good karma or bad, they would meet the fate that awaited them. Neko relaxed into his seat, feeling the thrumming vibration of the aircraft's engines. Letting himself sink into the rhythm, he found rest.

It would be time for action soon enough.

* * *

Glasgian had never known power like the crystal granted him. Since bonding it to him, he had felt wonderful, stronger than he'd ever been, capable of—well, of anything. No wonder Urdli had wanted to keep him from it; the *morkhan* must have wanted it all to himself.

The flight from Seattle had been exhilarating. To

ride the wind like that, to move under the power of his own will. Never had he known such freedom in this world. It was almost like journeying astrally. To will movement and have it happen, with no regard for flesh, no recourse to machines. It was marvelous.

He touched down briefly at the site where they had uncovered the crystal, just long enough to assure himself that the calculations were correct. The stone knew; he could feel it in the vibrations of the crystal lattice. The resonance was perfect, focused where it should be.

Glasgian laughed aloud. Vindication was wonderful, but what was to come would be even better. This was just the start.

With tonight's work done, they would see, they would all see, that he was right. *Now* was the time. *This* was to be the cycle that would see elvenkind triumphant. And Glasgian would continue to lead the way, as he had just done. There would be no place for laggards and faint hearts like Urdli. Let the old fossil crawl back under his rock and hide his head. The new order was coming. Glasgian's order. He would be a new Lojan, bestriding the world like a victorious colossus.

He flew with breathtaking speed to his destination, a stretch of nondescript forest. To the mortal, mundane eye the place would have looked ordinary. It might even have seemed ordinary to Glasgian had he been here a week ago. But no longer. Ever since he had bonded to the crystal, his senses were expanded, empowered. He saw all things more clearly than ever before.

As he brought the stone lower, the small life of the forest noticed his approach and began to scatter. "Run!" he called out to them. "Run and tell of the dawn of the new age."

He roved over the ground, studying the form of what

he had sought for so long. Running his astral senses along its boundaries, he felt its size and shape, perceived its contents. It was not as he had expected. It was larger, its form more irregular, and its content greater, but none of that mattered. With the crystal bound to his will, he had the key. The cache was his now to do with as he willed.

He brought the crystal down on a small rise just south of the structure. The south was appropriate; south was the home of fire, and fire was what he brought. Before he called that fire, he wanted to see his prize. Summoning an earth elemental seemed the obvious choice to lay it bare. Obvious and facile. An air elemental was a better choice. Earth shielded what he sought; let the opposing element rip bare the hidden treasure.

Having made the decision, he wasted no more time, summoning a spirit more powerful than he would have dared try to control yesterday. The branches of the trees rustled as if greeting the new arrival. The elemental would have been visible even to the unaided eye, its power a shimmering ripple in the air, but to Glasgian's heightened senses it was a glorious aurora of power swirling in a tight whirlwind. Such power, such beauty, and it had come to do his bidding. So, let it do that bidding.

He ordered the elemental to clear away the sediment that hid what he wished to see. Instantly, leaves and loose debris began to shift and skitter along the ground, moving faster and faster in a whirlwind tumble. Loose dirt and larger branches joined the tumult and the wind rose to a roar. The cyclonic effect grew until trees were uprooted and flung away. The tempest grew stronger still. Stones and massive clods of earth were ripped wholesale from the ground and swirled higher into the funnel. The soil was torn away, then the underlying rock strata fragmented under the erosional effect and was swept away as well.

Glasgian's senses tingled in harmony to a quiver in the crystal. The elemental's assault had awakened the magical defenses of the hidden cache. They trembled on the verge of acting against the elemental, almost activating. Those defenses were strong enough to scatter the arcane energy of Glasgian's summoning, but with the crystal in his power, those defenses belonged to Glasgian now. He willed them to stillness and watched gleefully as the elemental laid bare his spoils. When the deed was done, he dismissed the spirit and contemplated the newly uncovered spheres.

They were of many sizes and colors, variations on a theme. He might even have found the sight pleasant, had he not known what lay within. He selected one at random. It was larger than most, a pale yellow sphere speckled with a faint dusting of charcoal and umber flecks. With the power of his mind, he pulled it from its resting place.

The contact of his telekinetic touch and his heightened sensitivity told him that this one was almost ready to hatch; so ready that it might survive being broken free of the shell. In the interest of scientific experiment, Glasgian decided to see. He exerted pressure on the shell, delicately balancing the interplay of power so that he exerted enough force to crack the shell without completely crushing what lay within. Cracks ran across the surface in a jagged rush. The shards of shell fell away in a gush of amniotic fluid, but he did not let the embryo fall. Oh no, that was too easy.

He stared at the ugly thing, noting its leathery pale gray hide, the tucked and folded wings spiky with the beginnings of feathers, the wedge-shaped head bumpy with babyish horns, all blunt save for the now-useless egg "tooth" on its nose. It was every bit as vile as he had imagined, but at least he was in a position to do something about it. This one would never grow up. He bathed it in fire and laughed to hear its pitiful shrieks.

"Screech all you want, worm. You are mine. There will be no answer to your bawlings while I hold the key to the nest."

It turned its head to him when he spoke, its filmed eyes searching for the source of its torment. Glasgian did not believe that it really understood, but its affinity for magic would let it locate him as the source of the occult flames torturing it. It mewled, begging for relief.

With a gesture, he stopped the flames. The beast whimpered in relief. He let it enjoy the moment; then, with a wide sweep of his arms, rent it limb from limb while simultaneously crushing its rib cage. Dropping the torn and broken form like the trash it was, he reached for another.

* * *

"There he is," Rabo called as the polarity of the windows shifted to transparency. Already facing out, Kham could see the glow on the horizon. The sky outside the window looked like sunset, but the time was nearer to midnight. So, what Kham was looking at had to be hell.

Rabo put the Airstar into a long, banking turn that would give them a better, more protected angle of approach. The hellion in the cabin remained were he was, but The Weeze and Ratstomper crowded Kham. His window offered the best angle to see the flickering light show. The catboy only raised his head a little and cast a sleepy-eyed glance out the window.

The glow of Glasgian's magic pulsated as if the power were fluctuating, but Kham didn't dare hope that it might be so. The brighter bursts probably only meant that Glasgian was unleashing specific localized spells. Destructive spells, to judge by how much the

Airstar was being buffeted by rough air. It was almost like making an approach through triple-A. Those spells might soon be coming their way and it would get even a lot more like triple-A. Lethally like it.

To avoid that, Rabo took them down to treetop level, trying to get closer without revealing their approach to the elf. The rigger was supposed to find a spot close in, where they could unload. Once the passengers had debarked, the orks and hellions would close on foot and Rabo would wait for the assault, bringing the chopper in as fire support.

Beta got up as his partner came into the cabin, opening the main door while Alpha said something. The wind rushing in and the noise of the whirling rotors carried away the hellion's words.

The ground was quite close, and getting closer.

It was almost time.

"Lock and load, chummers," Kham shouted, loud enough so his voice could be heard. He slapped the magazine on his weapon to be sure it was snugged home, then worked the charger. He couldn't hear the sound of it slapping home, but the smooth feel of the action told him the weapon was ready.

It was time.

One by one they jumped from the hovering chopper.

28

Rabo had chosen a good spot, placing them so they were coming at the elf from behind and to one side. The woods were thick with forest giants, screening them from the elf's sight and muffling the low thrum of the silenced rotors. The hellions led the way, moving quickly through the benighted trees. Slipping starlight goggles down over his face, Kham improved his already excellent night vision. Fear of running into a tree was not going to slow him down. The other guys did the same, and the crew moved at top speed along the vector Rabo had given them.

After ten minutes, the hellions slowed and Kham gave the signal for his guys to do the same. While they might be able to see well enough to crash through the brush of the forest floor, their progress was too noisy. If they wanted to catch the elf unaware, they'd have to do it quietly. Reaching the edge of the woods, they hid among the piles of loose brush and fallen trees, feet sinking into soft earth that smelled freshly dug. Kham didn't like it at all, but then he rarely liked being out of the plex. Getting ready to take on a powerful elven mage didn't add much to his enthusiasm for loam and rotting leaves.

Alpha tapped him on the shoulder. ''Remove your goggles. They have insufficient compensators to deal with magical energy flares.''

''Swell,'' Ratstomper whispered harshly. ''Couldn't you guys at least get us decent equipment?''

''Is there a problem with your equipment?'' Alpha asked, turning cold metal eyes on her.

''Weapon's fine,'' 'Stomper said grudgingly.

''Nothing important to say, don't talk. It's almost time. The rigger is coming,'' Alpha told them before slipping away to rejoin the other hellion. Together they moved away from the orks, taking up a position from which they'd launch the second prong of the ground assault.

Looking out from his hiding place, Kham could see that the elf had created some kind of pit in the middle of the clearing. Most of the open area was a shallow bowl, starting at the tangle of debris that marked the edge of the forest and sloping down in a cutaway of soil and rock. Near the center the angle of the slope increased sharply, plunging to unknown depths.

Communing with hell? he silently asked the elf.

Glasgian stood on a stony rise about thirty meters to Kham's right. Though the air was still, the elf's coat whipped around him as if he stood in a gale. The elf was watching something that hovered, dark and writhing, over the center of the pit. At irregular intervals, Glasgian gestured and arcane bolts flew from his hand to lash at the thing. The elf laughed when the whatever-it-was screamed.

Suddenly the elf seemed to sense that he was no longer alone. He turned, looking directly toward where the orks were hiding. The thing over the pit dropped, landing with a faraway, soggy splat. There wasn't any more time for sneaking.

"Hit him!"

The hellions were firing before Kham got the second word out of his mouth. The elf reacted almost as quickly. He ducked low and a finger of stone rose between him and the hellions. As their tribarrels sent streams of ineffectual fire against the rock, the elf began to laugh wildly. The rock cut off Kham's line of fire as well. He led the guys around for a better angle.

Undaunted, the hellions separated, each trying for an opening. Secure behind his shield, Glasgian worked a greater magic. A wall of rock and earth erupted between him and the charging cyberguys, no mere pillar this time but a mass at least fifty meters long and half as many high. They scrambled back, narrowly avoiding the growing wall.

At that moment, the Airstar swept in at treetop level, guns formerly concealed in its fuselage deployed and firing. The guys cheered Rabo on as he raked the ground around the elf, bringing the deadly torrent of firepower closer to its target. Incredibly, the elf stood his ground, gesturing in the chopper's direction. For an instant, nothing happened, then Neko shouted, "The trees!" Kham didn't understand until the earth groaned beneath his feet and a half-dozen of the forest giants at the edge of the clearing flew upward, trailing clods of earth from their roots like a missile's contrail.

If Rabo saw them, he never reacted. The first tree sliced through the Airstar's tail boom, sending the craft into a crazy spin. The second would have hit the cockpit, except that it was no longer where it should have been. The whirling craft struck the bole of that forest giant and stove in, its blades chopping themselves to destruction against its bark. Only one more of the flying trees smashed into the battered chopper, but it was overkill. The Airstar dropped like a rock, falling in a tangle with the debris of its attackers. The unsuccessful wooden missiles dropped as well.

Glasgian turned his attention to the shouting, firing orks.

A sizzling ball of eldritch energy rumbled from the elf's cupped hands. Kham dropped, throwing himself into the raw earth at the pit's shallow edge. He hit shoulder-first and felt rocks beneath the surface gouge into his muscles—a minor price to avoid the magical blast. The others were not so lucky or quick.

The spell erupted in their midst. Furthest from the center of impact, the catboy was picked up and tossed away, flailing. The two orks took the brunt of the blast. The Weeze erupted in flame, screaming as her clothes melted to her skin. She fell to the ground, tumbling over and over as she rolled down the slope. Ratstomper's clothes ignited, too, but somehow she remained standing for a few seconds. Howling in rage and pain, she tried to bring her rocket launcher to bear. Then something, ammo or a grenade, cooked off. It blew her in half, her spasming arms flinging the launcher high in the air. It landed five meters in front of Kham.

He looked at the weapon rather than back at her. The elf's voice cut into his numbness.

"Your kind is such a tiresome bother, oh great trog leader. The children with the bigger guns were bigger threats and so required my more immediate attention. I hope you haven't been bored by the wait."

Kham raised his eyes, staring at his death gathering among the elf's fingers. His senses seemed abnormally sharp. He heard the flap of Glasgian's coat, the crackle of flames from behind him, and soft, pained moans from the pit. Savoring the melange of flavors from the grit in his mouth, he got a new salty-sour taste when he licked his dried lips. Then came the scent of his own sweat-soaked clothes as well as the smell of things he didn't want to put names to, things he'd smelled before and thought he'd grown used to. But his eyes were sharpest of all. Every fold of the elf's suit, every wrinkle in his coat, was apparent. The elf's smooth, perfect skin. His wide smile and perfect teeth. The wind-blown fineness of his pale silvery hair. The cold, frigid depths of his glacial blue eyes. All absolutely vivid.

Out the corner of his eye, Kham saw Alpha racing down the length of the earth barrier. Beta was heading in the other direction. Each had almost reached his end of the wall. Nice moves, but a little late.

For some reason Glasgian delayed blasting Kham. Almost in slow motion, the elf turned as Beta cleared the earthen obstacle, firing his tribarrel as he came. Glasgian unleashed the energy he had gathered for Kham's demise, bathing the hellion in scarlet fires. The metal guy grinned mirthlessly as the flames disappeared, but only for a second. His tiny eyes went wide, first with surprise, then with terror, as the magic began to take effect. Deep within he seemed to glow, the normal pallor of his skin taking on a ruddy look. Then any false promise of health vanished as the glow intensified. For a moment, he seemed a chrome-plated glass statue, confining a laser light show, then he began to smoke as what remained of his flesh caught fire and burned. His screams rose into the night, then stopped suddenly as something within his armor exploded and he flew apart in sparking, fiery bits.

Glasgian laughed wildly.

"And you thought yourself safe from magic. Consider it repayment for Madame Guiscadeaux, whom you so ignominiously killed. She was a promising student."

The other hellion didn't give the elf time to enjoy his triumph. Alpha rounded the far end of the wall. Like his partner, he came out firing, but unlike Beta, he no longer relied simply on his antipersonnel weapons. A quartet of rockets screamed away from launchers, shrouding him in a pall of smoke hellishly lit by the tracers from the tribarrel.

For his trouble Glasgian dumped the earth wall on the hellion, burying him.

But the elf hadn't acted fast enough to shield himself completely. Without the hellion's guidance, Alpha's rockets didn't hit the mage, but two of them blasted into the rise on which he stood. He was rocked from his perch, thrown clear of the crystal.

Some of the fire seemed to go out of him, and for the first time that night Kham saw Glasgian as vulnerable. But he'd be up soon. Already he was shaking his head, recovering from the stunning effect of the explosion.

Kham would have shot him at once, but his AK had disappeared. He glanced around for it, but the only weapon in sight was Ratstomper's launcher. Good enough. The hellions had shown that it would take heavy firepower to take down this mage, and the launcher was big bang. He scrambled up, staggered to it, and hefted it onto his shoulder. Glasgian didn't seem to know Kham was there. That wouldn't do. The bastard needed to know he was going to die.

"Freeze, weed-eater," he ordered as he trained the launcher on Glasgian.

Slowly, the elf focused on him. Although the elf eyed Kham malevolently, he did nothing. That made Kham wonder, for Glasgian had not been reluctant to unleash his destructive spells before. Suspicion flared, and Kham hesitated. Did the elf have some secret defense? Apparently sensing Kham's wavering resolve, Glasgian stared at him contemptuously as he rose and started back up the rise.

Toward the crystal.

Kham realized that through all the previous combat, Glasgian had been in contact with the rock. Maybe that was the key to the elf's amazing well of arcane power. It had to be. Whatever else it was, the crystal had to be a power focus. He shifted his aim, centering the pale rose stone in the cross hairs. He didn't know if the missile would damage it, but it was worth a try.

"No!" The tremor in the elf's voice told him that he had made a right guess. "You don't know what you'd be destroying."

Kham didn't have to know, beyond knowing that it would pain this elf, make him pay. "Move any closer to it and we can find out."

Glasgian froze. "Don't be a fool, ork. Don't listen to the dragon's lies."

"How do ya know what dat wizworm said?"

"I know he lies."

"Funny. It said da same about you."

Kham shifted his position so that he could easily switch targets from the crystal to the elf, but he still kept the weapon aimed at the rock. From his now slightly more elevated position, Kham found he could look past Glasgian and into the pit.

It was full of objects that looked like big eggs, shattered shells, and the things that must have come out of them. He didn't recognize much of it, except that one of the corpses looked something like a tiny dragon. With a shock, Kham realized that he was standing on the edge of a dragon's nest.

His reaction caused him to drop the muzzle of the launcher. Glasgian took advantage of Kham's distraction to make a break for the crystal. Snapping the launcher back up, Kham put a round between Glasgian and the stone. The concussion knocked Glasgian back, tumbling him over and rolling him back down the slope. Dirt and stones pelted down.

Towering over both of them, the crystal sat serenely, undisturbed by the violence around it. It was a promise of power, a gift of new life, and a harbinger of doom, all at once. Kham shivered.

"If this is left undone, there will be hell to pay," the elf said quietly.

"Price has been pretty high already."

"You cannot imagine how much more it will be. Your children will curse you, should they have tongues left in their heads. Your race and all mankind will vilify you, if you stop me from doing what must be done."

Doing what? Killing orks and breaking eggs. "Ain't never had much good said about me by norms. Less by elves."

"Other elves have been foolish. They have not seen your inner spirit, as I now have. The courage you have, the conviction you show."

"Can da drek."

"I understand your anger. But I did not know what I should have known from the first. I want to make amends. We need not be enemies."

"Wasn't my choice."

"Mistakes and misunderstandings. And not all on my part, either. You know that we elves are long-lived, that we have fine things, that we have magic, and you are jealous. You need not be jealous. You too can have such fine things, have your life eased by magic. I can see that you will live a long life, too. All you need do is extend a little trust.''

Could Glasgian do what he had just said? How could Kham trust this elf? ''Ya tried ta kill me and my family.''

''As I said, mistakes and misunderstandings.'' The elf smiled ingratiatingly, showing perfect teeth that glinted in a beautiful, though dirt-smudged face. ''I did not know the strength of spirit in you then. I do now. Let us work together. Let us sear this wretched place with fire and spread its ashes on the wind. Let us face the dragon together. With my magic and your spirit, we will surely conquer. We shall be as Lojan and Yasmundr, mage and indomitable warrior. They will sing our praises forever.''

Kham had always wanted to be a big shot warrior. That was the dream all orks had; being warriors was what orks did. So why did he have such a sour feeling in his stomach? ''Den what?''

''Then we will be the heroes. The world will be ours.''

''All for geeking one old worm? Ain't likely.''

''You think in the short term, a common failing of your kind. You must—you will—learn to think more clearly. To have perspective.''

A slight shift in the wind brought the stink of burnt flesh to Kham's nostrils. Perspective, huh? Maybe he was finally getting a little of that. ''I ain't no warrior hero.''

The elf looked disappointed. ''Perhaps I still misunderstand you a little. Perhaps the martial road is not your true concern. You have spoken of your family. Could it be that you only wish peace, to go home to them and live out your life?''

Yeah, it could be. Much the elf would know about that. "Maybe."

"Then peace can be yours. You need not be a warrior and face the worms, dying after a short, brutal life. I can make it different for you. And I will, if only you will let me use the crystal." The elf took a step up the slope. "I can bring a lasting peace to this world, rid it of the vermin." Another step. "You need only leave."

"So ya can come hunting me when ya feel like it."

"No. I will let you go. You and the other survivors." Glasgian gave him a sympathetic look. "Ah, you thought you were alone. Indeed, some of the others still live, but they shall not live long without attention. You dally. The crystal gives power, and power can heal."

Kham didn't know who was still alive, maybe no one besides himself. The elf was a proven liar, and the groan could have been one of his illusions. So why was Kham still listening? "And why should I trust you?"

"Because you sense that I speak truth. I will do what I have said I will do. Have no doubt of that. I am a prince of the true blood, and my word is binding. But you are not of my line, and you do not understand the bonds of the given word. So, for you, I will swear an oath. By the bones of the Mother and by my hope to see the beauty of harmony in the twilight, I will do as I have said. It is a solemn oath."

Kham didn't recognize the oath, but the sincerity in the elf's voice was persuasive. The fragger really wanted to get his hands back on the stone. Could he be trusted?

"I'll see that you live like a king," Glasgian offered as he took another step toward the crystal.

Crown the wise, the dragon had said. Was it wisdom to let the elf regain control of the crystal? Harry always said wisdom came with age, making it something Kham had little of. Nor was he likely to get a whole lot more wisdom; he knew an ork's life span. The elf's promises, even if they were good, were made to him and him alone. Once he was gone, what then? The elf would still be around to do as he pleased.

"What about my children?" Kham asked in a voice that quavered more than he expected.

Solemnly, the elf nodded. "They will live in a better world."

"Your world."

The elf took another step. "Yes, my world."

Act, or end as a slave, as your race was in ancient times, the dragon had said. So who was the liar?

Kham pointed the launcher at the stone.

"No!" The elf shouted.

Kham pulled the trigger.

"NOOOOO!" Glasgian's shout changed pitch, warping itself into a scream of agony. The rocket impacted the crystal and exploded. Impossibly, the elf's voice carried over the sound of the explosion.

An arc of blue-white energy sizzled from the smoking stump of the crystal and speared the elf in the forehead. He jerked as if he had been jolted with a trillion volts of electricity. Thunder rolled in a sky suddenly dark with storm clouds, and bolts of lightning crashed down, striking all around them. The rising wind tugging at him, Kham let go of the launcher and dropped to the ground. As the storm grew, Kham burrowed deeper. Each bolt set his muscles twitching.

Face-down in the dirt, he thought about Lissa and the kids, wishing, and almost praying, that he would see them again. Had he done the right thing? Had he just blown their futures to smithereens?

At length the tempest abated and Kham thought that it might be safe to look around. He raised his head. The clearing looked little different. A thin trail of smoke rose from where the Airstar had crashed beyond the trees. Had Rabo survived? A whimpering drifted to him from the edge of the deeper part of the pit. The Weeze. She was still alive at least. What a tough ork. As Kham stood up shakily, his gaze fell upon the elf.

Glasgian lay limp, draped over the broken crystal. The fragments of the stone were no longer tinted red, but had returned to the pale green color they had been in the cavern. The elf clasped one last rose-colored shard in a hand seared free of skin. As Kham watched, the color faded from the broken crystal.

The elf's expression was slack, spittle sliding down his cheek. His face was no longer youthful, no longer beautiful, and his hair, once full and fair, now only remained in patches of grungy gray. His lined and withered visage was barely recognizable. Incredibly, his chest still moved. He was alive.

He was also beyond helping anyone do anything, including himself.

"Not worth the killing."

Kham spat on him and turned away.

29

The Weeze was in pretty bad shape, but Kham thought she'd live if he could get her out of the Salish and back to civilization. He trudged up the slope and headed for the trees, figuring he could put some of the brush together into a litter. He wanted to get her out of the pit before anybody came to investigate. Whoever showed up, whether elf or dragon partisan or

Salish-Shidhe tribal, wouldn't be interested in being friendly with a couple of wounded and worn-out orks.

He found a couple of saplings for poles and pulled them up, feeling the ache in his own tired muscles. It'd be a long walk home. Rooting through the brush for something to tie the poles together, he almost didn't hear the stealthy approach behind him. He spun when he judged the time right, a heavy piece of wood in his hand.

It was the catboy, battered and bedraggled, but alive.

Neko backpedaled away from Kham, tripping over a tangle of sticks, and landing on his rump. Kham's swing missed and only then did he notice that the catboy's weapon was slung and his hands empty.

"Drek! Ya ought not do dat ta people. I coulda pulped yer head."

Neko looked up sheepishly. "Sorry. I thought you heard me. I was making enough noise."

"Come on," Kham said, extending a hand. "Get up."

The catboy took the offered hand and Kham lifted him to his feet without effort. When he released Neko, the catboy nearly fell again. Kham saw that he wasn't able to put any weight on his left leg. If it wasn't broken, it was badly sprained.

"Hurt bad?"

"I will live."

"More dan some people can say."

"True enough. I saw what you did."

"Did ya? Gonna tell yer dragon friend all about it?"

"If I had a dragon friend I might. But since I don't . . ."

The catboy left the rest hanging, making a statement without actually saying anything, leaving Kham to guess at just what he meant. Kham wished that for once Neko would just say things straight out. "Still claiming ya aren't working fer da wizworm?"

"Still."

Still evasive, more like, Kham thought.

A crashing sound from Glasgian's earth wall made them turn in its direction. Dust hung in the air around one end, shrouding the figure that was digging its way free from the rubble. Alpha's tribarrel was bent into a corkscrew, useless. The hellion was battered, his chromed armor dented, scratched, and begrimed. But he was still functional, another survivor. As Alpha emerged from the dust, Kham could see that the hellion was in bad shape. Gaps showed the internal workings of his cyberlimbs and he emitted grinding noises and jets of fluid every time he moved. The tubes that had run into his nose flopped against one shoulder, dribbling a dark fluid. One of his skull plates was dented deeply. The clashing sound of his movement stopped as he halted and stared at the shattered remains of the crystal.

"He doesn't look very happy," Neko commented drily.

"Well, if ya ain't gonna tell da worm, he's gonna have ta. I wouldn't be happy if I were him." Kham bent back to his work. "Come on, we gotta help The Weeze."

For a time, the only sounds were their own grunts of effort and the rustling of the springy twigs that Neko collected for binding material. They finished the litter as best they could, and began to drag it toward the lip of the deep pit. The broken-toy noises of Alpha's movement started up again, but Kham didn't bother to look; the litter had caught on something. Kham had just worked it loose with Neko's help when the catboy suddenly yelped and dropped his end.

Kham turned in time to see Alpha only a half-dozen meters away and closing. The tribarrel's motor sparked quietly and impotently. Then a clanging sound began as some kind of weapon tried to emerge from a concealed compartment in the hellion's forearm. The clanging stopped and black smoke began to pour from the half-open compartment. Rage burned hotly in the hellion's eyes; there was no mistaking his murderous intent.

"Traitor. Killer. Traitor," Alpha mumbled as he continued his slow-motion—for him—charge. The hellion was on Kham before he could get out of the way.

The ruined tribarrel swung up and Kham instinctively raised an arm to ward off the blow. Metal crashed down onto his arm, breaking the bone. Pain flared in the limb like a thermite explosion. Wrong arm, stupid! He fell backward into the litter, pinning Neko. Neko yelped as if he felt the pain Kham was holding inside. Feeling the squirming catboy pummeling him on the shoulder, Kham dimly realized that Neko was feeling his own pain; Kham had fallen on the catboy's injured leg.

The hellion raised the tribarrel for another strike, but Kham managed to roll aside, and the weapon muzzles buried themselves in the dirt. Kham rolled further away and scrambled to his feet, desperately looking around for the rocket launcher. The weapon still had another round when he'd dropped it; it'd be just the thing to stop this homicidal lunatic. If Kham could fire it with only one hand.

"Traitor, killer," the hellion chanted.

Despite all the damage Alpha had taken, he was still fast enough to keep up with Kham as he stumbled backward, unwilling to take his eyes off the hellion. But Alpha's reactions were well off from the uncanny responses of which he had been capable when uninjured. Kham managed to dodge the next swipe from Alpha and plant his own metal fist in the hellion's face. Alpha's head rocked back, saved from the full force of Kham's blow by his armored plates.

The hellion tried to encircle Kham with his arms, but Kham dropped and rolled away. He felt the bones in his arm grind, but kept the pain in. It was the price of getting clear. He knew better than to let the metal man get a grip on him; his flesh was no match for the crushing grip of Alpha's cybernetic limbs.

Alpha knew it, too. The hellion pivoted and closed again. Warier this time; he blocked Kham's shots. Still, the hellion wasn't fast enough anymore to launch his own attack and still block Kham's shots. Their fight became a dance: Kham twisting out of the hellion's reach with sudden changes in direction and Alpha shifting to counter each attempt to get past him. Every exchange took more of Kham's waning strength, and he didn't know how long he could keep it up. He was panting and the pain in his arm was starting to make him dizzy.

His hopes of getting off easy vanished when he finally spotted the missile launcher; it lay almost directly behind Alpha. Alpha's limbs were slowed but his brain wasn't. The hellion saw where Kham was looking, and began to herd him further and further away from it. Kham tried shifting the path of his retreat around, but the hellion shifted too, pressing Kham further away from the launcher.

Taking what he thought was his best chance, Kham tried to dart past the hellion as Alpha negotiated a rocky patch of ground. Unfortunately, the cyberguy still had too much speed. Alpha rocked back on one leg and lashed out with the other. The striking limb was stiff, but it had enough power behind it to slam Kham's leg muscles into numbness. He went down.

The hellion was on him instantly, pummeling him with both arms. Kham got his own cyberarm free and slammed a good shot home against the side of Alpha's head, denting the damaged plate further.

That was his chance. Kham started pounding on the plate. If he could warp it enough, get an edge to grip onto, he might be able to rip it away. Without the armor's protection, the hellion would take Kham's blows with real effect. Kham might be able to knock the hellion senseless or, better still, crush the bastard's addled skull.

Alpha pounded him mercilessly. Blows he could have blocked impacted with terrible power. Kham felt a rib go, but he kept on. A seam on the metal man's head plate ruptured, and Kham's fingers locked onto the edge.

At last, Alpha seemed to realize his danger. The ruined tribarrel snapped across and knocked Kham's arm away. But Kham kept his grip, and the armor plate ripped away bloodily. But it was no good. The hellion got Kham's arm pinned against the ground. With the weight of the hellion on him and his only functioning arm trapped, there was nothing Kham could do to exploit the opening he had made.

Alpha lifted his left arm limb above his head, then stopped, blinking. Kham figured the removal of the cyberguy's armor plate had loosened a few connections and, for a moment, he dared think that the hellion might be stunned. Then the cyberguy tilted his head down and stared into Kham's eyes. There was a terrible lucidity in Alpha's eyes.

"You failed the master, trog. That releases me to do what should've been done before." The hellion smiled viciously. "If it weren't for your meddling, Beta and Gamma would still be alive. They were my chummers, trog."

As Alpha cocked back his raised hand, a wide steel blade slid out from his wrist, gleaming faintly in the pre-dawn light. Alpha angled his arm, pointing the tip of his blade toward Kham's throat.

"This is for my chummers, trog."

Then Alpha's face exploded. The chatter of a submachine gun filled Kham's ears as bits of bone and brain splattered him. Instead of disgusting him, the gory shower brought relief.

He was alive.

It was not Kham, but the hellion who had died. Alpha's arm remained upraised, frozen in place. The razor-edged steel glinted in the starlight, pointing heavenward. Kham's eyes followed the line of the weapon and ended up staring into the night sky.

Was there somebody up there to thank?

Kham let his gaze drift down again and saw that there was indeed somebody to thank down here. Neko stood just beyond Alpha's immobile shoulder. The catboy still held his Colt in firing position, aiming at the back of Alpha's skull, at the opening Kham had ripped in the armor plate.

Time slipped back into motion, and Kham watched Neko lower the muzzle of his weapon and eject the empty clip. The fixed expression on the catboy's face softened, slumping down through relief into exhaustion.

Kham heaved at the dead weight pinioning him to the ground. It took great effort to get that weight off him. When he did, he lay exhausted, his strength finally spent. Kham stared at the holes pocking the hellion's back; they were the marks of small-caliber shells that could not penetrate the armor. If Kham hadn't ripped Alpha's skull plate free, Neko's bullets would have been ineffective. And if the catboy hadn't shot the hellion, Kham would have been meat. It had taken the two of them to beat the metal man.

Neko limped over and looked down at him. There was a half-smile on his face, a questioning look. But the catboy said nothing.

"Guess maybe I did figure ya wrong, catboy."

"Guess maybe you did." Neko held out a stout stick. "You'll need this for your arm. I'd help you up, but I don't think I can take the extra weight."

"S'okay." Kham got himself painfully to his feet and took the offered stick.

Neko pulled a strap out of his pocket, checked to see that Kham's arm was straight, and started to wrap the splint in place. A little surprised, but definitely pleased, Kham let the catboy bandage the arm.

"Da two of us don't look much like winners."

"Three of us. There's still The Weeze and we haven't checked on Rabo yet. But winners? This is one time when what you look like doesn't matter. All that matters is that you're still breathing."

Kham looked at Neko and frowned. "Weren't you da one talking about souls ta Harry?"

"If you are still breathing and do not have your soul, you have got no business breathing."

Shaking his head, Kham said, "Maybe someday, catboy."

"Maybe what?"

"Maybe someday I'll figure ya out."

But first he had some figuring out to do about himself.

While they dragged the litter down to The Weeze and got her on board, Kham did some of that thinking. He did more as they dragged her to the shelter of the woods, where they did what they could for her before going to check on where the Airstar had crashed. To Kham's immense surprise and relief, they found Rabo alive but pinned among the wreckage. It took their combined strength to pry him loose, but in the end they managed. They even salvaged some medical supplies from the wreck, enough to dull the pain of the two seriously injured orks so that they could sleep. It took them the better part of an hour, but they got themselves away from the nest.

At one point some kind of aircraft passed overhead, but nobody bothered them. Kham was glad. He was in no shape for another tussle. With luck, Rabo would be mobile in a day or two, and the three of them could pack The Weeze out. Till then, they'd make do in the woods.

Mostly the catboy kept quiet. So did the woods. No searchers came looking, or gunning, for them. Kham wondered about that, but he saw no reason to complain.

It gave him some more time to think.

This had been the toughest run he'd ever been knocked around on. Too many people lying to too many other people, manipulating them to their own ends. And he'd fallen into the middle of it because of needing money. Running only for money had driven him straight into the hands of the manipulators. He vowed inwardly that it wasn't a position he'd ever end up in again.

"Ya know, catboy. I'm tinking about getting outta da business."

Neko looked him up and down with an evaluating gaze. "Unlikely. You were born to run biz."

"Life's short, catboy. Too short ta waste running somebody else's errands. Dyin' fer dem."

"But you're not really thinking of giving up the shadows, are you? You need their freedom too much."

No, Kham realized. He wasn't thinking about giving up. In fact, he was thinking thoughts entirely too strange. "I got a family, catboy."

"And?"

And what? This run in pursuit of the dream of living longer had revealed sides of himself he'd not paid attention to before. Some of it he liked. There were a lot of feelings bumping up against habits and stray thoughts in his head. Still, a couple of things seemed clear.

"Da suits, even when dey're dragons, wanta own ya. Ain't right. Da only way ta keep 'em from doing dat is ta work fer yerself. Ya gotta stand against 'em, fight 'em when ya have ta, and turn dere plots against 'em every chance ya get.''

The catboy gave him that look again. ''You make a very ugly David.''

''David?''

''The shepherd boy with the sling who fought Goliath.''

''But he slew da giant and became king when he grew up, didn't he?''

Arching an eyebrow, Neko said softly, as if to himself, ''Crown the wise.''

Now Neko was talking like the dragon, too. ''Don't know dat I can be called any kind of wise.''

''Wisdom itself.'' Neko chuckled. ''I suppose it doesn't really matter. What kind of king could you be, anyway? The world has outgrown that sort of thing.''

What kind of king, indeed? By now Kham had figured that the dragon's proverb wasn't meant to be taken literally. He shrugged. ''Magic came back.''

''So it did.''

''Well, it's not like I gotta boss odder people around. Don't know dat I wanta. But I can leastways always rule myself. If I can't beat 'em, at least I'll never bow ta 'em. And sure as fragging hell is hot, I ain't gonna join 'em.''

Kham looked down at the diminutive catboy. The Biblical David was a shrimp, too. ''Ya gonna keep playing dere games, catboy? Or are ya brighter dan ya look?''

RoC
SF
ADVANCE